DISTRBUTION CITY
A novel by Boss Fred

Library of Congress Control Number 1-249480681

ISBN 978-0-615-32980-2

Printed in United States of America

Distribution City
Bankroll Ink P.O. Box 50532
Minneapolis, MN 55405

cover design Sick Graphics
author Boss Fred A.K.A Frederick Moore

www.distributioncity.net

This book is dedicated to the life and memories of

Carleton Elijah Lamar Temple,

R.I.P "Face"

&

Augustine Togba Jr.,

R.I.P. "Stine"

About the Author

Boss Fred is from and currently resides in minneapolis minnesota. Distribution City is his debut novel and the first release from Bankroll Ink.   Bankroll Ink is a publishing\ distribution company founded by Boss Fred upon his release from prison in 2008. Boss Fred Created Bankroll Ink so he could Boss up on the literary world and get paid in full for his book Distribution City. Boss Fred wrote Distribution City while serving time in a Federal Prison for a trumped up weapons charge. Just like his music, distribution City and the Distribution city series were created for entertainment purposes and to make money and were not in any way shape form or fashion designed to give lames the game. Author note "If any of my work entices or encourages you to embark or take part in any type of illegal activity I suggest you learn the STATE and FEDERAL laws on the subject before its to late! Words of advice 'dont do the crime if you cant do the time.' and 'STOP SNITCHING.'" PEACE and LOVE to all those who purchased my product and or support my movement. 100%.

DISTRIBUTION CITY
Somewhere in the Midwest

"Pop, pop, pop, pop, pop." Gunshots rang out. Saheed ducked; without hesitation he pulled out his 10 MM Glock and returned fire – with each pull of the trigger there was a loud "boom" that followed every hollow-tipped slug out of the large caliber pistol. One of the slugs found its mark, hitting the shooter in the mouth, instantly lodging several teeth into his brain and knocking a patch out the back of his skull, spraying the driver of the drive-by vehicle with blood and brain matter. As the terrified driver sped away, Saheed continued to "bust" at the vehicle, emptying the clip. As the car turned the corner, Saheed cursed himself out for letting him get away.

The driver was Polo, a long-time enemy of Saheed's. The shooter had to have been one of Polo's little homies, although Saheed didn't recognize the boy. He assumed whoever he was; he just became another statistic, another dead black man, and another victim to inner-city violence. Just another notch under his belt. He assumed right.

Saheed walked around the corner, got into his black Cadillac DTS, and drove away, putting distance between him and the neighborhood-turned-warzone, doing the speed limit as he made his way to the freeway. He wanted to be as discreet as possible, knowing that police were on their way to the block to investigate the shots fired.

20 minutes later Saheed pulled into the garage of one of his houses. He sat in his car thinking hard about the situation at hand. He had just gone to the "hood" to pick up some cash that one of his workers owed him. He parked around the corner like he always did. That way he wouldn't pick up any heat from the dope spot in case the police were watching. Through his rearview mirror, he noticed a green Chevy Caprice driving slowly across the intersection behind him. That set off an alarm in Saheed's mind because Black, Saheed's partner in crime, had just told Saheed the day before he saw Polo riding in a green Caprice. Saheed wasn't trippin' because he stayed strapped and was ready for gunplay at all times. So as Saheed stepped around the corner, almost to the D-Spot, the green caprice tried to creep up on him. Saheed turned around just in time to see the shooter coming out of the window with what looked like a tec-9 – that's when the gunfire erupted.

With his brain racing, he planned his next moves carefully. First he had to get rid of the gun because forensics was no joke in this day and age, and he wasn't the one to get caught up like that. Even though the 10 mm was his favorite "bitch," he had an arsenal of weapons and he knew he could get another if necessary. Second, he needed to create an airtight alibi in case investigators ever tried to tie him into the shooting.

On that thought, Saheed went into the house. He was greeted by Kiesha. Kiesha was Saheed's "ride-or-die, down-for-whatever bitch." She gave him a kiss on the cheek and said "what's up Daddy, did you bring the groceries?" He replied, "Do you see any muthafuckin' groceries?"

"Damn, nigga, excuse me."

"Keisha, listen to me. You hear me?"

"Yes, Daddy."

"If anyone ever asks, I was here with you all morning, since last night. You *hear* me?"

"Yes, Daddy. Is everything all right? You come in here like you killed somebody."

"Watch your mouth and be careful what you say, you hear me?"

"Yes, Daddy."

Saheed then walked over to the fireplace, put some wood in, and got a fire going. Then he stripped off all his clothes and threw them in the fire. That's when Kiesha understood the seriousness of the situation. She knew Saheed stayed on some hi-tech shit. Knowing Saheed loved his marijuana and always wanting to please her man; she rolled a blunt and brought it to him. He took it and walked into the bathroom without lighting the blunt. She watched as he took some rubbing alcohol and poured it onto a rag and began rubbing his face and body down – the reason he did this was to get rid of any traces of gunpowder that the glock may have left on his skin.

Then he got into the shower and started to scrub his skin like crazy. Kiesha, watching from the other room, was turned on from seeing her man naked, dick swinging. She stripped her clothes off as fast as she could and went into the bathroom to join her man. Saheed saw her walking towards him and forgot what he was thinking. He was hypnotized by the sexy image of this milk chocolate colored beauty, with the body of a goddess and a face from heaven getting into the shower with him. She dropped straight to her knees and began kissing "Big Killa," her pet name for his penis. She wrapped her lips around him and continued to give him a "Presidential" blow job, making his dick harder than a rock. After several minutes of this, Kiesha pulled her face away. Taking him into her hand, she gently caressed him; she rubbed her breasts against his tip as she stood up. She then turned around and bent over, keeping a firm grip on "Big Killa." She began rubbing her apple shaped ass against him. Saheed weakly protested as she slid him inside of her. Saheed was "Mr. Safe Sex" and had never had unprotected sex with Kiesha, even though he had been hitting that for two years. For two years Kiesha had wanted to have Saheed's child, he just wasn't ready to be a father.

Now he was deep inside of her, feeling all the heat of her body and loving every minute of it. He continued to stroke her as she cried out his name and told him she never wanted him to stop. With the hot water hitting him in his chest, trickling down his body onto hers, he felt himself about to "cum." Caught up in the moment and unable to pull out, he came inside of her, struggling to keep his rhythm as her body drained him of everything he had.

Slowly pulling out, he and Kiesha finished washing up. After getting out of the shower Kiesha looked at Saheed with a scandalous grin and said "that was the best sex ever," paused, and then said, "I'm pregnant." Saheed replied "quit playin', if you are you're getting an abortion."

"Whatever, nigga! I would never kill my baby."

Then Kiesha walked out of the bathroom. Saheed lit the blunt Kiesha had rolled him. Upset he let her catch him in the shower without a raincoat. He decided he would deal with her later; he had more important issues to address, like getting rid of Polo for good. All this public disputing, shoot-outs in broad daylight were bad for business. Polo had to go ASAP. Saheed took a pull from the blunt and the smoke made him cough hard. The weed was some Purple Kush, probably the best in town – he grew it himself.

CHAPTER TWO

The beef between Polo and Saheed started four years prior. They had been cool at one point in time but Polo secretly envied and was jealous of Saheed. Where as Saheed always seemed to have more cash than a bank and enough hoes to run a brothel, Polo was always struggling to get his money up and was constantly getting dissed by the ladies, even the hoodrats couldn't stand him. Polo hated everything about Saheed – from his light-colored skin to his long hair that he kept braided and the women loved. Most of all, he hated the respect Saheed got everywhere he went. Polo was a dark-skinned ugly motherfucker with nappy hair that wouldn't grow. A snake that wasn't to be trusted. A fake ass nigga with no respect for anyone, not even his own mother.

One night at Club Millennium, Polo was getting drunk with his crew when Saheed walked in with a boss hooker named Diamond. Diamond was a platinum blond with light blue eyes and had "ass for days." She would have fit right in at the Playboy Mansion. Polo had tried to get at Diamond several times but she always brushed him off. Drunk off Hennessey and hating the way Diamond was all over Saheed; Polo said to his crew, "yo, fuck that nigga, Saheed. We need to stick that nigga up." He then added "I already peeped his operation "Homeboy," got stupid cash." One of his crew spoke up, "if we do that, we gonna have to ice that man. Saheed's known for killing and we don't need him gunning for us." Polo replied "With all the money we gonna make, it will be worth taking his life."

Standing nearby, Saheed's homie, Black, overhead these drunk-ass niggas talking loud and plotting on his boy so he walked around the club until he found Saheed, then told him what he overheard. Saheed snapped when he heard what Black told him, saying "it's always some bitch-raised motherfucka who tries to test a man. I ain't never done nothing but look out for that nigga. I see I gotta make an example out of him." With that said, Saheed called up some of his soldiers and told them to come down to the club. When they got there, it was like they brought the whole northside with them. Then Saheed and his entourage walked up on Polo. Polo said, "Saheed, what's going down?" like everything was cool. Without saying a word, Saheed punched Polo in his jaw, breaking it instantly. Saheed's squad followed suit and started beating on Polo's people. When the fight kicked off, the music stopped. You could hear women screaming and glass being shattered as some turned bottles into weapons. The club security tried to break up the fight and got beat down.. In the end, there were broken bones and blood everywhere. Polo was on the floor and he looked dead, with shoe prints all over his face. His face was disfigured to the point where his own mother wouldn't have been able to recognize him. But he was still breathing.

It's been on ever since. Fist fights and gunplay with soldiers being murdered on both sides, even some innocent people lost their lives from the gang violence that started as a result of one man's jealousy . . .

CHAPTER THREE
Meanwhile, across town . . .

Polo was shaken, he just got his homeboy June killed. He had dropped the body off outside of the Emergency Room and sped off, already knowing June was dead. The only reason he did this was because he knew he would be the next one to die if June's family found out that June died because Polo had him on some bullshit that didn't even concern him.

June's uncle was O.G. Tank, the leader of the Southside Blood gang. Polo knew the Bloods didn't play no games – every time they had a problem, people wound up dead, *every time*.

Now Polo had to go to Tank and tell him that his nephew was dead. So he went to Tank's spot on the southside. Once inside he told Tank "June just got shot in the head. I don't think he's going to make it." Of course, Polo already knew June was dead but he wasn't about to tell Tank that. Tank said "what the fuck you just say?" Polo lied and said "man, me and June were at a traffic light on Broadway, rollin' in my Caprice, when that bitch ass nigga Saheed pulled up on the right side of us and started dumping." He continued, "I recognized his Cadillac and caught a glimpse of his face before I pulled off." Tank said nothing but if looks could kill Polo would have been a dead motherfucker. Polo kept talking. "I dropped June off at the hospital Emergency Room downtown and came straight over here. That nigga Saheed gonna pay with his life, that's my word," Polo said convincingly, hoping Tank bought his bullshit story. He needed Tank and the Blood gang to step up and help him fight his war against Saheed and them Northside Niggas that he ran with. He knew they would be coming at him hard after his failed attempt on Saheed's life.

Polo was a member of the Black Mob, but with so many members dead or in prison they were only a fraction of the force they used to be.

Tank didn't associate with anyone who wasn't part of his organization. He told his nephew June he shouldn't either. But June was his own man and had known Polo for years. Now June was dead. Tank thought to himself if that hard-headed lil' nigga would have just listened he would still be alive. Tank was trying to make sense of the situation but something just didn't feel right. He knew about the problems between Saheed and Polo and now he was caught up in the middle of it, with his nephew dead. All he knew was somebody had to pay. He didn't trust that shady-ass nigga Polo. Matter of fact, he didn't trust anyone. With that frame of mind he had built the most dangerous and feared gang in Distribution City. Under his leadership the Bloods had taken over the southside and were getting money like they were part of corporate America.

As he looked at Polo, Tank snapped out of his thoughts. He said to Polo, "I'll be in touch with you. Let me know if you find out where this cat Saheed is at. I have to go tell June's mother what happened." With that said Polo got up and left the building. Tank turned to his Lieutenant Smoke and said "put the word out we got $50,000.00 in exchange for Saheed's life." Without a word, Smoke went to follow his boss' orders.

CHAPTER FOUR
North Side, Distribution City

It was a busy night inside Saheed's gambling spot, with big pimps, major hustlers, and professional gamblers all under one roof. The stakes were high and with the house getting a 5% cut of every bet on the craps table (players gambled against eachother) they would make a small fortune this night, with all the proceeds going straight to Saheed. He had to pay his security – he kept two guys at the front door with big guns in sight and two at the back door with shotguns at the ready. Every gambler who came in had to check his weapons at the back door and get past the handheld metal detector before they were allowed to gamble.

He had to make sure his customers felt safe. He went out of his way to make sure they were comfortable by supplying them with free alcohol and food, and he kept at least one of his whores in there sucking dick for $100.00 a pop. The reason for all this was the longer people stayed the more money he made.

Downstairs he had two craps tables and two black jack tables; he even had three slot machines that were rigged so they never hit the jackpot. On top of that, the house took bets on all professional baseball, football and basketball games. Saheed's operation was real serious.

Black was in the house tonight and he was winning big. He was up $20,000.00 and about to make his exit. Before he left he went to talk to Saheed. He pulled him to the side and asked "how much of that Kush you got left?"

Saheed replied, "got whatever you want, my nigga."

Black said, "can I get five pounds for this $20,000.00 I just won?" knowing Saheed wanted $5,000.00 firm for each pound.

"You know I can't short myself like that, Black," adding "its business, not personal."

"Yo, when you gonna let me get that dro connect? I need your plug player."

What Black didn't know was Saheed was his own connect; he had three houses in Distribution City with hydroponic systems set up inside growing marijuana. The money he made off each house was all profit, he could have made much more but he kept the number of plants at each house to a minimum in case police ever stumbled across one, that way the feds wouldn't pick up the case. Police could never find out about the houses unless someone snitched. That's why Saheed never told anyone about his weed operation. It was his bread and butter; it was how he came up. No one knew his money grew on trees.

He looked at Black and remembered his cocaine supply was running low. Black had a Mexican connection on them bricks. The only problem was Black had been out of "work" for a few days. He asked Black "did that shipment come in?"

Black answered, "Not until tomorrow."

Saheed said, "Look, I will give you four pounds of 'purple' plus twenty G's for two them 'thangs'." (kilos)

Black thought about it, and then said "let's do it." Then Black asked Saheed, "Why do you risk your freedom selling cocaine when you got bitches breaking bread daily and you're making more than enough money off ya gambling business? You always got pounds of bomb green; I can't understand why you fuck with dope?"

Saheed replied, "somebody gotta do it, dope always gonna sell and I gotta make mine." With that said they agreed to meet the next day.

They met at Black's crib the next day. The transaction was made and they went their separate ways. Inside his dope spot, Saheed took one of the kilos out of the sealed package and saw what he was looking for – 1,000 grams of Peruvian flakes, pure coke. He then took 1,000 grams of creatine and blended it with the cocaine, put it in a compressor, and pressed it back into a brick. Just like that he turned one into two. Next he took the other 1,000 grams of cocaine and a different cutting agent that when cooked with cocaine all "came back" to crack cocaine. If he used any more than 500 grams of "comeback" on the second kilo, it would have messed up the drug and made it no good. If he had used the same cut on the second kilo that he had used on the first one, when it was cooked into crack all the cut would dissapear and he would have been left with what he originally had. Saheed had more varieties of cut then he could count, all were a white odorless powder and most could be found at the local nutritional shop.

Saheed started with two keys, now he was at the table with three and a half "bricks" (kilos). The two bricks with Creatine in them would go to customers who snorted the drug. The one and a half would go to people who cooked the coke into crack. When the three and a half kilos get sold, Saheed will have tripled his money. That's why he sold cocaine – it was an investment.

The drugs continued to flow like a River through Distribution City: Cocaine, Heroin, Methamphetamine, Ecstasy,

Marijuana, PCP,LSD, Prescription Drugs and more, all this could be found on the streets. Everyone seemed to be getting high, even children. Hustlers were getting paid and the FEDS were watching.

CHAPTER FIVE
City Hall, Downtown Distribution City

"We have to do something *now!*" screamed Mayor Bucks. "The crime in the city is out of control, violent crime has doubled since my election into office. This years murder rate is up 18%, robbery 27%, rape 9%, and drug-related arrests have sky rocketed. Our county jails are full, state prisons are full. I propose a joint effort between federal and state law enforcement agencies to clean up the streets of Distribution City."

He was speaking to the U.S. District Attorney, Mr. Herbert C. Dicks. Mayor Bucks continued, "We need your office prosecuting these smaller cases. Most of these guys are repeat offenders, they are in the streets raising hell, and they are going to cost me my re-election next year."

"I understand completely, Mayor, and I agree. With my office prosecuting we can enforce these federal laws on these low-level offenders and have them locked up for the next decade or two."

"Exactly," said Mayor Bucks.

"Furthermore, with all the time they'll be facing, these guys will be more than happy to allow us to use them as bait to catch the bigger fish!" said Prosecutor Dicks, with an evil grin on his face.

They talked some more and from their discussion they came up with "Operation F.A.L.C.O.N." – Federal and Local Coalition Overtaking Narcotics. They shook hands and the United States Attorney Herbert C. Dicks left the Mayor's office. After he left, the Mayor got up and locked the door. He sat back down at his desk, pulled out an envelope from the bottom drawer, then removed a small plastic bag containing Cocaine from inside the envelope, emptied the contents onto his desk, pulled out a hundred dollar bill and rolled it up. "God bless America," he said to himself, then put the bill to his nose and inhaled the Cocaine.

CHAPTER SIX

Saheed's cell phone wouldn't stop ringing. People had been calling him all day for this and that. Even when he didn't feel like talking, he always answered just to keep things running smoothly. So as his phone sung him a song he looked at the caller ID and saw it was LaTasha calling. LaTasha wasn't good for anything but sucking dick – when it came to that she was a pro. She could deep throat the dick without any gag reflex. Saheed had been trying to put her down, he wanted to make some money off that "B.Z." but she was one of them chicken heads who would rather fuck for free than get paid for it – it didn't make sense to him.

Thinking about the way she liked to swallow his seed made his dick hard so he answered the phone. "Yeah, what's up?"

"What it do, Saheed?"

"LaTasha, you already know what it *do*, every time I hear your voice my dick gets hard."

"You're so nasty, Saheed. But listen, that's not why I'm calling. I got something important to tell you."

"What is it?" asked Saheed.

"I don't think we should talk about it on the phone. Come over and smoke a blunt with me and I'll tell you what's popping."

"O.K., baby, I'll be through."

Saheed hung up his phone.

Pulling up to LaTasha's town house, Saheed grabbed his 45. out of the stash spot. LaTasha's whole family were Bloods and she was on some gang-banging shit too. Saheed wasn't a member of any gang. He chose at an early age to be all about "getting money" instead. He did business with hustlers all throughout Distribution City, it didn't matter to him what you represented, as long as your money was good.

Knocking on the door, LaTasha let him in and led him to the living room couch. They sat down and Saheed rolled a blunt of purple. They were kicking back, smoking, when LaTasha put the blunt out. Saheed said, "I thought you had something to tell me." She replied, "I do," then reached for Saheed's belt and unbuckled it. Saheed knew what time it was and set the 45. on the table.

LaTasha eased Saheed's pants down then pulled out his "wood," took him into her hot mouth, and had him down her throat instantly. Saheed couldn't handle it and bust a fat nut that made his body jerk a lil' bit. When LaTasha came up for air, she had her hand inside the couch cushion. When she pulled it out she was holding a chrome pearl handle 22. She had it pointed right in-between Saheed's eyes. He was frozen, scared to move. He didn't know what this bitch was on but he was caught with his pants down, literally. His gun was on the table out of his reach.

"LaTasha, baby, what are you doing?" pleaded Saheed.

"Nigga, shut the fuck up! You kill one of my people then come around me like shit's sweet. Now you gotta pay and I'm about to get paid."

"Baby, put the gun down, I haven't killed nobody."

"Nigga, I *said* shut the fuck up!" yelled LaTasha. She swung the pistol at Saheed in an attempt to pistol whip him . . . big mistake. He moved quick and caught her arm in mid-swing, brought his knees up hard into this crazy bitch's stomach, knocking the air out of her. At the same time, he wrestled the gun away. With the gun in his hands, he got up, pulled his pants up and grabbed the 45. off the coffee table.

"You silly ass bitch, this is how you pistol whip a motherfucker," Saheed said through clenched teeth, and then swung the barrel heavy 45. as hard as he could hitting LaTasha in the temple, knocking her unconscious.

When she woke up, she realized she was in her bed, ass-naked, spread eagle and tied to the bed post. Saheed was standing over her with a hot curling iron in his hand. "Bitch, you got some explaining to do."

"Saheed, please don't hurt me – I'll tell you everything," cried LaTasha. She told him as fast as she could about the $50,000.00 bounty out for him and how it was said he shot June when he was trying to get Polo.

Now everything made sense to Saheed. June was the cat rollin' with Polo. June was a Blood and now he was dead, and they wanted revenge for their dead homie.

Saheed looked at this sad, sorry bitch who, 30 minutes earlier, was going to kill him or have him killed. He felt no remorse for her. He took the curling iron, plugged it in, and turned the heat on high. After it was hot he shoved it hard and deep into her pussy. LaTasha let out a bone-chilling scream as the curling iron cooked her insides and mutilated her vagina. She screamed, bucked and thrashed until she passed out from the pain. Saheed removed the curling iron, wiped his prints off everything he touched, and went to leave. Before he did, he picked up LaTasha's cell phone and called Tank, who he knew from around town. Tank answered "what's up Boo?"

"I got your Boo, tied up and half dead. You need to come check on her," replied Saheed. He then hung up the phone. He had called Tank because even though Saheed felt LaTasha deserved to die for what she pulled, he wanted her to survive and suffer. He wanted Tank to know he knew about the contract out on him. Before he left, he picked up the blunt from the ashtray and lit it, then walked out the door, leaving the place smelling like Purple Kush and burnt flesh.

CHAPTER SEVEN
Underworld Studio, Warehouse District, Distribution City

Saheed parked his Cadillac in front of the Jackson Building, which was home to Underworld Entertainment, Saheed's record/promotion company. Inside he had an office and recording studio. As he walked in he heard one of his artists, Young Mac, recording a song from the booth. *"We got crack cocaine in Distribution City, we got Methamphetamines in Distribution City, we got ecstasy in Distribution City, we got what you need in Distribution City."*
His voice was coming through the state-of-the-art sound system in the studio. The volume was up and the bass was pounding. Saheed walked past his producer, True, and hit the power button. When he did this, everything shut down. Caught off guard, True just looked at his big homie, Saheed. Young Mac came out of the booth and said "what the fuck happened?! I was almost done."
"Saheed erased everything we just recorded, that's what the fuck happened," True said with an attitude.
Young Mac hollered "that's bullshit, homie! I've been working on this song all day."
"Fuck that, y'all can re-record that shit later. Right now we about to get our hands dirty."
Saheed told them about what just went down and the situation with the Bloods. True and Young Mac were ready to kill after they heard about the hit the Bloods had on Saheed. Saheed was like a father to them, so they wouldn't hesitate to do anything he told them too. He instructed Young Mac to go steal a car and meet him in the hood in an hour. When it came to stealing cars, Young Mac was a professional, that's how he ate before Saheed taught him how to hustle. He kept a pocket full of money ever since. Saheed and True went to True's house to grab the "choppers." Saheed kept eight Assault rifles over there; he had five A.K. 47s over there, and three A.R. 15s. They put two A.K.s and one A.R. 15 into the stash spot then drove to the hood to meet Young Mac. Young Mac was already there waiting on them, sitting inside of a 1980-something Suburban.
Saheed's plan was to fire bomb the Party Lounge and when people ran out to escape the fire they would be gunned down. The Party Lounge was the Bloods' base of operations/hang-out, disguised as your neighborhood bar. If you weren't a member of the Bloods, you didn't go in there. If you did, you would regret it

later. The Bloods didn't like strangers amongst them. Saheed knew the Bloods would be deep in there at this time of night.

They loaded the choppers into the Suburban. They all had gloves on, careful not to leave their prints on anything, not even the choppers. Saheed then prepared the Molotov cocktails, pouring gasoline into glass bottles then stuffing pieces of a ripped up towel into each. He told Young Mac to follow him over to the southside – Saheed drove alone in his Cadillac. Young Mac and True were in the steamer. (a stolen vehicle.)

Saheed parked his Cadillac on a quiet street seven blocks from the Party Lounge and got into the Suburban. They drove up the alley behind the Party Lounge. Saheed and True got out and lit the Molotov cocktails. Saheed threw his through the back window; True's hit the back door, setting the place on fire instantly. They sped around to the front of the Party Lounge. People were starting to come out in a panic. Young Mac and True opened fire with the AK's – *"blam, blam, blam, blam blam,"* was all you could hear. Women were screaming but their voices were drowned out by the gunshots. Saheed had gotten out of the truck with the A.R. 15 and began shooting, aiming every shot with precision, catching bodies left and right. Young Mac and True had recklessly emptied their clips and were hollering "let's go!"

Saheed jumped back into the steamer and Young Mac hit the gas. Around the same time, someone came out of the Party Lounge, pistol blazing, every shot tearing into the Suburban. As Young Mac turned the corner, a bullet popped the tire. None of them were hit. They drove on a flat tire back to Saheed's Cadillac. As planned, they left the assault rifles in the stolen vehicle, since they couldn't be traced back to them. They jumped out of the Suburban. True lit the last Molotov cocktail and threw it inside the truck, setting the interior on fire instantly and eliminating any traces of evidence they may have left behind. The three of them piled into Saheed's Cadillac and drove off into the night.

CHAPTER EIGHT
North Side, Distribution City

Saheed was lying in his bed watching the 6:00 a.m. news. The anchor woman was saying "last night at the Party Lounge on Distribution City's southside, bar patrons were savagely gunned down after the bar was set on fire. Apparently the rear exit was set on fire and when the occupants tried to escape the burning establishment they were caught in a hail of bullets. Details are few at this time. What we know is police confirmed five people are dead and nine were wounded. Several are in critical condition. Witnesses say the gunmen had blue rags over their face and fled in a dark colored Suburban. The Party Lounge is a known hang-out for the Southside Blood gang leading to speculation that this is the latest in an ongoing gang war between the Bloods and the Crips. Police are asking for the public's help. Anyone with any information should contact the Distribution City Police Department."

Saheed shut off the television as Kiesha entered the room with nothing but a towel on. She was fresh out of the shower and getting ready to go to work. Saheed was fresh out of the shower and getting ready to go to sleep. "Big Killa" was wide awake.

"Kiesha, come talk to me."

Looking at his erection, Kiesha knew he wanted to do more than talk.

"Daddy, I have to go to work."

"I need you to take the day off, Boo."

"Saheed, you know how important my job is to me. I . . ."

He cut her off in mid-sentence with a passionate tongue kiss. The way he kissed her got her juices flowing immediately. He removed the towel from around her curves then he palmed her soft, round ass with both hands, pulling her body against his. Saheed then laid his woman down on his king-sized bed. Kissing her neck, working his way down to her firm breasts, he started teasing her nipples with his tongue, causing her to start breathing heavily. She pushed his head towards her love as he drug his tongue across her body, around her navel, until he came in contact with her clitoris. When he did, he kissed it, and then licked it, before taking it into his mouth. This caused Kiesha to moan with pleasure. Saheed was treating her body like it was the best thing he ever tasted. Kiesha was rotating her hips in a circular motion when Saheed slipped two fingers inside of her.

This triggered an orgasm like she never felt before. It seemed like her eyes rolled into the back of her head as her legs and body shook uncontrollably. Kiesha was in heaven on earth, Saheed had never done that to her before and she never wanted him to stop. Saheed eased back on top of Kiesha and started tongue kissing her, at the same time using one hand to guide himself inside of her. Slowly he moved back and forth, inch after thick inch, until she was filled with pleasure. Taking both of her legs and placing them on one of his shoulders, Kiesha began moaning as he seemed to go even deeper. With her voice exciting him, he started stroking her faster. With a firm grip on her legs, he plunged into her harder with every stroke. Kiesha cried out "fuck me, Saheed! This is *your* pussy! Oooh, Daddy!" At that instant he exploded inside of her but he didn't stop – they continued to have sex in different positions for the next hour.

When they were done, Saheed rolled a blunt of Purple Kush and smoked the whole thing by himself. Kiesha laid there and studied him while he smoked. Amazed at how good he made her feel, she was thinking to herself how she would do anything for him, when he said to her "Kiesha, if anyone ever asks, I came home at 10:00 p.m. last night and passed out drunk. You were with me all night. You hear me?"

"Yes, Daddy. Is everything okay?"

" Don't ask me no questions, I wont tell you no lies."

CHAPTER NINE
South Side, Distribution Center

"It's all out war! Motherfuckers wanna fuck with me; I will bring it to this entire city." Tank spoke with authority. He was talking to his Lieutenant Smoke. "I can't believe them Crip niggas. They came to us with that peace treaty shit, talking about a cease fire; stop the violence and all that. Then turn around and try to snake us. We done fell for the forty-four fake-out."

"You read the D.C. Tribune? They dubbed this thang the Southside Massacre, community leaders are calling for peace, the Mayor is pushing for a crack-down and the Police Chief is promising arrests. Our soldiers can't even make a move with police pullin over every car in sight. Shit, them motherfuckers are sitting down the block right now with binoculars. We can't even make any money," said Smoke.

"Dig this, with this Party Lounge drama I didn't even get a chance to tell you about LaTasha. Turns out Saheed was fucking that girl and being the gangstress that she is she tried taking the nigga out for us Blood, she wanted that $50,000.00."

"What you mean tried'?" asked Smoke.

"Like I said, *tried*. The nigga ended up taking her gun, beating the shit out of the bitch, then stuck a hot curling iron up her pussy. Then, before he left, he had the nerve to call me from her cell phone and talk crazy."

"Yeah?"

"Yes, nigga, so I strike over to her town house – front door's wide open. I find her tied up to her bed; the room stunk like burnt flesh. I thought she was dead until I noticed she was still breathing. I rushed her to the Emergency Room. She's in Intensive Care now. The doctors say she's going to make it."

"Damn," replied Smoke.

"She was able to tell me what went down. Saheed knows about the money we got on his head and that makes me wonder if he was the one who hit the Party Lounge."

"That makes sense, Tank. The way I see it, we lay down this Saheed cat and the Crips too, fuck 'em all. I will do it myself, that's real talk, Blood," Smoke said with tears in his eyes and anger in his voice. His older brother was one of those who got killed in the drive-by, he was full of emotions. Everyone who was hit were members of the Blood gang except for that sexy freak from Texas – she lost her life just hanging out. Smoke was at the Party Lounge when the shit popped off. When he saw his big brother on the ground with half his face missing, he went crazy and ran outside shooting. The reality of what had happened still hadn't completely come to Smoke. He couldn't bring himself to accept the fact his brother was dead, not to mention three of his homies.

"Just like that, Smoke, we gonna put in work and ask questions later. We're gonna lay our Blood Brothers to rest, let the heat die down, then handle our business."

CHAPTER TEN

North Side Distribution City, Two Weeks Later

Saheed and Black were inside Saheed's gambling house smoking blunts and relaxing. They both had lost money tonight. The only time Saheed lost money was when he himself chose to gamble. On this night, he chose to shoot dice with the rest of the gamblers. He lost everything the house made plus $15,000.00. His pimp friend, Icy Waters, was the big winner. Only the Lord knew exactly how much he won but it was a lot.

Black spoke up, "that man Icy Waters ain't no joke. He came in here, took my cash, your cash, and your bitch. Rose was the finest hoe I ever seen you with, Saheed, you gotta be upset about him knocking off your bitch."

Rose was one of Saheed's whores. Icy Waters had got in her head and she decided she would rather roll with him.

"Let me tell you something, homie. I run through hoes like pounds and keys. I don't give a fuck about that bitch!" Saheed lied through his teeth. Rose had made him more money than any woman he ever had and he knew he would miss her. Black knew his boy was frontin' but didn't press the issue. Instead he hit the blunt and said "yo, did you read today's paper? Five bodies found inside suspected crack house – that was those Crip niggas' spot over Southeast. My lil' cousin run with those boys. He said them was his partnas who got murdered."

"That's fucked up," said Saheed.

"Yeah, it's fucked up. Their other homie, Fat Loc, just got killed the other day. Now them niggas is on bullshit, they're riding around over south right now talking about they popping every Blood they see on sight."

"Man, them young niggas out here don't be giving a fuck," said Saheed. He continued, "ever since them Crip niggas shot up the Party Lounge, the block been hot as hell. Young Mac was in the hood when police did a sweep, caught the lil' nigga with a quarter ounce crack hard." (7 grams)

"Is he still locked up?"

"Naw, I had to bail him out earlier today. His bail was $40,000.00; I had to get 'em out."

"Damn, $40,000.00 for a quarter ounce? That's crazy!" stated Black.

"I know it's crazy. My bail bondsman says he's lucky the feds didn't pick up the case, told me the feds have been picking up every gun and petty crack case that's come down for the past week. And then he tells me don't be surprised if they step in and take it."

Just the thought of the feds snatching up Young Mac fucked with Saheed's mind. He had plans for that lil' nigga to blow up with this rap shit. If he went federal, he would be looking at a mandatory minimum of five years with the crack laws. In a state court, he was only looking at probation. That would definitely fuck up his plans. He wasn't worried about Young Mac saying anything to the police, Young Mac was solid. But after the so-called Southside Massacre, Young Mac had been acting differently. It was like it seemed to be eating at his conscience. He knew Young Mac had never killed anyone before that night and that was most likely the problem. He thought about the lives he had taken throughout the years and how he had never told a soul. He always did it by himself. Just like his O.G. had taught him. His O.G. had always stressed to him "why do you need someone with you when you're going to kill somebody? So they can tell on you? Eventually you're gonna have to kill them. You don't need that – do your dirt by yourself." His O.G. would stress the point over and over to him. Not even his homeboy Black knew about the work he put in.

"Saheed . . . *Saheed!*" Black yelled, snapping Saheed out of his thoughts.

"What's up, nigga? You ain't gotta shout, I ain't deaf," said Saheed.

"You act like that kush got you zoning. Like I was saying, I'm about to ride out." Black stood up to leave.

"Alright then my . . . "Saheed was cut off by the sound of gunshots and his front window shattering. He and Black both dove for the floor at the same time as a barrage of bullets tore through his house. It sounded like several automatic weapons were being fired at the same time, like they were in Iraq or Afghanistan or some shit. The shooting seemed to go on forever. Black and Saheed were crawling towards the back of the house. Saheed didn't want to look back, fearing that his friend may have been hit. Finally the shooting stopped. He looked at Black, Black looked at him. Black asked "you get hit?"

"Nah, you?"

"I'm good," replied Black.

They pulled their weapons and went out the back door. Looking around there wasn't a car in sight. They walked around the front and saw the street littered with bullet casings. The front of the house had more holes in it than a sponge. As they walked back inside, Saheed noticed blood on Black's sleeve and said "say, you got blood on your arm."

After further observation, Black realized he'd been grazed by a bullet.

"Kiss my black ass. I was starting to think I was bullet-proof," joked Black.

"This ain't no time for jokes, homie."

"Yo, I'm serious," Black said with a grin, happy he only got grazed. Then he asked, "don't you still got those cameras posted up outside?"

Caught up in the moment, Saheed hadn't even thought about the surveillance cameras.

"Yeah, let's go check the tape."

When they did, the tape showed two cars pulling up, then niggas with guns hanging out of every window started shooting at his spot. They had what looked like handguns, assault rifles, and even a 12-guage. They seemed to fire every bullet out of every gun before they smashed off into the night. The first car looked like a small Lexus or a Toyota or something. They didn't recognize it; it didn't matter. The second car, a green Caprice, was undeniably Polo's.

"That pussy ass nigga gotta go," said Saheed.

Just then they heard sirens. "D.C. police are running late as usual." Said Black. Saheed hurriedly put the guns and the surveillance tape in the stash. He hid the tape because he wanted to keep his beef in the streets. When Polo gets what he gots coming he didn't need the law investigating him.

When the police arrived they took pictures and asked a few questions. Saheed and Black played ignorant like they didn't know who did the shooting or why. They offered Black medical assistance but he declined. They collected the shell casings – 92 in total. Approximately 80-something bullet holes were in the front of the house. The police finished their report and left the scene.

CHAPTER ELEVEN
South Side, Distribution City

"Oh God, fuck me, Smoke, I love your dick!" cried Desire.

Desire is a local stripper who catered to those with money or anyone else she found attractive. She herself was beautiful with her light skin, long hair, green eyes, large breasts, and big ol'ass. All the hustlers wanted to fuck. If they found out what she knew they would change their minds. Desire is HIV positive and she's on a mission to infect as many people with the disease as possible. She feels like if she has to suffer and die from AIDS then she would bring as many people as she could along for the ride – misery loves company.

"Oh . . . Smoke . . . I love it . . . take the condom off," she said between deep breaths. Smoke was laying his dick game down and loving the pussy. Even though the pussy was good, Smoke wasn't trying to run up in Desire raw. He had a wife at home and he knew she would chop his dick off if he gave her a STD, so he ignored her request, slapped her on the ass, and kept hitting it from the behind.

"Smoke, I want to feel you. Take off the rubber," moaned Desire. Then she reached back and tried to take the condom off herself. Smoke realized what she was doing, grabbed her wrist and said, "What the fuck are you on, bitch? You're crazy as hell!" and he kept on stroking her.

Just then he heard a loud bang from the front of the house. Smoke pulled out of the pussy and went for his 357. He was in a crack house and assumed somebody was trying to rob him. Before he could get to his gun, the bedroom door flew open and two masked men were pointing guns at him. One was holding a 12-guage and the other had what looked like a 9-millimeter. They yelled for him to get on the ground. He could barely hear them over Desire's screams. He did as they told him and lay down on the floor. Smoke figured as long as he complied he would live. He had a half a kilo in the stash – he would give it to them, no problem.

"Nigga, where that shit at?" said the man holding the pistol. Smoke thought he recognized the voice. At that instant the man with the 12-guage stomped on the back of Smoke's head, driving his face into the floor.

"Talk, nigga," he said, putting the cold steel of the shotgun against the back of Smoke's neck.

"It's inside the closet, Nike shoe box on the top shelf," replied Smoke.

Desire was crying and the man with the 9-millimeter put it inside her mouth.

"Shut up, you funky bitch!" he told her as he reached down and fondled her breast. "Maniac, get the shoe box, Cuz," said the man with the gauge.

Smoke heard the name Maniac and knew he was in trouble. He and Maniac had been enemies forever. Ever since he flipped from a Crip to a Blood, Maniac had been trying to kill him. Maniac was a member of the Riverside Crips. He hated Bloods with a passion and hated Smoke for switching sides.

Maniac looked at his homie Lil' Skitzo and wanted to shoot him for saying his name. He planned on killing Smoke, now he had to kill this pretty bitch of his too. Something told him not to smoke that wet (PCP) with him earlier that day, now Lil' Skitzo made a crucial mistake. Knowing he wasn't going to leave a witness, Maniac took off his mask. Looking at Maniac, Smoke almost shit on himself. He knew this crazy ass nigga was going to kill him. Maniac seen the fear in Smoke's eyes and laughed. He walked over to him and kicked him in the mouth, knocking out his two front teeth. He took some duct tape out of his pocket and taped Smoke's hands behind his back. He heard Desire crying and turned his attention back to her.

"Didn't I tell you to shut the fuck up? I'll give you something to cry about, bitch," Maniac said as he walked up to her and put his gun to her temple. With his free hand he pulled out his dick. Desire was still naked on the bed. With his gun still up against her temple, he mounted, and then inserted himself inside of her. She continued to cry as he raped her for the next few minutes. After ejaculating inside of her he got up and grabbed the Nike box in the closet. Inside the shoe box he found the crack. Desire let out a scream. When Maniac came out of the closet he saw Lil' Skitzo had removed his mask and was sodomizing the girl.

"You like this, bitch?" asked Lil' Skitzo. The only consolation for Desire was that she knew both of her attackers would contract HIV from her as neither had put on a condom.

Smoke realized these niggas were preoccupied with Desire and seized the opportunity to escape. With his hands taped behind his back he managed to get to his feet. He ran towards the window, lowered his head, and dove through it asshole naked. With his body sliced up from the broken glass, he got up and ran down the block. Maniac ran to the window and saw

29

Smoke running away. He raised his gun but Smoke was out of view before he could shoot.

Maniac turned around. This crazy motherfucker Lil' Skitzo was still raping the bitch. He tucked the crack and started to shoot both of them but decided not to.

"Skitz, we gotta go."

"Hold on," replied Lil' Skitzo.

Maniac fired his gun into the floor, bringing Lil' Skitzo back to reality.

They left the house, leaving Desire alive but traumatized.

CHAPTER TWELVE
East Side, Distribution City

Saheed was inside one of his grow houses. It was time to harvest this crop. He was in a good mood – growing marijuana was his favorite hobby and this was the best part of it. He looked around the room. It was as if he was standing in the middle of a forest. Big buds were everywhere and it smelled like a skunk had sprayed the room with its scent. Saheed estimated he would get about six pounds off of this crop.

He had multiple strains of weed growing at each house. He had a strain called Skunk #1 – that's what was causing the skunk smell. That strain definitely lived up to its name. He had a strain called blueberry. When smoked, it tasted like blueberries and that was its natural flavor. He also had a strain called Kryptonite. It was the most potent strain of marijuana that he grew. The dark green bud was strong enough to break down Superman – that's how it got its name. The only problem with the Kryptonite was that the plants didn't produce as much as the other strains. That's why he rarely sold any of that. If he did, the most he would sell would be a $50.00 bag and it would only be a blunt's worth. All of his bud was top of the line. He had smuggled all of his strains from Amsterdam years earlier in the form of seeds. He had gone there on vacation. While there he learned how they grew it and was turned out instantly. Now he was a master of the game. He cloned all of his plants from his other plants so he no longer had to deal with seeds. His plants didn't even grow seeds because there were no male plants around to pollinate his females.

Sometimes he would order new strains off the Internet. When people smoke the same weed repeatedly they can get burnt out on it. So he went out of his way to keep variety. It took him all day to cut the plants, trim and hang the buds. It would take at least two weeks before it would be dry and ready to smoke.

He moved his clones into the flowering room where he had just cut down his last crop. At each of his grow houses he kept two grow rooms – one for the vegetative cycle and one for the flowering (budding) cycle. In the vegetative rooms the grow lights would be on 24/7, allowing the plants to grow leaves and get big. When the plants were big enough, he would take clones from them, and then move the plants into the flower room, where the lights came on and off every 12 hours, forcing the plants to grow buds. After 60 days in the flower room, the plants would be ready to harvest. This was how Saheed managed to keep a never-ending supply of Hydro.

As he finished up with his plants he decided he was done selling cocaine. He would leave that to Black and the rest of the hustlers willing to take that risk. He told himself he would open a couple of more grow houses to make up for the money he would lose from his cocaine business.

He told himself he would teach True and Young Mac the game, it was getting to be too much work for one man anyway.

After Polo shot up the Gambling Spot, he shut that operation down until he could find another house. Although he continued to take bets on the sports games, even that was getting to be too stressful. One day he would profit $10,000.00, the next he might lose $30,000.00. Only his weed was for sure and even that wasn't guaranteed. A crop could go bad at anytime, just like a bitch.

Saheed's cell phone rang. He answered, "Yeah?"

"Saheed, the FEDS got an arrest warrant out for Young Mac."

When Saheed got the phone call from True telling him the United States Marshalls were looking for Young Mac, his brain started racing instantly. This changed everything. He wondered why things could never go as planned. He felt bad for his lil' homie because the boy was caught red-handed and Saheed knew he would have to do some time, unless he could get off on some kind of technicality, which was highly unlikely being that he was caught during a task force raid on the block.

Young Mac's album was almost finished – they would have to get that out of the way ASAP. Young Mac had a club song called "Shake it Baby" that was banging and it was radio friendly. They had planned on using that for the first single and to promote the album. He decided he would still move forward with the same plan. They needed to move fast, time was running out.

Saheed jumped into his rental car and made his way over to the studio to go meet Young Mac and True. Saheed had put the Cadillac up until things cooled down in the streets. He had several cars to his name but he didn't want to take the chance of being recognized by anyone.

He pulled up to the Jackson Building and went into his studio/office and was greeted by True, Young Mac, and the smell of Kryptonite. Young Mac passed him the blunt and after the handshakes and hugs they got straight to business.

"Man, them people hit my momma's house looking for me. Got her all worked up and worried about me. I can't go home, I don't know what I'm about to do," said Young Mac.

"Don't even trip, my nigga. Listen and do what I tell you to and everything's gonna be straight," said Saheed. His words were of little comfort.

"Easy for you to say, you ain't looking at a mandatory five years."

"Nigga, if you would have kept the dope in a stash spot like I told you to, instead of walking around with the shit in ya pocket like a damn fool, you wouldn't be in this position."

"I know," replied Young Mac pitifully.

"It is what it is. This is what we're gonna do. Finish them last songs you're working on, then we can get your album mixed and mastered. I want that out of the way in case the feds manage to catch up with you," said Saheed.

"The album is done, we finished it last night. I had Black's cousin Lil' Skitzo drop 16 bars on the '6 Feet Deep' track," True said, jumping into the conversation.

"Did he go hard?" asked Saheed.

"The nigga's lyrics were on point," said Young Mac.

"He was talking about raping bitches and all kinds of sick shit!" added True.

"O.K., I'll check that shit out later. True, take everything over to Magic Studios so they can work their magic. Tell them to mix and master "Shake it Baby" before anything else. I want to get that song to my contacts down at the radio station as soon as possible. Young Mac, I got a spot you can chill at until we make our next move. You gotta lie low for now."

"I know. *Damn*, I fucked up!" said Young Mac.

"Yeah, you fucked up. Life's about the decisions we make. When we make the wrong ones we have to suffer the consequences of our actions. Most importantly we gotta stay strong and handle any situation life throws at us like men," Saheed said, speaking like the role model he was to these young cats. Then he added, "That $4,000.00 I put up for your bail is gone. Feds get their hands on you; you might not get a bond. My lawyer is paid in full. I always give him some 'just in case' money. He's the best, we'll have him represent you but I'm not going to bring this to his attention until the time comes. He will want you to turn yourself in and this ain't the time for that, ya dig?"

"I can dig it," replied Young Mac.

They smoked another blunt and went their separate ways. True took Young Mac's album over to Magic Studios to get mixed and mastered. Saheed took Young Mac back to the weed house he just left from on the east side of town.

When Saheed and Young Mac stepped inside the house, the first thing Young Mac said was "it smells like dank up in here."

Saheed laughed and said, "let me show you something, little homie."

He took him up into the attic where he had hung his buds up to try earlier in the day. When Young Mac saw the buds hanging from wall-to-wall, taking up the whole attic, he thought he died and went to heaven. Young Mac was a "weed-head" for real.

"What's this about 20 pounds?" he asked.

"Naw, it's only gonna be five or six pounds when it dries. It looks like a lot more than it is."

"Saheed, where you get all this shit?"

"I grew it."

"Stop lying."

"When have you ever known me to lie?"

"If you grew this, you're gonna have to teach me how it's done."

"That's the reason I brought you over here. All the bomb we've smoked or sold over the past few years I grew. Why you think I always had the best Chronic?" Saheed said.

On their way down to the basement, Young Mac couldn't believe what he just saw. When they got to the basement and Young Mac saw the hydroponic system, he almost pissed in his pants. The grow lights were so bright they almost blinded him. Saheed handed him a pair of sunglasses. Young Mac was speechless. Looking at the rows of small marijuana plants made him a believer.

"Nigga, you could sit in this house and not leave for years and the FEDS would never find you. When you stepped back outside you'd be a millionaire!" Saheed joked, breaking the silence, even though what he said was true.

"Saheed, you should have been shown me the game."

"Well, you're in training camp now. I'm going to teach you everything I know about this shit, but first things first. You can't call none of your people from here especially your mom's house. The FEDS might have her phone tapped. Second, don't bring anyone over here – not your brother, not your lover – you hear me?"

"Yeah, yeah, I hear you."

"Third, don't tell a soul about this, not even True. I'm going to give him the game when he's ready for it. You hear me?"

"Yes, sir," joked Young Mac, saluting Saheed. "I won't speak on it."

Time went by. Young Mac continued to lay low. His single "Shake it Baby" was a local hit and was getting played on the radio daily. It was a smash hit throughout the clubs in Distribution City. Promoters were calling, wanting Young Mac to perform. The only problem was he had the federal warrant out for his arrest. His album was ready for release. Underworld Entertainment was officially in the game.

CHAPTER FOURTEEN

Mayor Bucks was in a meeting with the D.C. Task Force and the United States Attorney, Herbert C. Dicks.

"We've put together the report you've asked for, Mayor Bucks," said Agent Wilson. Agent Wilson was the officer in charge of operation F.A.L.C.O.N. He had been employed by the D.E.A. for the past 15 years. He had locked up more criminals and innocent people than he could count. He didn't care if the person he arrested was guilty or innocent as long as they got convicted.

On several occasions throughout the years, he'd been forced to plant drugs on suspects to ensure their convictions. He was corrupt. He was also a racist. He believed in white supremacy. He hated blacks more than any other race. Ever since his wife left him for a black man, he'd hated blacks with a passion. When his daughter gave birth to a little black baby, he disowned her and vowed to his white brethren in law enforcement that he would "lock up every nigger possible."

Agent Wilson spoke. "Inside the report we've detailed what we are investigating. We have inner city blacks controlling the crack market, Asian gangs importing ecstasy pills by the millions from overseas, and the Mexican Mafia has a firm grip on heroin, Methamphetamines, cocaine and the marijuana trade." He paused to clear his throat, and then continued. "We got independent drug smugglers bringing in high grade marijuana from Canada, nothing like what the Mexicans are importing from Mexico, its way more potent. Last, but not least, we are finding an increase in people growing pot hydroponically in their houses, right here in Distribution City and throughout the suburbs."

Having waited his turn to speak, U.S. Attorney Dicks interjected "the Task Force has made hundreds of arrests since the start of Operation F.A.L.C.O.N. Of those arrested, many have supplied valuable information to our office. Thus far we've secured hundreds of indictments with many more sure to follow."

Mayor Bucks stood up and said "O.K., gentlemen, I, along with the good citizens of Distribution City appreciate the hard work and effort. Let's keep up the pressure and take back control of the city. Anything else?"

"Yes, Mayor. We have drug dealers from all across the country and overseas doing business in D.C. The reason for that is we apparently are living up to our name. This is a distribution city, meaning drug dealers are getting more for their product here than almost anywhere else in the country. Operation F.A.L.C.O.N. may turn into the biggest drug sweep ever, reaching from coast to coast, and may stretch all the way to China," added Prosecutor Dicks.

"Alright (sniffle), this meeting is over (big sniffle). Mr. Dicks, please stay so I may have a word with you."

After the Task Force left Mayor Bucks said, "This thing is bigger than we imagined, at this rate I'm guaranteed re-election (sniffle)."

"Not only that, Mayor, but with the success of this operation I will be a prime candidate for the Senate."

"Yes (sniffle), this is definitely a win-win situation for us."

"Got a cold, Mayor?"

"No, it's just allergies," replied Mayor Bucks.

The men went their separate ways. Mayor Bucks returned to his office and locked the door, took his envelope containing cocaine out of his desk, emptied the last of its contents onto his desk top, and snorted the drug. He was relieved to have his daily fix. He was upset because he was all out and had to go through the trouble of getting more.

CHAPTER FIFTEEN

Saheed was talking on his cell phone with Black.

"What did you say, Black? My phone's breaking up."

"I said I think I'm being followed."

30 seconds later the truck that was following Black turned a corner.

"Oh, never mind, they turned. I be trippin' sometimes. Dat skunk be having me paranoid."

"Shit, you can't be too safe, my nigga," Saheed said.

"Real talk. Yo, Saheed, I'll be there in a minute."

They both hung up. Saheed laughed to himself about the way Black talked, he was always saying "yo," like he was from New York or some shit. As far as Saheed knew, the nigga hadn't ever even seen the East Coast.

Saheed was waiting on Black to bring him a kilo of cocaine. Even though he was getting out of the game, the demand was still there. One of his customers wanted to buy two keys. So he planned on buying one brick from Black and turning it into two. When he was done he would profit $20,000.00. Saheed looked at it as a quick flip – a power move – all in a day's work. He figured he would check that paper, and then take Kiesha down to the Seafood Room for dinner. He needed to talk to her about her being pregnant. At first he thought she was bluffing, but when he had her take a test it confirmed her pregnancy.

Black pulled his truck behind Saheed's Cadillac. Even though he still had the rental car, he drove the Cadillac because he had an electronic stash built inside of the back seat. Saheed put on the emergency brake, hit a few buttons on the dash in proper sequence, and the back seat folded down, revealing a secret compartment big enough to hold a few assault rifles. From the stash spot Saheed grabbed a bag that had $20,000.00 cash – all $20.00 bills inside of it. At the same time, Black jumped into the Cadillac, holding a bag of his own.

"What's up, Black?"

"What is it, Saheed?"

"$20,000.00, all twenties inside," Saheed said as he handed Black the bag of money. Black passed Saheed the bag with the kilo of cocaine inside of it. Saheed looked inside the bag and noticed the kilo had been vacuum-sealed shut. This was done to keep drug sniffing K9's from smelling the product. Satisfied, Saheed put the bag inside the stash and closed it. Black was the only one who knew about the stash.

"Saheed, when you gonna hook me up with your guy who builds them stash spots? I need one for the truck ASAP."

"Anytime, homie. I'll call him later and tell him you're going to call," said Saheed. Then he gave Black the man's number. "Let me get out of here, I got a tight schedule," Saheed said.

Quickly they shook hands and Black got out of the car. Saheed pulled off with Black following him, at the end of the block Saheed took a left and Black turned right. A few moments later Saheed was driving down Main Street when he noticed a blue Explorer behind him. When Saheed came to his turn, the Ford Explorer turned also. Saheed picked up his cell phone and called Black.

"Say, what kind of car was following you earlier?"

"A blue truck."

"I got a blue truck on my heels right now . . ."

Before Saheed could say anything else the lights started flashing on the Explorer. "It's the police, cousin, they pulling me over. I'll call you back."

"Call me back," Black said and Saheed hung up. He pulled over with the police truck behind him. Two men got out of the truck. They were aiming pistols and yelling for Saheed to put his hands outside of the window and slowly exit the car. He did as he was told and within moments he was in handcuffs and placed into the back of the truck. The two officers were searching his Cadillac. Saheed was nervous. His heart was beating so fast and hard it felt like it was going to jump out of his chest, even though he had the drugs stashed. He was spooked because they had no reason to pull him over or search him. The only reasonable explanation for the search was somebody had to be snitchin'. The only person who knew what he was on was Black. Saheed couldn't bring himself to believe that Black would snitch on him. Things weren't making sense. He told himself just be cool and see how the situation plays out.

The officer with the red face and the beer belly came back to the truck and yanked Saheed out of the vehicle, punched him in his gut, then demanded *"where are the guns and drugs?!"*

"I don't know what you're talking about, officer," replied Saheed. The officer then reached inside of Saheed's back pocket and pulled out his wallet. Taking out Saheed's driver's license and reading from it he said, "Corey James. Or shall I just call you Saheed?"

When the cop mentioned the name Saheed, he knew someone was snitching. Saheed's government name was Corey

James. Saheed was the Holy name his father had given him. His father explained to him Corey James was a slave name and that's why a Holy name was necessary. Saheed was also his street moniker and what people knew him as. When it came to the government and official business, he was known only as Corey James. Being that this pig knew his alias was proof somebody was talking to them people, but who, Saheed wondered.

"The K9 is about to be here. Make it easy on yourself and tell me where the dope is, you drug-dealing Motherfucker," the officer said, with a country accent, before punching Saheed in the stomach for the second time. Saheed had the wind knocked out of him from the blow. When he caught his breath he spit in the cop's face and said "suck my black nigger dick, you punk bitch."

Saheed's verbal assault on the officer was cut off in mid-sentence with a blow to the jaw that knocked him to the ground. With his hands cuffed behind his back, Saheed hit the concrete face first. The cop didn't stop there. He started kicking and stomping on Saheed as hard as he could.

"Wilson, what's going on?" asked Agent Wilson's partner.

"This black pile of shit spit in my face!" he hollered back and kept kicking Saheed, who was curled up in the fetal position, trying his best to block the blows from his attacker. Never one to miss an opportunity to beat on a nigger, Agent Wilson's partner approached Saheed and kicked him in the back of the head, knocking him semi-unconscious. The crooked cops continued to pound Saheed and he thought they were going to kill him. Out of nowhere a feeble voice said "hey, what's going on here?"

Saheed glanced up and saw an elderly white woman holding a pen and notepad.

"Official police business ma'am, go back in your house," ordered Agent Wilson.

Acting on instinct Saheed yelled, "Miss, please call the police. They're trying to kill me; they're not the real police."

The old woman spoke to Agent Wilson, "give me your badge number; I'm calling 9-1-1." She looked at the other cop and said "I need yours too."

The officers looked at each other with confusion written all over their faces when Agent Wilson said to the elderly woman, "here's my badge number, but I assure you that's one of the bad guys," and he pointed at Saheed, then went on, saying "he tried to attack me."

"That's nonsense. I've been watching since you pulled him over." She wrote his badge number down and said, "I'm going

inside and calling 9-1-1. That man needs medical attention."
She turned and walked towards her house. Agent Wilson was so
angry he felt like shooting the old bitch and the nigger in
handcuffs. He turned to Saheed and said, "Looks like it's your
lucky day," and then spit in Saheed's face; the spit mixing with
his blood, then kicked him one last time before removing the
handcuffs. Walking back to his truck he said "see you soon,
Saheed," over his shoulder. The cops got back into the Ford
Explorer and drove away.

Even though he was in excruciating pain, Saheed was happy
to see the truck pull away. He was glad they didn't find his dope
and he was thankful he was still alive. Dragging himself to his
feet he thanked the Lord for that Angel disguised as an old
woman.

Saheed got into the Cadillac and drove home. When he got
there he went straight to the medicine cabinet and grabbed a
bottle of syrup (Promethizine with Codeine). Removing the top,
he swallowed the half-empty bottle in one drink and went and lay
down. He fell asleep instantly.

Saheed awoke to Kiesha giving him a sponge bath. At first he was confused, and then he remembered everything that happened.

"Baby, what time is it? He asked, catching Kiesha off guard by his words. Kiesha just looked at Saheed for a moment, relieved that he regained consciousness; a tear fell from her eye.

"It's 5:00 p.m. You have been asleep since I got home from work yesterday, Saheed. Tell me what happened to you."

"The police beat my ass," as he said this he realized his head hurt in the worst way.

"Oh my God, I've been so worried. Look at your face," Kiesha said as she held up a hand-held mirror.

"Damn," Saheed said, looking at his two black eyes, lumped-up face and slightly crooked nose. "Them pussies broke my nose." Looking at his face, his anger started to build – the longer he looked the madder he got. He moved to get out of the bed and pain shot through his body.

"Kiesha, I need you to get me some more syrup when you go to work." Kiesha worked in the pharmacy down at the hospital. She was able to get anything she wanted when it came to prescription drugs.

"What you need to do is go down to the Emergency Room. When I came home yesterday, I noticed the empty bottle and figured you would want some more so I grabbed a bottle for you today before I left work."

"Would you fix me a glass, baby?"

"Anything for you, Daddy," she said, and she meant it.

Saheed wanted some more syrup ASAP, he knew the codeine inside of it would take away some of the pain. Kiesha came back into the bedroom holding a glass of Sprite. She set the glass down on the dresser and removed the bottle of syrup from her purse and began pouring some into the glass, causing the Sprite to turn purple in color. She handed the glass to Saheed and he took a sip, lifted the glass back to his mouth, and drank it all. Saheed loved the taste of syrup and had a tendency to abuse the stuff. Kiesha watched him drink it all and shook her head saying, "that's a dam shame, you're lucky you're hurt." She didn't approve of him drinking syrup or smoking weed but she knew she couldn't stop him.

"Lucky I got you," he replied.

"Daddy, you need to go see a doctor."

"Baby, you're my doctor." This made her blush and she lay down next to her man and told him she loved him. "Kiesha, do me another favor and hand me my cell phone and roll me a blunt."

"Yes, Daddy. I turned your cell phone off because it wouldn't stop ringing," she said and handed him the phone. When he turned the phone on he had 17 new voicemail messages and ten text messages. The majority of them were either from Black or people trying to buy some green. There was a message from Kross Kountry Distribution – they wanted to set up a meeting and possibly give Underworld Entertainment a distribution deal. With the response Young Mac's single "Shake it Baby" was getting, a distribution deal was guaranteed.

Kiesha handed Saheed the blunt she had rolled him. He lit it and started smoking.

"Kiesha, take my phone and write down all my contact numbers."   knowing he had over 100 numbers in the phone and Being lazy she replied "I can't right now, I'm busy."

This surprised Saheed, he was expecting her to say "yes, Daddy," like always. He asked "busy doing what?"

"Pleasing my man," she responded and kissed him on his neck. Then she began flicking her tongue down his chest, across his mid-section. "Hi, Big Killa," said Keisha, talking to Saheed's dick like she always did. He was hard as wood and even though he was in pain he was ready for some action. Kiesha was working her tongue back and forth between his sack and his shaft. And when she finally put him in her mouth he forgot about the pain. Saheed thought to himself that he had his own personal porn star.

Then he started thinking about what he had to do. Being that someone was snitching, he had to get a new cell phone. Same for the rest of his inner circle. He decided he would call a meeting so they could figure out what's going down and what to do about it. He wasn't going to risk selling the coke he had, he knew Black wouldn't give him a refund. So he'd just "front" the kilo to True, even though True never had that much dope, he should be able to handle it with no problem. He told himself if he ever gets the opportunity he would kill that cop Wilson for beating him like he did.

He thought about how much money he would make when Young Mac's album dropped. If it sold like he was expecting it to, he planned on retiring completely from the dope game; although he would still grow marijuana for his own personal use.

Saheed's thoughts were distracted by the tension building inside of him. Kiesha was doing her thing and he couldn't take it anymore. He felt an explosion as Kiesha drained him of everything. She moaned "mmmm . . ." as she swallowed every drop without breaking her rhythm and kept on going like she was the Energizer Bunny. Saheed hit the blunt one more time and set it in the ashtray. Kiesha didn't stop until he fell back asleep.

CHAPTER SEVENTEEN
Downtown Distribution City

Saheed, Black, True and Young Mac were lounging inside of Lucy's Cabaret. Lil' Skitzo was supposed to meet them down there to discuss performing with Young Mac at his album release party. A few weeks had gone by since Agent Wilson's assault on Saheed. Since then, Saheed had managed to secure a distribution deal with Kross-Kountry Distribution with Underworld Entertainment bringing home $8.00 for every compact disc sold. Young Mac's contract agreed to a $2.00 per album cut, with Underworld Entertainment (Saheed) banking the remaining $6.00.

A stripper named Desire was giving them a table dance. She had the undivided attention of Young Mac, True and Black. Saheed's attention was diverted to the stage where Rose, Saheed's ex-whore, was working her body like the professional she was. Between the old white men and the young hustler who were making it rain $1.00 bills, the stage was covered with money.

When the song ended, Desire climbed down from the table and sat on Black's lap, caressing his dick. She asked if he wanted to go to the VIP booth – seconds later they were on their way.

Inside the booth, Black sat on the couch and Desire went straight to work, rubbing her big ass against Black.

"Desire, I'm trying to fuck, what's good?" asked Black.

She responded "$200.00, Big Daddy," then she stepped out of her thong so Black could get a good look at her dripping wet pussy. He pulled two one-hundred dollar bills off of his large bankroll and gave them to her. "I don't have any condoms," said Black. He never carried condoms; he was one of those cats who liked it raw.

"Then it's gonna cost you $400.00," said Desire with a smile, happy she had herself another victim.

Black gave her an additional $200.00 and pulled out his dick. She bent over and began sucking him to full erection. When satisfied, she climbed on top of him, riding his dick to the best of her ability. As she rode him she was thinking about how fucked up she was for passing around HIV like it was candy, but she reasoned someone gave it to her so it's only fair.

"Oooh, Black, you feel so good," said Desire.

Black was feeling himself about to cum and said "stop, I paid to fuck you, not get fucked." He pulled himself out of her, turned her around, and slid back inside. After ejaculating all over her ass cheeks and back, Black got dressed and left the VIP booth without saying a word to Desire.

As he entered the main room, he saw his cousin, Lil' Skitzo, talking to Young Mac and True at the bar so he joined them.

Saheed was at the table still, sipping on some Hennessey and Coke while having a conversation with Rose. She was saying "I miss you, Saheed."

"What the fuck you telling me for?" was his response. He was thinking about how dumb she was and he knew she wanted to come home.

"That motherfucka Icy Waters locks me inside his house every day. The only time I get to leave is when it's time to get money. He told me if I try to leave him he will kill me and my mother."

"What the fuck are you telling me for, Rose? I saw Icy the other day flossing in a new Mercedes Benz and he told me your pussy paid for it, so unless you're trying to see me driving a Rolls Royce that you paid for, there's nothing left for us to talk about," Saheed said with a cold expression on his face.

With tears in her eyes, Rose pleaded, "Please help me, Saheed. I'm sorry. I never should have left you. I'll do anything you want me to, just get him off my back."

Just then Icy Waters walked into the club with one of his pimp friends. When he saw Rose talking to Saheed he went straight over to the table and said to Rose, "Bitch, you're out of pocket. Get your shit and go get in the car."

Rose started to get up but Saheed put his hand on her thigh and stopped her. Then Saheed said to Icy Waters, "the bitch is leaving with me. It's over for you pimpin'." What Saheed said caught Icy Waters off guard. Rose continued to sit and was staring at the floor. Icy Waters said, "Rose," when she ignored him he realized what time it was and said "Saheed, you can have that bum bitch back. I got badder bitches paying me daily."

He then shook Saheed's hand and left as quick as he came, upset that Rose went bad on him. Saheed and Rose were at the table laughing. Rose was happy to be through with Icy Waters, Saheed was laughing because he knew Icy Waters didn't want no problems with him.

It was Rose's turn to get up on the stage. She went and got on the stage and Saheed joined the others at the bar. Black said to Saheed, "I see you got your bitch back."

"You already know," replied Saheed.

"Yo, that slut Desire got some fire pussy!" Black said.

"Yeah? She let you hit it?" asked Saheed.

"Pussy good," Black responded.

"I hope you used a rubber," said Saheed, knowing his friend hated condoms.

Just then Desire walked up and asked Black to buy her a drink. Black looked at her crazy and said "I think you can afford your own."

Desire replied, "Whatever, nigga," and told the bartender to bring her an Apple Martini. Desire turned from the bar and saw Lil' Skitzo staring at her. She recognized him instantly as one of the niggas who raped her. Lil' Skitzo was so high when he raped Desire that he didn't recognize his victim, he was only staring at her because he thought she was beautiful. He smiled at her and she mugged him back. His smile made her want to cut his throat; she wanted to hurt him like he hurt her. When Lil' Skitzo approached her and asked "hey, sexy, what's your name?" she realized the nigga didn't recognize her and if he did he was a good actor. She decided to play along and got his phone number.

The music stopped and the DJ said into the microphone, "Ladies, make sure y'all show some luv to Young Mac, one of Distribution City's finest. Be sure to thank him for blessing us with his presence and the hottest strip club anthem ever!"

Young Mac lifted his drink in salute to the DJ. Then the DJ pressed "play" and Young Mac's single "Shake it Baby" started pounding through the speakers. The club was packed and everyone seemed to be singing along with the chorus as it went, *"dancing-like she's in a video, shake it baby; I love the way you work that, shake it baby; you got me hypnotized girl, shake it baby; turn around, don't stop, shake, shake it baby."*

Rose was on the stage and the way she was moving made her ass look like it was having a seizure. This was driving the tricks crazy and they were tossing piles of money on the stage. At the same time, the other strippers surrounded Young Mac. They were dancing and shaking their asses in unison while True and Black were making it rain with what looked to Saheed like thousands of dollar bills. Ever since Saheed gave True that kilo, he'd been running around thinking he was Scarface or somebody. Saheed watched True throw away money while thinking about the $10,000.00 True still owed him. He looked at Lil' Skitzo, who was mean-mugging Young Mac like he hated the man. Saheed thought it must be jealousy or envy and made a mental note to watch him. They continued to kick it until 4:00 a.m., when it was time for the club to close. Black, Young Mac and

True said they were going to Black's house – they had five strippers down for "whatever." Lil' Skitzo had left earlier with Desire. Rose had given Saheed everything she made that night (almost $3,000.00) so he decided to take her to a hotel and come up with a new game plan.

CHAPTER EIGHTEEN
Distribution City, Southside

Lil' Skitzo and Desire were riding through the southside with Desire behind the wheel of Lil' Skitzo's Tahoe. Lil' Skitzo had purchased the truck with the drug money he made after he and Maniac robbed Smoke.

"This is a nice truck," Desire said.

Lil' Skitzo didn't reply. His head was spinning from all the alcohol he drank at Lucy's Cabaret. He felt like he was about to throw up, so he rolled down the window. The fresh air helped clear his head and he regained control of himself.

"Are we almost there?" Lil' Skitzo asked Desire. He was ready to bust a nut and go to sleep.

"Almost," said Desire, thinking how she would like to cut his dick off and stuff it into his mouth. Only problem with that was she didn't think she could go through with it. Back at Lucy's Cabaret, Desire had called Smoke and told him the situation. He instructed her to get the nigga alone and bring him back to the spot – the same house where she was raped. Her and Smoke stopped kicking it after that incident but they still kept in touch. She didn't like Smoke's plan but she was high off the two ecstasy pills she had taken earlier that night and went against her better judgment.

Smoke had told her to bring the nigga into the house, that the door would be open. When she pulled up to the crack house, Lil' Skitzo was asleep. She started caressing his dick and he woke up.

"Come on, let's go inside." They got out and were walking up to the house when Lil' Skitzo recognized the house from the robbery. He looked at Desire and realized he had raped her.

"Hold on, I forgot something in my truck," Lil' Skitzo said as he turned to leave. At that instant, a man came from around the side of the house, dressed in black with a red rag covering his face. He was holding a 357. Without saying a word he opened fire. The first bullet caught Lil' Skitzo in the temple and tore a hole in his forehead, killing him instantly. Desire started to scream when she was cut off by a hollow-tipped slug to the chest. Smoke blasted a few more rounds into each body, and then disappeared into the night like a shadow in the dark.

*****

West Side, Distribution City

Black, True and Young Mac were all enjoying themselves, as were the five strippers that followed them back to Black's house. After the DJ introduced Young Mac to them at the club, they were all on his dick; they were all competing for him. Young Mac spoke up saying "Ladies, I understand it's not every night that you're in the presence of a rap star, but it ain't as fun if the homies can't have none. Show them some luv. We all big fish."

Black walked over to a stripper named Juicy, took her hand and said, "Come upstairs with me, I need to talk to you." She followed him to a bedroom upstairs. Juicy was impressed with Black's house and the way it was furnished. The master bedroom where Black brought her was ultra-plush. She knew what Black wanted and decided to let him have his way with her. Without saying a word, Black grabbed hold of Juicy's long ponytail, pulling her head back and exposing her neck. Then he bit her softly and started sucking on her neck.

"Nigga, what kind of freak are you?" she asked playfully with a Southern accent. Juicy was a dime piece with a body other women would kill to have, and a few men died fighting over her. Black just wanted to fuck. With both hands on her thighs he raised up her skirt revealing the prettiest pussy Black had ever seen. Black laid Juicy down on his king-size bed and started undressing.

After getting undressed, he dimmed the lights and got in the bed.

"Black, I want you to eat my pussy," Juicy said, seductively. Black, being the freaky motherfucker that he was, had no problem with that and went straight to work, diving in head-first. Black was working his tongue like the professional he was, causing Juicy to have multiple orgasms and she couldn't stop cumming. Living up to her name, Juicy's juice was flowing and Black was drinking it up like Kool-Aid. He even licked her asshole before he was done.

Black told Juicy, "turn around – I'm a gonna hit it from the back."

"Put a condom on," she told him.

"If you insist," Black replied, and walked over to the dresser, cursing to himself. Taking a condom out of the drawer, he put it on in front of her. Climbing back on the bed he got behind her, pulled the condom off, and entered her. They both let out a moan at the same time. Juicy's stuff was so hot and tight Black told himself he'd never had any better. Unable to hold back,

Black came, releasing his semen inside of Juicy. Juicy felt Black cum and could feel the semen inside of her. Black tried to keep going but she pushed him off of her. When she saw he wasn't wearing a condom she said, "oh, hell, no! Nigga, you bogus!"

Black just laughed and said "the shower's in there," and pointed towards the bathroom. Juicy went and got in the shower, ready to cry because Black came in her and she didn't want to get pregnant. An STD didn't even cross her mind. Black went downstairs without bothering to put some clothes on. When he entered the living room, everyone was naked and having sex. Young Mac was lying on the couch with one of the strippers riding his dick and the other was riding his tongue. True was sitting on the recliner getting some head from an Asian stripper named Chyna. Black had wanted to fuck Chyna for a long time, so he got behind her and just stuck it in – with a mouthful of dick she couldn't protest. Black didn't know it, but he was HIV positive even before he had sex with Desire.

*****

Downtown, Distribution City

Inside the Marriot, Saheed and Rose were lounging in a Jacuzzi, sipping on champagne and having a good time reminiscing. The conversation became more serious when Saheed said "everything is different now, Rose. I shut down the Gambling Spot after it got shot up, niggas is getting murdered every day and night out here in the streets, Underworld Entertainment is about to blow up, Young Mac's album is going nationwide."

Rose just sat there looking dumb, and then said "I didn't know the Gambling Spot got shot up, that's crazy. Listen, Saheed, there's something I want to tell you. That bastard Icy Waters has a suitcase full of money hidden at his house on the southside."

She then told Saheed the address and where the suitcase was, and how easy it would be to steal it. Saheed made a mental note, and then changed the subject. "Rose, I'm sending you down to Miami. My partner's got a high-class escort operation popping down there. Every call will be for $1,500.00 or more, we need to be getting some of that money, you dig?"

Rose had always wanted to go to Miami; the thought of it brought a smile to her face. "I'm down for whatever, Saheed," she replied.

Saheed got out of the Jacuzzi and went and lay down on the bed as the air dried him. Rose came out a moment later and was dripping sex. She took a condom out of her purse and approached Saheed. Watching her walk had him rock hard. Rose took the condom from the package and placed it in her mouth. Without using her hands, she put the condom on Saheed's dick and rolled it down, using her lips. She didn't want to use a condom with Saheed but she knew he wouldn't have it any other way. She sucked on him through the condom for awhile, then climbed on top of him and started riding him backwards, loving every inch of the big dick inside her. She then leaned forward and started bouncing her ass like it was a basketball. They continued to fuck until they were both exhausted and couldn't take any more.

CHAPTER NINETEEN
South Side, Distribution City

Saheed, Young Mac and True were riding in Saheed's Cadillac, discussing the death of Lil' Skitzo and Desire. They were on their way to go check out the address Rose gave Saheed.

"I can't believe they're dead," said True.

"I know. That's crazy. We were just kicking it last night," said Young Mac.

"That boy Black is shook right now. He told me his auntie, Lil' Skitzo's mother, had a nervous breakdown when they told her that her son was murdered. He told me there weren't any witnesses and the police don't have any suspects," added Saheed.

"It had to have been those Bloods, I can't understand why he would even go in their neighborhood, the man was slipping," said True, shaking his head.

"I told him to ride out with us. Chasing that bitch Desire got that nigga killed," Young Mac said.

"That's what happens when you think with your dick. We all need to learn from his mistake. So what went down at Black's house?" asked Saheed.

"It went down. I fucked two of them hoes," bragged Young Mac.

"I hope you used a condom, all them bitches do is sell pussy all day," said Saheed.

"You already know," replied Young Mac.

"I couldn't hit nothing, I didn't have any rubbers so I just got some head and went to sleep," said True.

"I'm surprised you didn't go bareback, horny ass nigga," Saheed said to True.

"I can't be out here slip-sliding in the raw. That shit's dangerous, people catching AIDS and shit. I don't need that. But your boy Black's a fool. I had that Asian chick giving me some head and this nigga creep up behind her and just started fucking with no condom," True said, as he laughed about it.

"That cat's burnt out. He's known for doing shit like that," Saheed said as he slowed the car down and started looking at the addresses on houses he passed.

"That's the house right there – that's Icy Waters' Mercedes in the driveway."

He kept driving, and then said "I think we should go in now. True and Young Mac didn't have any objections, they both trusted Saheed's judgment. Saheed pulled over and opened his stash spot, removing three pistols and ski masks, handing one of each to his young soldiers. His dick got hard just thinking about the suitcase full of cash money. Saheed looked up and saw Icy Waters' Mercedes drive through the intersection.

"This may be easier than I thought," said Saheed.

They all got out of the car and started walking around the corner towards Icy Waters' house. It was after dark so nobody noticed the three strangers walking through the neighborhood. As they approached the house they pulled the ski masks over their faces and ran to the back door. Leaning against Young Mac for support, Saheed kicked the door locks as hard as he could and it flew open. They heard a beeping sound, indicating an alarm system and a dog started barking as they stormed into the house. They were barely inside when a giant Rottweiler blocked their path. The dog was growling and baring its teeth. Saheed was about to shoot it when True fired his gun, striking the beast in its torso. The dog let out a whimper and limped away, dripping blood. They went into every room in the house to make sure nobody was home. After securing the house, Saheed rushed to the bedroom where the suitcase was supposed to be. Just like Rose said he would, he found the Gucci suitcase in the closet. A quick peek inside revealed what he was looking for. Snatching up the suitcase, Saheed yelled for the others to "come on," they followed him out of the house. In and out. They ran back to the car as fast as possible, knowing the police were probably on their way to respond to the alarm. Inside of the car, Saheed quickly put the guns, ski masks and money in the stash spot. He had to take the cash out of the suitcase to make it fit. Young Mac and True couldn't believe their eyes, watching Saheed fill the stash with cash. Closing the stash spot, Saheed put the car in drive and drove off. Doing the speed limit and being careful not to break any traffic laws, they were only a few blocks from the freeway when the police got behind them.

Just as Saheed was going to get on the freeway, the police car turned its lights on. Saheed pulled the Cadillac over and told the others to be cool. After a few minutes, the officer approached and asked for a driver's license and proof of insurance. Saheed handed the officer what he asked for and the cop returned to the squad car. A moment later another squad car pulled up and Saheed started wishing he never pulled over. Young Mac was scared. Even though Saheed had helped him obtain a fake ID, he had never used it and wasn't sure if it would work. Plus, he was thinking about the money in the stash and wondered if it was too good to be true. The officer returned to the window and handed Saheed his driver's license and insurance card. Then the officer commented "we had a burglary in the neighborhood, do you mind if we search your car?"

"Yes, I mind. I do not consent to a search," replied Saheed.

"Get out of the car," said the officer.

"I said, 'I do not consent to a search'."

"Get the fuck out!" the officer commanded as he drew his gun. At the same time the other officer on the scene pulled Young Mac and True out of the car. All three were placed in handcuffs and put in the squad cars – Saheed in one, Young Mac and True in the other. Saheed watched in silence as the pigs disrespectfully dug through his car and trunk. He wasn't worried because his stash spot was built professionally and he was sure they wouldn't find it. Young Mac was in the other squad sweating hard. He was scared they would find out his ID was false and, even worse, find the money and guns in the stash. The cop came and let Saheed out of the squad and took his handcuffs off, then said "we're going to run a warrant check on your friends and then you guys will be free to leave."

Saheed was relieved they didn't find anything. He went back to his car and started cleaning up the mess they made. While he was cleaning his car he said a short prayer for Young Mac, asking the Lord to not let them find out about the fake ID.

A few minutes later the police let True and Young Mac out of the second squad car and removed the handcuffs. One of the officers noticed Young Mac's shirt was wet from perspiration and noted, "You boys are up to something. Consider yourself lucky because you got away with it for now."

Without responding they walked to the Cadillac and got in with Saheed, put the car in drive, and 15 minutes later they pulled into the garage at the grow house Young Mac had been staying at. Saheed grabbed the money from the stash and they went in the house to count and divide it. Saheed dumped the money on the floor and everybody just looked at it for a moment. It was separated in stacks. They counted the cash - $190,000.00 in total, all in ten and twenty-dollar bills. Saheed took the lion's share ($90,000.00) for himself and gave Young Mac and True $50,000.00 each. They were happy with that. He had told them before they left that he would be taking half of whatever they made that night.

Saheed rolled up a blunt. As they were smoking they talked about the night's events. Everyone was in a good mood. Saheed showed True his hydroponic system and gave him the game. True was amazed, as was everyone who had never seen a marijuana operation. He told True he could keep the $10,000.00 he still owed for the kilo. Then they made plans to open up weed houses for True and Young Mac. Saheed knew Icy Waters had a lot more money than what he found because there were only ten and twenty-dollar bills. He wondered where he kept all the fifties and hundreds.

CHAPTER TWENTY
Downtown, Distribution City

Agent Wilson was inside the Federal Building talking to the U.S. Attorney, Herbert C. Dicks.

"Did you hear about the bodies that were found on the southside last week?" Agent Wilson asked.

"Yes, I read about it in the D.C. Tribune," Mr. Dicks replied.

"Well, the young man who was murdered just happened to be a prize informant of mine."

"No shit? Killing a federal informant, somebody's going to jail for life," stated Dicks.

"See, that's the problem. We don't have anything to go on. No clues, no witnesses, no evidence. His name was Andre Williams. He was a member of the Riverside Crips. This guy had problems with everybody. Other than him being killed on the Bloods' turf, we got nothing," Agent Wilson said with a disgusted look on his face.

"I assume his death damages part of your investigation?" asked Prosecutor Dicks.

"Well, Mr. Williams had made a few controlled buys for us, nothing major. But he was giving us information on some dealers from the northside of town that are supposed to be big time. He said he knew all about their operation because one of them was his cousin."

"Did he make any controlled buys from these alleged 'big time dealers'?"

"Unfortunately, no. We were working on that before he passed unexpectedly. Although I have made contact with one of them. They call him Saheed. He's a dirty shit bag. I will be more than happy when we lock his ass up," said Agent Wilson.

"I wonder if it's the same Saheed I've been hearing about. A few informants have brought up the name but none of them could give me anything solid."

"If it's the same guy, I won't rest until he's doing twenty years in a Federal Penitentiary."

"Bring me some concrete evidence against him and I'll get him locked up for life."

True and Young Mac were debating on what they should do with their share of the money they had stolen.

"I know Saheed says we need to invest the money, but I got the urge to go treat myself to something nice," said Young Mac.

"I'm feeling the same way. We need to do it big, we deserve it," said True, thinking what he could spend his cash on.

"Let's go down to Jimmy's Jewelry and see what he got for sale," said Young Mac.

An hour later they walked out of Jimmy's Jewelry with matching Date-Just Rolexes with the diamond face and iced-out bezels. They spent $7,500.00 each on them. Young Mac dropped an additional $5,000.00 on a gold chain and cross medallion with ten carats of Princess-cut diamonds. True spent another $2,000.00 on a pinkie ring. From there they went to the mall where they both spent thousands on new wardrobes.

Young Mac's album release party was coming up in a few days and they were ready to get their shine on. Saheed had rented out Club Millennium for the party. The local DJs were promoting the album's release and the club was expected to be filled to capacity.

It took a long time for Young Mac to record his album and everyone was ready to reap the rewards. Since True had produced the album, Saheed agreed to give him $1.00 for each album sold.

When Saheed saw their jewels he just laughed because he knew they would go spend their money on something foolish. Then he told them they should have each put that money down on a house. Saheed told them to hold the rest of their cash until he talked to his realtor; he wanted them to be growing their own marijuana ASAP. The demand for the stuff was so high there was never enough to go around. As soon as Saheed would harvest a crop, it would get sold instantly.

Lil' Skitzo's funeral was going to be held the same day as Young Mac's album release party. Lil' Skitzo was supposed to perform with Young Mac.

"It's a shame we never got to do the show together. 'Cuz had some talent," said Young Mac, thinking about his dead homie.

"That's how it goes in the hood – here today and gone tomorrow, just like that," said Saheed.

"I hate them Blood niggas, them cats swear they're hard. I'm mad enough to take another ride to the southside," stated True.

Nobody said anything in response. They were all thinking about the Southside Massacre.

The silence was interrupted by the ringing of Saheed's phone. It was Rose calling from Miami. She told Saheed everything was cool, the money was being made and she was stacking it like he told her to. He told her he wanted to see her soon, and then hung up the phone. He decided at that moment he would take True and Young Mac to Miami after they handled all their business in D.C., but he didn't let them know what he had planned.

They decided to go for a ride. Saheed had stopped renting cars now that he had gotten the Cadillac painted. It had been black, now it was cocaine white with a black tint on the windows. Even though the police knew he drove it, he figured he was safe because of his stash spot. He loved that he had the electric stash spot in the Cadillac. Other than that he didn't give a fuck about the car. Saheed could afford to drive anything he wanted but believed in keeping a low profile. They were cruising down a backstreet when they spotted Polo's Caprice parked in front of an apartment building. They knew it was Polo's by the design on the chrome 22" rims on the car. Saheed's heart rate started to rise as he devised a spur-of-the-moment plan to X-Polo out of the game. He drove up a block and parked, watching the Caprice through the rearview.

He still had the guns and ski masks in the stash. He opened it and gave both True and Young Mac a pistol and a mask, also grabbing one of each for himself. The guns he gave them were both 9 mm Rugers. He was holding his 45. Smith & Wesson, the same one he pistol whipped LaTasha with. He circled around the block and parked about 100 feet behind Polo's Caprice. He didn't want to have True and Young Mac involved in his shit, but after they put in that work on them Blood niggas with him he knew they could handle it.

The plan was to wait until Polo came out of the building and when he got in the car they would drive along-side him and open fire. They waited, waited and waited . . . no Polo.

Three hours later, True and Young Mac were talking about how bad they had to piss. Saheed needed to shit so they pulled off and looked at it like Polo's lucky day.

Back at the house they took turns relieving themselves. Afterwards, Saheed rolled a couple of blunts and they all got high. Sitting around high and knowing where Polo may be was driving Saheed crazy. Young Mac and True passed out from the Kryptonite. Saheed decided to go back and see if he could catch that nigga Polo slipping. On his way out the door, True saw him leaving and asked "where you going?"

He answered, "I'll be right back," and walked out the door. True knew exactly where he was going.

Back on the block, the Caprice was still parked in front of the building. Saheed parked in the same spot he had been in earlier that day. The sun had set and it was dark outside, the cover of darkness made Saheed's job that much easier.

He had been sitting there for 45 minutes when he saw Polo emerge from the apartment building; his face and silhouette were lit up from the lights on the front of the building. Watching Polo walk to the Caprice, Saheed took the Smith & Wesson off safety; he already had one bullet in the chamber. Then he put on his ski mask.

When Polo got in his car, Saheed made his move. He put the car in drive. As he rolled down the passenger side window and eased up alongside the Caprice, he had his 45. in his right hand and his left was on the steering wheel. Slowing to a stop, Polo's face came into view and Saheed squeezed the trigger. *"Bang, bang, bang,"* barked the 45. There was a light tint on the Caprice's windows which kept the window from shattering but there were three holes in the window, and the window was covered with blood. Saheed saw Polo's body slump to the side so he emptied his remaining five shots through the driver's door and drove off as if he hadn't done anything.

Polo was hit in the back of the head from the first shot – the next two missed. When the bullets started coming through the door, he was hit in the chest, stomach and legs. He was wearing a bullet-proof vest, which stopped the slug that hit his chest from penetrating his heart.

Police and paramedics responded quickly and he was rushed to the hospital. The surgeons operated and he was placed on life support. When the police first arrived and found Polo bleeding to death, they found nine ounces of crack cocaine in his pockets and a semi-automatic pistol on his waist. They assumed it was a drug-related shooting and wrote it off as a drug deal gone bad.

Thunder could be heard in the distance as heavy rain pounded the pavement. Inside the First Baptist Church, mourners wept and were grieving over the death of Andre Williams (a.k.a. Lil' Skitzo).

The first four rows were filled with Lil' Skitzo's relatives. Black was seated in the front row next to Lil' Skitzo's mother. The remaining rows were taken by friends and acquaintances, mostly gang members. It seemed like every Crip in the city showed up for their dead homies funeral. A lot of people had to stand because all the seats were taken.

Saheed, True and Young Mac were among those standing. The preacher was finishing up with the eulogy when he started speaking out against gang-banging and black-on-black violence. He seized the opportunity and asked the gang members in attendance to come forward and give their lives to God.

The family was forced to have a closed casket service due to the damage that was done to Lil' Skitzo's face when he died.

After the service ended, people started making their way to their vehicles. The sound of thunder drowned out Lil' Skitzo's mother's sobs. The people in the church quickly realized that it wasn't thunder they were hearing – *it was gunshots!* The preacher told everyone to get on the floor and started praying loudly.

The shooting stopped and there was mass confusion inside and outside of the church. People were moving in every direction, women were screaming, and police sirens could be heard in the distance. Someone had done a drive-by.

Outside three members of the Crips were on the ground bleeding, all of them were conscious and yelling out in agony. Black and Lil' Skitzo's cousin, Kendra, were sitting on a bench crying, she had been shot in the thigh. She was standing in front of the church talking to Maniac when a car pulled up, someone inside shouted, "what's up, Blood?" then started shooting. Maniac had been hit also; he was rolling around on the ground holding his stomach.

When the police arrived, Kendra told them everything she could remember before she was put in an ambulance and taken to the hospital. She was the only witness willing to talk to the police. Everyone else who saw what happened were Crips and they weren't saying anything.

Maniac and the others who were wounded were all taken to the Emergency Room and were expected to survive.

Even with all the pandemonium, Lil' Skitzo still had to be laid to rest. After all the drama, his body was transported to the D.C. cemetery, along with a police escort, where he was buried without any further disruptions.

CHAPTER TWENTY THREE
Club Millennium, Downtown Distribution City

Young Mac's album release party was jumping hard. Everybody who was somebody was in the house. The club was filled beyond its capacity. Saheed had quadrupled the money he spent on renting the club out by charging $15.00 a head at the door. It was $50.00 for VIP.

Club Millennium had a room called the Plasma Room. It was actually the whole third level of the establishment. They called it the Plasma Room because of the giant plasma TVs that were set up. The TVs showed the stage where Young Mac was set to perform later that evening. Some showed live video of what was popping in the VIP section on the second level. Others showed what was going down on the dance floor on the main level. The Plasma Room had its own private bar and if you weren't on the list security wasn't letting you in.

Tonight the Plasma Room was reserved for Underworld Entertainment and its affiliates. Everybody in there had a bottle of champagne. Blunts of hydro were being passed around between the ladies and gentlemen, the ballers and shot-callers, the pimps and hoes, and the niggas and bitches.

Saheed was lounging on a couch with Kiesha sitting next to him. He didn't want her to come but she begged him and said she wanted to see Young Mac's show. He agreed to let her come but told her she had to leave after the performance because she was pregnant with his child and he didn't want her caught up in the middle of a fistfight. His real reason for not wanting her to come to the party was he knew the place would be packed with women and Kiesha was extremely jealous. She knew Saheed was a whore master since before she met him, but that didn't stop her from hating the game. After seeing the Rolexes True and Young Mac had purchased, Saheed decided to go splurge on himself. He went and bought an all gold Presidential Rolex with the diamond face, diamond bezel and diamonds on the band. It cost him $24,000.00. He bought two pinkie rings that were full of ice – these set him back $9,000.00 total, and he was wearing his gold chain with the diamond encrusted Underworld Entertainment emblem. The man had on so much ice he looked like a walking igloo. When women looked at him all they could do was shiver. Keisha saw the other women eyeing her man and, as always, she was ready to fight a bitch.

It was 11:00 p.m. and Young Mac was scheduled to take the stage at 11:30 p.m. Saheed and Young Mac had come to the conclusion that the FEDS didn't know Young Mac's true identity and therefore it would be safe to make public appearances – they were wrong.

Black was at the bar drinking drink after drink when he stood up and shouted, "Excuse me, can I have everyone's attention? As most of you know, my cousin, Lil' Skitzo, was laid to rest today. I want you to take a drink of whatever you're drinking, followed by a moment of silence dedicated to my little cousin and everyone else who lost their life in the streets."

Holding up his double shot of Remy Martin Louis the 13th, everyone in the Plasma Room put their drink in the air, and then Black downed his drink, followed by everyone else. After a minute of complete silence he said, "thank you," and the party resumed.

Saheed said to Young Mac, "you ready?"

He replied, "I'm focused."

It was time for him to take the stage. Saheed glanced at a plasma showing the VIP and saw it was filled with women and players from the D.C. Professional Basketball and Football teams and their entourages, along with a lot of Crips. They were all doing it big.

The VIP had a balcony that overlooked the stage and dance floor section of the club. Saheed decided to go down there to watch the show. On his way down he glanced at the plasma showing the dance floor and thought he saw LaTasha. He hoped it wasn't her.

"What's up, Distribution City?!" yelled Young Mac as he stormed the stage, microphone in hand. True was right behind him operating as his hype man.

After the crowd calmed down, Young Mac said "Will all the sexy ladies in the house raise their hands?" it seemed like every woman in the building put her hand up. That's when he spotted Juicy and Chyna in the crowd and pulled them up on stage. He picked them because he knew they could dance. From there he jumped right into his hit single "Shake it Baby." The ladies went crazy and started getting their groove on as Young Mac did his thing. One threw her panties on stage. Chyna and Juicy didn't let Young Mac down as they danced on the stage like the professionals they were. They looked so good on stage that when the song was over they were escorted straight upstairs to the VIP so they could hang with the ball players. From there, Young Mac performed his song "Six Feet Deep" in tribute to Lil' Skitzo. Then he performed "Knock 'em out," and this drove the thugs into a frenzy, causing a fist fight to break out on the middle of the dance floor.

After security broke up the fight, Young Mac told the hyped up crowd he would perform one last song. He told the crowd they had a choice – he would either do "Quick and the Dead" for the street niggas or "She's a Dime" for the women, depending on who made the most noise. The women easily won. As he was starting into "She's a Dime, he saw about ten white boys with badges around their necks pushing through the crowd. He first thought was they probably were there because of the fight, but he quickly realized that didn't make sense. When they got on stage and surrounded him and True, he felt like his life was over. He knew right then that he fucked up. The redheaded cop looked at a picture in his hand, then looked back at Young Mac and told him to put his hands in the air. When Young Mac didn't comply, he pulled out his taser and said "I'm not going to tell you again."

Young Mac replied "fuck you."

His microphone was picking up the exchange of words. Without saying anything else, the U.S. Marshall shot Young Mac with his taser right there on the stage. The crowd started booing and yelling obscenities at the officers. A couple of people threw beer bottles at them. True was being restrained as the officers handcuffed Young Mac, who was in bad shape from being tased. They then stood Young Mac to his feet and walked him out of the club as quick as they came.

True regained his composure and before he got off the stage he thanked everyone for coming out and showing love for Young Mac. He let them know Young Mac's album "Death Before Dishonor" was in stores and encouraged everyone to go out and buy it or buy it online at www.UnderworldEntertainment.com.

Saheed looked on from the balcony of the VIP, upset that he had allowed this to happen. He turned to leave and bumped straight into that crazy bitch LaTasha. She was obviously drunk and was staring at him with hate in her eyes. Saheed hoped he didn't have to hurt this bitch in front of everyone. He thought to himself he should have just killed her for that bullshit she pulled. He walked past her and she didn't say anything. She just kept looking at him crazy. Kiesha was right behind Saheed and followed him back to the Plasma Room. Once there, Saheed informed Kiesha it was time for her to go home and that he would be right behind her. Her response was "you're trying to go fuck with that bitch down in VIP, ain't you? I saw the way you were looking at her. You think I'm stupid, don't you?"

"Kiesha, go home. I'll be right behind you. Get off that bullshit."

"Whatever, nigga," keisha said as she stomped out of the Plasma Room. This made Saheed want to slap some sense into her. He couldn't stand when she caught an attitude with him. He had to get his thoughts together so he fired up a blunt of Kryptonite as True joined him on the couch in the Plasma Room.

"Damn, I fucked up, True. I should've known this would happen," said Saheed, looking at the plasma TVs. The club DJ had put some music on and the party was back popping.

"We did our thing tonight, though, the crowd loved us. Let me hit that blunt," said True, reaching for the cigar. Saheed passed him the blunt then said, "I'm calling my lawyer first thing in the morning."

True was coughing from the marijuana smoke so he didn't reply, but he pointed at a plasma showing the VIP section as it was showing a fight in progress. The Crips appeared to be jumping somebody as True, Saheed and others in the Plasma Room looked on. After stomping whomever, that somebody was unconscious. Two guys picked him up in the air and started walking towards the balcony. Security was nowhere in sight.

True yelled "they bout to throw him over the balcony!"

Just as he said this, they threw him over the balcony head-first; he landed on top of some fat girl who was on the dance floor getting her groove on. They were both lying in the middle of the dance floor and appeared to be unconscious. All this could be seen on the plasma TVs, which meant the whole incident was recorded.

"Shit's crazy, let's ride out, True," Saheed said. As he got up to leave he looked back at the plasmas and saw police and security had things under control and were shutting the party down. On their way out, they ran into Black, who informed them that old boy who got tossed out on the dance floor was a Blood and that's why the fight broke out.

Outside, Black saw Chyna and Juicy getting into a Cadillac Escalade with some of the ball players from the VIP.

"Look at those sluts, they both got some good pussy," said Black.

"You fucked Juicy? I've been wanting to hit that," said Saheed, thinking to himself he didn't want to fuck her anymore.

"What y'all niggas on? I got some cum freaks that are trying to get fucked," said True.

"It's all over for me; I gotta go deal with Kiesha's crazy ass then get up early and check on Young Mac."

"We can take 'em back to my crib," said Black's horny ass, always down for some new pussy. They shook hands. Saheed headed home, Black and True left to go kick it with the cum freaks.

CHAPTER TWENTY FOUR

LaTasha was sitting in her car waiting for Saheed to come out of the club so she could blow his brains out. She didn't give a fuck who witnessed the act.

Ever since her ordeal with Saheed, she had been living in hell on earth. She wished he would have killed her instead of doing what he did to her. The only thing that kept her from committing suicide was the thought of revenge.

Her life was pure misery. The burns from the curling iron would not heal completely because they kept getting infected, causing her vagina to constantly be in pain and drip a white-colored pus that stank terribly. Antibiotics didn't seem to help and the stupid doctors in D.C. didn't know what to do next. They told her she would probably have to fly to California to see a medical specialist for treatment – something her insurance didn't cover. And to top it off her coochie looked like Freddy Kruger's face.

When she decided to go to Club Millennium, it was only an attempt to take her mind off the misery she was suffering. She had heard the song "Shake it Baby" enough times on the radio to know every word of the song's lyrics. She had forgotten that once upon a time Saheed told her he owned a record company called Underworld Entertainment. At the time she thought he was bluffing, trying to impress her. When she saw him tonight, it all came back to her. And if he thought he was gonna get rich and live happily ever after he had another thing coming. LaTasha swore to herself that she'd see to that.

It was while she was waiting for Saheed to come out of the club that she noticed that bitch he was with come walking out of the club and get into the driver's side of a late model Honda Accord. As the car pulled out of its parking space, LaTasha decided to follow the bitch, telling herself if she could find out where the bitch lived she could catch Saheed slipping – coming or going from her residence. She reasoned that way she wouldn't be going to jail tonight for murder.

LaTasha followed the Honda to the edge of Distribution City's northside, being careful to keep her distance. She watched as the car pulled up to a house with an attached garage. The garage door lifted up, and then the Honda pulled into the garage as the door shut behind it.

LaTasha pulled down the block and parked her car. She was watching the house through her rearview mirror, as she dialed

Tank's phone number on her cell phone. When Tank answered she started explaining the situation to him. As they were speaking, LaTasha noticed a car pull up to the house. When she saw Saheed get out of the car she got excited and started speaking rapidly into the phone saying, "the nigga just pulled up and walked into the house."

"OK, this is what you do – sit tight while I get the dogs together, we on our way. You just keep your phone on."

"I'm waiting for you, just hurry up."

"LaTasha, you did a good job, but stay in your place and remember who you're talking to," Tank said with authority.

LaTasha rolled her eyes and said, "I'm waiting."

"We're on the way, keep your phone on."

They both hung up. LaTasha impatiently waited as she watched the house. She fantasized about returning the favor and sticking the hot curling iron up Saheed's ass.

*****

Inside the house Saheed and Kiesha were arguing. It seemed to Saheed that that was all they did since she became pregnant.

"Bitch, if this is an indication of what the next 18 years are gonna be like, you need to hurry up and get an abortion," said Saheed, upset because Kiesha kept nagging at him about petty issues. Instantly he regretted saying that – he was actually starting to look forward to being a father.

With tears in her eyes, Kiesha said "fuck you, nigga, you need to leave. I'm tired of your shit."

Saheed laughed at her and said, "Bitch, you must've forgot whose house you in and who runs this motherfucker, but I'm a do you a favor and leave before I hurt you."

As he turned to leave Kiesha cried out, "please don't leave. I'm sorry, Daddy, don't go."

Her apology caught Saheed by surprise but he didn't feel like playing her game. Looking Kiesha in the eyes he said, "fuck you in your stankin' ass, bitch. I'm outta here."

As he walked towards the door Kiesha said, "You think you're slick. I know you going to go fuck with one of them hoes from the club. I hope that pussy's good because I won't be here when you get back."

Saheed walked outside without closing the door behind him. As he was getting in his car he could hear Kiesha crying in the background. He drove away thinking to himself, "fuck that bitch," as he lit the blunt that was in the ashtray.

*****

Meanwhile . . .

LaTasha had driven around the corner to meet with Tank and whoever else was with him. She parked behind the van they were in and jumped in with them. Inside the van was Tank, Smoke, and two young cats she didn't recognize but to her they both looked like killers. Everyone was dressed in black and ready to handle business.

Tank said, "Show me where the nigga's at."

They drove around the corner and LaTasha pointed the house out.

"*Fuck,* the car he pulled up in is gone; he had to have just left."

Tank parked then said, "Maybe he ran to the store. Let's wait a few minutes and see if he shows."

After 15 minutes of waiting Smoke said "I say we go up in there and make that bitch of his talk. We could kidnap the bitch if we have to."

After a short debate they agreed with Smoke's plan.

"LaTasha, you wait in the van, we don't want this bitch to recognize you," Tank said as he tied a red bandana around his face. Smoke and the other men followed his lead and did the same thing. They all checked their weapons and made sure they were ready to fire. Smoke was the first one out of the van; the others followed him to the front door of the house. As he went to kick the door open, something told him to see if it was unlocked first. He twisted the knob and it swung open. Immediately he saw a woman asleep on the couch, her body illuminated by the television. Smoke pointed his gun at her as the others went from room-to-room to see if anyone else was in the house. Suddenly Kiesha woke up and said, "Saheed?" as she rubbed her eyes, looking at the figure pointing a gun at her.

Not believing what she was seeing, she thought she had to be dreaming.

"Say something else and I'm a shoot you, bitch."

Not recognizing the voice she knew it wasn't Saheed. She realized she wasn't dreaming. When the man with the gun and red rag around his face grabbed her by the hair and threw her on the ground face first, Kiesha started crying, "Please don't hurt me. I got money, you can have it, just don't hurt me."

Smoke replied "shut the fuck up, Bitch," then he kicked her in the ribs.

The others came back into the front room. Tank said "nobody else here."

He looked at Kiesha and the first thing he noticed was her fat ass. He heard her crying and said "stop that crying. Just tell us where Saheed's at and we won't hurt you.

Kiesha replied, "I don't know where he's at."

Tank slapped her hard in the back of the head, then said "bitch, ain't nobody playing with you."

Then he slapped her again. Tank looked at his two lil' homies and said, "rip this place apart and see what you can find. You can split whatever you come up with."

They went straight to work, looking for anything of value. He then turned his attention back to Kiesha and said, "Listen, bitch. Do what the fuck I tell you and we won't kill you. You try and play me, your gonna die tonight."

Unable to keep her emotions in check, Kiesha began to cry hysterically and Tank smacked her again on the back of the head. "Crying ain't gonna help you, bitch. Call that nigga Saheed, maybe he can help you," Tank said, then he picked up Kiesha's cell phone off the table and handed it to her.

Without hesitation she called Saheed. The phone rang a few times then went to voicemail. She tried again and got the same result. She realized Saheed was pushing decline and sending her to his voicemail. She couldn't believe this was happening to her. She tried calling him again, this time the phone wouldn't even ring – he had turned the power off. She hung up and tried to dial 9-1-1 but Tank saw what she was trying to do so he snatched the phone away and punched her in the jaw.

"You're a silly-ass bitch, ain't you?" said Tank as he pulled Kiesha's arms behind her back. Without Tank saying a word, Smoke knew what to do. He pulled some handcuffs out of his pocket and placed them on Kiesha's wrists.

"Bring me a pillow case," Tank said to Smoke.

Smoke left the room and returned with a pillow case and the two young Bloods who had been tearing up the house. They had found a few pounds of marijuana in the bedroom and several pistols throughout the house. Tank took the pillow case and put it over Kiesha's head. He told Smoke to pull the van into the driveway. Smoke went outside and did what he was told. Smoke was used to calling the shots but Tank was in charge here and Smoke knew not to test his boss. Tank tied the pillow case around Kiesha's neck. When the van was in the driveway, he put Kiesha over his shoulder as she continued to cry and carried her out to the van, his goons right behind him.

Tank usually wouldn't involve himself in a mission like this, but this was in retaliation for his dead nephew, June. It was personal and he was going to make sure this cat Saheed got dealt with accordingly.

Saheed ended up over at Black's house with Black, True and the "cum freaks." It was 5:00 a.m. in the morning and True was passed out in one of the bedrooms. Black and the females were all wide awake, a side effect from the ecstasy pills they had taken. When Saheed arrived, the three cum freaks, as True had referred to them, were having a threesome as Black recorded them getting it on with his camcorder.

"I see you're making a movie. How come you ain't in it?" Saheed asked Black.

"Yo, I'm supposed to be starring in this muthafucker but I took an ecstasy pill and my dick won't get hard."

Saheed laughed and said "I thought that shit was supposed to be better than Viagra."

"So did I," said Black. He was frustrated because his dick wouldn't get hard.

"Here, blaze this blunt up. Maybe that will help," said Saheed, handing Black his last blunt of Kryptonite. Black lit the blunt and immediately started coughing from the potent smoke and passed the cigar to Saheed, who took a puff and started coughing too.

The men coughing, combined with the smell of the smoke, got the women's attention. They stopped licking on each other and one of them asked "can we smoke with y'all?"

Saheed took another pull from the cigar and passed it back to Black, exhaled the smoke, then said to the females, "y'all probably used to smoking that regular weed. I don't think you could handle this."

The vocal woman approached Saheed. As she walked towards him he saw how bad she was with her high yellow skin, large breasts and hair that hung down damn near to her waist. Saheed assumed she was Native American. She looked Saheed in his eyes and said, "nigga, I can handle anything."

She grabbed his dick, caressed it, and repeated, "Anything."

"Let Pocahontas hit the blunt, Black," said Saheed.

Pocahontas took the blunt and inhaled more smoke than Saheed had ever seen a woman inhale, held the smoke for about ten seconds, then exhaled so much smoke that her mouth looked like a muffler on a raggedy-ass Chevy. She did this without coughing or choking and Saheed couldn't believe what he just saw – no one had ever hit the Kryptonite and not choked. Had to be the ecstasy, he told himself. Pocahontas had passed the weed to her girl, who was in the process of coughing up a lung. As the weed began to relax Saheed, he realized his erection was about to tear through his jeans. Pocahontas had him going, so he grabbed her by the arm and told her "we need to talk."

"Talk about what?" she asked.

Saheed led her by the hand into the bathroom. Once inside he didn't have anything to say. He just undid his pants and Big Killa burst through. Pocahontas looked down in amazement at the size of Saheed's penis and said, "ooh, it's so big," as she put her hand on it and started playing with him.

"You think you can handle *that*?" asked Saheed.

"I told you, I can handle anything," Pocahontas replied, and dropped to her knees. She went to take him inside her mouth when Saheed said, "hold on." He pulled out a Magnum rubber and put it on.

"Give me this," said Pocahontas, grabbing Saheed's dick and making it and the condom disappear in her mouth like she was some kind of magician.

Saheed couldn't believe she had him all the way down her throat. Watching her deep throat him, he thought of LaTasha for a brief second only because she was the only other woman he had been with who was able to swallow all of him.

Playing with her clit as she sucked him off, Pocahontas brought herself to an orgasm and started moaning loudly with his dick in her mouth. He loved the feeling.

When she stopped moaning, Saheed grabbed her by the hair and pulled her to her feet.

"I wasn't done," she said.

Without replying, Saheed reached down and rubbed her clean-shaven sex. She was dripping wet and ready. He put her arms around his neck and picked her up. Placing both of his arms under her legs as she wrapped them around his waist, with both hands he palmed her soft ass. Pocahontas reached down and slid him inside of her and let out a loud moan as he went deep. This excited Saheed and he began lifting her up and down his shaft as he thrust in and out of her, keeping a firm grip on her ass.

"You're so strong and you feel so good," Pocahontas managed to say, and dug her fingernails into Saheed's muscular back.

"You can't handle this," said Saheed as he picked up the pace.

"Ooh, I . . . I . . . I can handle anything," she said, breathing heavy.

74

Saheed started banging her as hard as he could, causing Pocahontas to scream with joy as she came, releasing her cream all over Saheed's dick. He kept pounding away, causing her to have multiple orgasms, something she had never experienced. She was digging her nails deep into his back and he knew she probably drew blood, but this only made him fuck her harder.

As he came he said, "Damn, you got some bomb pussy!"

Still holding her in the air, he turned around to see Black standing in the doorway holding his camcorder.

"What the fuck? You dirty muthafucka . . ." Saheed said as he set Pocahontas on the counter and tried to snatch the camcorder from Black's hands.

"Nigga, you a porn star," said Black and started laughing along with the other girls.

"How long you been standing there?" Saheed asked Black.

"I got it all on tape."

Saheed looked at Pocahontas and said "you watched him record us." She just smiled at him innocently and shrugged her shoulders.

"I'm a put that on the Internet," said Black.

"You got me all wrong, homie, give me the tape," demanded Saheed.

"I'm just playing dog. Chill out."

"Fuck what you talking about? Give me the tape."

Black handed him the camcorder. Saheed pushed rewind and watched himself in action, while Pocahontas looked over his shoulder.

"We look good together," she said.

"You're right, we do," he replied, then pushed the eject button and removed the tape. He started pulling the film out of the cassette. After pulling it all out, he flushed it down the toilet as the others looked on disappointed.

"You shouldn't have done that, that was a classic," Black said.

"Whatever, man, I'm about to leave. Pocahontas, give me your phone number."

She gave it to him and he stored it in his cell phone. He would definitely call her, she may be down to get some money, he reasoned with himself. Then he thought about Rose. He told himself he better start paying Rose more attention before he lost her again. He told Black to holla at him tomorrow and left to go home. On his way to the house he hoped Kiesha was asleep and didn't hear him come in. He needed to take a shower because he knew he smelled like sex and didn't want to hear her mouth. He reflected on the night's events – they were bittersweet.

On the sweet side, he had made money. Young Mac's album release party was a success and he had some of the best sex of his life.

On the bitter end, Young Mac was in federal custody and that was making him sick. LaTasha was back in the picture and he knew he would have to deal with her eventually. The man getting tossed from VIP could file a lawsuit and include him. Even though he had insurance on the party, he didn't need the headache, and Kiesha kept stressing with her bullshit.

When he pulled into his driveway he noticed the front door was cracked open and said aloud to himself, "This bitch is trippin'."

Walking in the house he saw it was a mess but before he could get past the living room the 7:00 a.m. news came on and the top story was about Club Millennium. The anchor woman was saying "last night at Club Millennium a local rapper by the name of Young Mac was hosting a party for his album's release when a team of U.S. Marshalls moved to arrest him on an outstanding warrant. According to our sources, he didn't comply with the marshalls and they were forced to use a taser in an effort to handcuff him, causing the crowd to react and throw bottles at the officers. They became combative and at some point a man was tossed over the balcony onto the dance floor, where he landed on a woman, breaking her neck. The man suffered severe head trauma. Both are being treated at D.C. County Hospital."

Saheed walked back to his bedroom and saw it tore apart. "This bitch lost her mind," Saheed said to himself, thinking Kiesha made a mess of his house. He looked in the closet and saw his Hydro was gone – he had three pounds in there and had planned on selling it the next day.

"I'm a hurt that bitch," he said to himself again.

He lifted the mattress off the bed and saw his 45. Smith & Wesson was gone. He looked in the dresser drawer and saw his 44. special was missing. He remembered Kiesha saying she wouldn't be home when he got back and got nervous. He went to the floorboard in the kitchen where he kept the majority of his money. Even Kiesha didn't know about that, but he went to check anyhow. Removing the floorboard he let out a sigh of relief as his eyes took in the sight of big plastic bags of hundred dollar bills vacuum-sealed shut. "Thank you, Lord," he said, still talking to himself.

He told himself mentally that he had to invest that money somehow or figure out a better place for it. Walking back into the living room, he noticed Kiesha's purse next to the couch. This set off an alarm in his head because he knew Kiesha didn't go anywhere without her purse.

He bent over to pick it up and noticed some blood on the floor. That's when he got worried. He knew Kiesha was upset but she would never harm herself, no matter how mad or upset she was. He looked in her purse and saw everything that was supposed to be in there – cell phone, make-up, ID, credit cards, cash, and her car keys. *Car keys!*

Saheed ran to the garage and saw the Honda parked in the same place as always during this hour. Saheed's head started spinning and he thought he was going to faint. If something happened to Kiesha he would go crazy.

He had to sit down and think. He was missing something. He took his cell phone out of his pocket. The power was off. He forgot he had turned it off when Kiesha was calling earlier.

Turning the phone back on, he saw he had two missed calls from Kiesha and had new voice messages. Calling his voicemail he got excited when the electronic voice indicated the message was from Kiesha. Then he heard her crying and male voices in the background. Then the message ended abruptly. He listed to it approximately 20 times, trying to make out the voices in the background. Unable to come up with anything he called Black.

"Yo," Black answered, obviously still awake.

"Black, I need you and True to get to my house immediately."

"Can't it wait a few hours? I just got my man's back in action."

"This shit is serious, dog. I think Kiesha's been kidnapped."

"What? O.K., homie, we on our way."

CHAPTER TWENTY SIX
South Side, Distribution City

After being kidnapped from her home, Kiesha was driven to a dope house on the south side of D.C. It was the same D-spot where Smoke was robbed and Lil' Skitzo and Desire were killed in front of. Only now it was no longer a crack house, Smoke used it as a place to store his drugs. He and Tank agreed that it was the best place to bring Kiesha, being that nobody ever came there.

Kiesha was still handcuffed with her hands behind her back. She was laid down on her stomach on top of an old pissy couch in the basement. As the smell of stale piss invaded her nostrils, Kiesha pleaded with her captors. "Please let me go, I haven't done anything. I don't know anything." She wasn't lying. Saheed kept his women on a need-to-know basis. His reason for that was what they didn't know couldn't hurt him. To him, pillow talking was some sucker-shit.

"Ho, you know sumthin'," said LaTasha, "and you gonna tell us everything you know about that bitch ass nigga you call your man." The pillow case had been removed from Kiesha's head and when she looked at the voice talking to her, she instantly recognized LaTasha's face from inside Club Millennium.

"What do you want to know?" asked Kiehsa.

"Bitch, tell us where he lives," spat LaTasha as Tank, Smoke, and the two goons stood in the background.

"He lives with me," said Kiesha, as her voice quivered. She was scared to death and swore to herself she was through with Saheed if she made it through this. She couldn't believe he had mixed her up in his shit.

"This is what you're gonna do, bitch, you're gonna call that Muthafucka and tell him to come and get you."

Kiesha was far from stupid. She realized they wanted her to set Saheed up. Were they going to kill him? She thought about the fetus inside of her and the pain she felt since that nigga kicked her in the ribs back at her house. She hoped her baby was all right.

"I'll do whatever you say, just don't hurt me," said Kiesha.

"Everybody come upstairs," Tank said. He went up the stairs and everyone except Kiesha followed him.

Once upstairs, Tank said to LaTasha, "that's a beautiful plan, I like the way you think, LaTasha. I want you and these two niggas to stay and watch that bitch. Smoke's gonna run me across town right quick. We gonna work out the details and handle this nigga Saheed. As far as that fifty grand, you got that coming."

"Tank, it's not even about the money anymore. That Muthafucka destroyed me," LaTasha said as her eyes teared up.

"I understand, but you got that coming anyway. Y'all just hold down the spot until we get back. Don't answer the door for anybody."

"All right, O.G.," said LaTasha.

"Blood gang," replied Tank.

"Blood gang," the others replied in unison.

Tank and Smoke left the house; LaTasha locked the door behind them. She then said, "Let's go torture this bitch."

Back downstairs, LaTasha lit up a blunt of Hydro and stood over Kiesha. Blowing smoke in her face she said, "we're about to have us some fun, bitch," then dumped ashes on her face. "Bitch, you think you're pretty, don't you?"

"Please, I'll do whatever you want me to, just don't hurt me," said Kiesha as she started crying again.

"Say 'Blood'," said LaTasha, looking at Tank's goon Raw Money, who was looking at Kiesha's butt. "I see you studying this ho's ass. Go on ahead and get you some."

"My thoughts exactly," said Raw Money. As he held his dick he approached Kiesha and squeezed her ass. Kiesha's reaction was to kick him. She got lucky and caught him in the balls, sending him to the floor in pain. Seeing this, LaTasha passed goon number two the blunt and walked up to Kiesha and stomped on her head. Kiesha screamed and LaTasha stomped her again.

"Now listen, tramp. You try anymore slick shit and we gonna kill you," hollered LaTasha.

By this time Raw Money was back on his feet. "Bitch, you like it rough, ha?"

Kiesha was still in her pajamas and he snatched her bottoms down to her ankles, and then pulled them all the way off, exposing her nakedness. Looking at her curves made him super hard. He pulled out his oversized dick and climbed on top of her as she cried hysterically, too scared to fight back. He spread her legs and savagely entered her from behind, causing her vagina to tear and Kiesha screamed again.

LaTasha took a big pull from the blunt, making the tip red hot, and burned Kiesha on her temple. "Scream again, bitch," said LaTasha, feeling no remorse as she watched Kiesha being raped.

Kiesha could feel the rapist's dick inside her stomach as he fucked her as hard as he could.

"Please stop, I'm pregnant. You're going to hurt my baby," begged Kiesha.

"Fuck your baby, bitch," said Raw Money, then he bust a nut inside of her.

Kiesha's words were music to LaTasha's ears. Instantly she felt the need to kill Saheed's baby.

As Raw Money pulled his dick out of Kiesha, he looked at goon number two and said "you better get you some of that good pussy."

"I'm cool, enjoy yourself," goon number two replied, with a look of disgust on his face. He didn't approve of what was going down. He was sorry for Kiesha but felt powerless to stop the attack.

"It's my turn anyway," said LaTasha, as she stood behind Kiesha with a broom in her hand. She looked at the semen dripping from Kiesha's ass and said to Raw Money, "nigga, you didn't use a condom," then looked at him like he was stupid.

"For what?" asked Raw Money.

"Nigga, are you crazy?" she asked, and then realized he must be crazy if he's down for kidnapping, rape and robbery. Kiesha's cries interrupted their conversation.

"Keep crying, bitch," said LaTasha, right before she jammed the end of the broom handle into Kiesha's coochie, causing her to scream at the top of her lungs. LaTasha seemed possessed as she kept shoving the broom handle as hard as she could in and out of Kiesha.

"*What the fuck you doing?!*" came a deep voice from behind. LaTasha turned around to see Smoke at the bottom of the stairs with a gun in his hand. LaTasha just stood there for a second looking dumb. When she turned back around, she saw blood leaking from Kiesha on the couch and Kiesha's body was convulsing as if she was having a seizure. LaTasha removed the broom and it was covered with blood. At the same time, blood started pouring out of Kiesha like a faucet.

"Bitch, you fucked up big time," Smoke said to LaTasha.

"Who you calling a bitch?" said LaTasha impulsively.

"You, bitch!" Smoke shouted. "Now say somethin' else and that broom gonna be up *your* pussy."

LaTasha stood there furious but didn't say anything. Turning to his lil' homies, Smoke said "why would y'all let her do this?" He pointed at Kiesha without turning around. Out of the corner of his eye he saw LaTasha raising a pistol in his direction. Like the veteran gun slinger he was, he spun around and shot LaTasha in the neck, a split second before she blew out his brains. She fell to the floor and he kicked the gun out of her hands.

"This bitch tried to sneak me," said Smoke.

The three men stood there staring at the two women bleeding to death.

"Change of plans, y'all," said Smoke to his two goons with his brain racing. Smoke pulled a switch blade from his pocket and handed it to Raw Money. "Cut that bitch's neck," he said and pointed his pistol at LaTasha.

Without a second going to waste, Raw Money grabbed LaTasha by her hair, pulled her head back, and cut her neck. He didn't give a fuck about killing. He had already killed twice for his gang. He didn't feel a thing – it didn't bother him.

"Give him the knife," said Smoke. Raw Money passed the knife to goon number two.

"Do her the same way, Blood," Smoke said to goon number two.

Goon number two stood over Kiesha with the bloody knife in his hand. His hesitation was obvious.

"What you waiting on, Dog?" asked Smoke.

When goon number two didn't answer, Smoke pulled back the hammer on his gun and pointed it at him. "Don't play with me, Blood," said Smoke.

Goon number two knew he would be killed if he didn't do as he was told. He said a quick, silent prayer, asking the Lord to forgive him. With tears in his eyes he reached down and sliced Kiesha's neck from ear to ear.

"Good man, I knew you had it in you. Now drag them bitches upstairs."

Following his orders, they did as Smoke told them. Smoke ran to the garage and came back inside with a gas can. The two dead bodies were on the living room floor. Raw Money and goon number two were covered in blood. Smoke looked at his own shirt and noticed blood spatter. He grabbed some changes of clothes from the bedroom and told his goons to wash up and change clothes. After that they carried all the drugs inside the house out to the van.

Going back inside they dowsed the bodies in gasoline and poured the rest throughout the house and basement. They started a fire in several places and fled the murder scene.

CHAPTER TWENTY SIX
North Side, Distribution City

By the time Black and True showed up, Saheed was stressing hard over Kiesha's disappearance.

"Yo, what the fuck was you saying about Kiesha being kidnapped?" asked Black.

"Nigga, I didn't stutter. I think she was kidnapped. Listen to this," replied Saheed. Then he called his voicemail and put his speaker phone on so True and Black could hear the message from Kiesha.

"Listen to the voices in the background; tell me if you recognize them."

They listened to the message several times but nobody could match a face with the voices, or even make out what they were saying.

"Whoever it was took a couple of my guns and a few pounds of Purple. But fuck all that. My only concern is Kiesha," stated Saheed.

"Yo, you gonna tell her family?" asked Black.

"I'm the only family she has."

"What about the police?"

"I don't know what I'm going to do. Stop with all the questions and let me think for a minute."

"Damn, whoever it was tore ya house up," said True. Then he sparked the blunt he just finished rolling up. As they sat on the couch, a rerun of the morning's news headlines came on the television.

"Say, check this shit out," said Saheed," and let me hit the blunt."

True passed him the weed without taking his eyes off the TV. After the anchor woman got done talking about Club Millennium, True said, "We need to get a copy of the video of the Marshalls using that taser on Young Mac. That shit was excessive force."

"I was thinking the same thing. I'm going to call the Sicilian in a minute and get him on the job."said Saheed. The Sicilian was Mike Soprano, Saheed's lawyer and one of the best criminal defense attorneys in the country. He was rated in the upper half of the Top Ten Super Lawyers in America. He had earned his reputation representing different factions of the Italian Mafia and anyone else with some big money.

"How much you think he's gonna charge to represent Young Mac?"

"Somewhere around twenty thousand – that seems to be his favorite number," said Saheed.

"That Dago charged me fifty large when I got hit with that conspiracy," added Black.

"Yeah, but it was worth beating the case, wasn't it?" asked Saheed.

"My freedom is priceless. The thing is, it was a cakewalk for him. They didn't have anything on me. A Public Defender could have won that case," Black answered.

Saheed took another puff from the blunt, and then said "you should have gone with a Public Defender then."

"Yo, fuck all that, I can't work with a Public Defender."

Just then their conversation was interrupted by a breaking news report on the TV.

"Yes, this is Ron Richards reporting live from D.C.'s southside. I'm at the scene of a house fire on 38th and 2nd Street. The firefighter in charge has told me upon their arrival that the house was completely engulfed in flames and the only thing they can do is let the fire burn itself out and keep it from spreading to surrounding residences. Police on the scene have informed me that 3830 2nd Street has been a problem residence and is being treated as a crime scene at this time. We at Channel Four will be sure to keep you updated as this story develops. Ron Richards reporting live, Channel Four News."

"Yo, that's the house where Lil Skitzo was shot in front of!" said Black, jumping off the couch and pointing at the TV.

"Sure the fuck is," said True. "You think it's related?"

"We probably won't know. Them bitches don't know how to solve a murder," said Black, with anger in his voice.

In reality, Distribution City had some of the best crime scene investigators in the country, along with the most advanced technology.

Saheed looked at his Rolex. It was still early but he decided to call his lawyer and see if he could catch him in the office.

"Soprano Law Office," answered his secretary.

"Mike Soprano, please."

"Who's calling?"

"Corey James," said Saheed.

"One moment, Mr. James."

"Corey, what's up," said Mr. Soprano.

"Mike, did you hear about the incident at Club Millennium last night?"

"Yeah, what about it?"

"The guy arrested on federal drug charges is like my little brother. I need you to represent him."

"What's his name?"

"Cortez Mack."

"I'll make some calls and see what's going on. I'll be back in my office at 3:00 p.m. Call me then."

"Yes, sir," replied Saheed. Then he hung up the phone.

"What did he say?" asked True.

"He said to call him at 3:00 this afternoon."

"Yo, what we gonna do about Kiesha?" asked Black.

"What can we do? I gotta sleep on it and try to figure something out," said Saheed.

"Have you tried calling her?" asked True.

"Her cell phone is here, along with everything else she owns. Something ain't right. She would never leave without her ID and cell phone. I haven't been to sleep yet. Y'all look tired, too. Let's get some sleep. Then we can think some more with our minds clear," Saheed said, then went to his room and fell fast asleep.

*****

When Saheed woke up he looked at his Rolex and saw that it was 2:58 p.m. He immediately called Mr. Soprano to see what was happening. Instead of calling the office, he dialed his cell phone.

"Mike Soprano," Mr. Soprano always stated his name when he answered his phone.

"Mike, its Corey."

"Here's the deal. Cortez Mack has a bond hearing at 9:30 tomorrow morning in front of Magistrate Janklow at the Federal Courthouse downtown."

"Can you be there?" asked Saheed.

"I can and I will be there. I already rescheduled a Pretrial Hearing I had for another client of mine. I need you to come to my office so we can take care of the paperwork." What he meant was, "I need some cash."

"I can be there at 4:00."

"I'll be here until 5:00."

Saheed hung up and counted the money in his pocket. He had a bit over five G's.

"It will have to do for now," Saheed said, talking to himself.

He walked into the front room and saw Black passed out on the couch and True was sleeping on the love seat.

"Wake up, Niggas!" Saheed shouted in an attempt to wake them up. Saheed rolled a blunt and thought about his weed houses. He hadn't been to check on them in a couple of days. Even though everything operated on timer, he needed to check on them daily to make sure everything was functioning properly. When growing marijuana, minor issues can cause major problems.

Saheed lit the blunt and the aroma from the marijuana woke Black and True up immediately.

"Let me hit that blunt," said True, half asleep and still tired.

"Y'all need to get up so we can go down to the Sicilian's office."

"Yo, Saheed, I got some things I have to do, homie. I'm going to run and handle my business. Just call me if you need me," said Black, thinking with his dick again.

"You ain't got nothing to do but go get some pussy. Just keep your phone on, I may need your help," replied Saheed.

Black went on about his business, while True and Saheed went downtown to Mike Soprano's "office in the sky."

Inside Mike's office, Mr. Soprano was saying, "my fee will be $25,000.00, anyone else it would have been $50,000.00." This was his favorite saying, Saheed thought.

"I got five for you right now and I'll get you the rest." Saheed never paid him in full all at once because to him lawyers were greedy and if you did that they would try to get more money out of you.

"I trust you, Corey, your word's good with me."

"Listen, Mike, I have another problem," Saheed said.

"What is it?"

"My girlfriend disappeared last night. I think she was kidnapped." Saheed let him hear the message on his voicemail and went on to tell him the circumstances surrounding her disappearance.

"You're going to have to notify the authorities. If she has in fact been kidnapped, the FBI will be involved."

"I assumed that," Saheed said.

"This is what you do. Remove anything illegal from your house, then call the police and make a missing person's report. If they determine there is foul play they might search your house. You may even become a suspect."

"This is fucked up."

"If it happened like you've told me, they won't be able to touch you," said a serious-faced Mr. Soprano.

"O.K. sir I'll see you at 9:30 tomorrow morning," Saheed always showed the old man the upmost respect.

"9:30," replied Mr. Soprano.

The men shook hands and Saheed and True left the office building. Saheed dropped True off, then went and removed his stash from his house and put it in the stash spot in the Cadillac. The Cadillac had been parked in a storage locker ever since he had shot up Polo. He had no plans of moving it any time soon.

Things have been moving so fast the past few days that Saheed hadn't even thought about Polo – didn't know if he was dead or alive.

Taking his lawyer's advice, Saheed reported Kiesha missing. He left out his assumptions about her being kidnapped, nor did he let them hear the message – he didn't want the FBI all in his mix. The police officer wrote up the report and told Saheed they would get back to him.

CHAPTER TWENTY SEVEN
County Hospital, Downtown Distribution City

As Polo lie sleeping in an induced coma, Dr. Stanchfield and Agent Wilson were having a conversation about him as they stood outside his room in the Intensive Care Unit.

"We've taken Mr. Smith off of life support as he's able to breathe on his own now," said Dr. Stanchfield. Dr. Stanchfield was the surgeon who operated on Polo (a/k/a Quincy Smith) when he was rushed into the Emergency Room, inches away from death.

"You said on the phone you were bringing him out of his coma today. What time will this happen?" asked Agent Wilson.

"Well, we've taken him off the anesthesia, now it's just a matter of time until he wakes up."

"Did he suffer any brain damage?"

"A bullet did pierce the back of his brain, although it's hard to say at this time. I expect he will make a fair recovery from his injuries."

"You mean his bullet wounds?"

"Yes."

"I need you to notify me immediately once this man becomes conscious, Doctor. Understand, he's looking at federal firearm and drug charges," said Agent Wilson.

"Poor kid. First he gets shot in the brain, now he has to deal with you people."

"Believe me, he's far from innocent, doctor. This man is a career criminal and he will probably end up serving life in prison under the violent offender three strikes law. By the time we are done with him, he'll wish he were dead," said Agent Wilson, laughing like it was a joke.

"That's a shame. Well, if you give me your number I will notify you personally of any updates on Mr. Smith's condition."

Agent Wilson handed him his card and said "be sure to call when he comes to. I have to put a man up here to guard him, can't allow him to escape."

Dr. Stanchfield put the card in his shirt pocket and walked off. He didn't like this Agent Wilson character. Actually, he didn't like the Feds period. His favorite nephew was doing 15 years in a federal prison on a trumped up drug charge.

*****

88

Downstairs in the depths of the hospital, the D.C. County Medical Examiner was performing autopsies on the flame-broiled remains of Jane Doe No. 1 (Kiesha) and Jane Doe No. 2 (LaTasha). The Medical Examiner dissected Jane Doe No. 2 and found a bullet lodged in her neck. He already determined the first body had been dead before the fire because there wasn't any sign of smoke inhalation inside the lungs, although the cause of death was inconclusive.

After finding the bullet lodged in Jane Doe No. 2, he recorded her death as a homicide. Then he took DNA samples from both bodies with the hope of possibly being able to identify the two deceased women. He took pictures of their teeth and noted that Jane Doe No. 1 was pregnant and suffered injuries to her fetus due to blunt force trauma prior to the time of her death.

*****

After receiving his discharge papers, Maniac was walking out of the hospital when he ran into Agent Wilson.

"Jamal Sanders," said Agent Wilson, blocking Maniac's path.

"You're in my way," said Maniac through clenched teeth.

"I heard you got shot. I was kind of hoping you would die."

"Man, fuck you, you bitch ass cracker. You gonna see a body bag before me!" replied Maniac.

"Listen here, you nigger mother fucker. That shit bag you're wearing is going to be the least of your fucking problems when I catch up with you."

"Man, fuck you," said Maniac, as he pushed past Agent Wilson.

"We'll see who gets fucked," Agent Wilson said to Maniac's back as he walked away.

The D.C. task force had wanted to arrest Jamal Sanders ever since a drug house they had under surveillance was robbed right in front of them. When they attempted to intervene, the criminals opened fire on the task force. When the shoot-out was over, a known gang member of the Riverside Crips was dead and a member of the task force, who happened to be a good friend of Agent Wilson's, was shot in the lower spine and paralyzed from the waist down. The other two perpetrators involved in the gun battle got away.

When the task force cracked down on the Crips, a snitch told them he overheard Maniac bragging, saying that he was the one who shot the cop. The only problem was the informant's word alone wasn't enough to charge Maniac with the crime. This took place over three years ago and Jamal Sanders had been on the task force's hit list ever since.

CHAPTER TWENTY EIGHT

United States Courthouse, Downtown Distribution City

It was 9:15 a.m. Saheed was talking to Mike Soprano outside of Magistrate Janklow's courtroom.

"Let's use that 'just in case money' I gave you towards your fee for representing Cortez," said Saheed.

"You sure you want to do that?"

"Like I said, Mike, this cat is like my little brother."

"OK, then my fee is paid in full – 25 big ones."

"I won't be needing a receipt," joked Saheed.

Mike Soprano never gave a receipt unless you asked for one; even then you were lucky if he gave it to you. Saheed assumed this was done for tax reasons. Saheed and True followed Mr. Soprano into the courtroom. They sat in the back row. Mr. Soprano went and spoke to the prosecutor.

Saheed felt someone staring at him. When he looked to his left, Agent Wilson was across the aisle mean-mugging with hate in his eyes. Throwing his middle finger up and displaying the only sign language he knew, Saheed turned to True and said "that's the pig who beat my ass."

"Which one?"

"The red-faced bitch over there who's trying his best to look hard," said Saheed.

"Here comes Young Mac," said True, pointing at Young Mac as he was escorted into the courtroom by a United States Marshall. He looked stressed out in his bright orange county jumpsuit. He was seated at the defense table with Mr. Soprano.

A few minutes later the same U.S. Marshall who escorted Young Mac into the courtroom said "All rise for the Honorable Judge Janklow," announcing the Judge's entrance into the courtroom.

"Thank you, you may be seated," stated Judge Janklow.

After reading through the papers on his desk, Judge Janklow said "this hearing is in regards to the matter of the United States of America versus Cortez Mack. Counsel, please state your names for the record."

"Benson Swingum, Assistant United States Attorney, said the prosecutor.

"Mike Soprano, counsel for the defense."

"Today I will hear from both sides on the issue of a bond. Mr. Swingum, you may begin," said Judge Janklow.

"Thank you, Your Honor. On behalf of the United States Government, we move to keep Cortez Mack detained in the custody of the U.S. Marshalls pending the outcome of this case, reason being that upon the warrant being issued for his arrest, Mr. Mack did not turn himself in, forcing the Marshalls to track him down and arrest him, leading us to believe he may be a flight risk," said Prosecutor Swingum with a smug smile.

"Mr. Soprano." Judge Janklow said as he stared at Young Mac.

"Your Honor," Mike Soprano began as he stood up, "my client is not a flight risk, I can assure you. If you look at his record it is clean. He's never been in trouble. The only reason he did not turn himself in is because he was unaware of the warrant for his arrest. He was under the belief that he had to appear in state court next month for his pretrial hearing. My client is not a risk to the community, nor is he a threat to society. He is an entertainer, not a criminal. If you look at the arrest papers you will see he was arrested on stage during a performance at a local night club. At this time the defense asks the court for a signature bond and the immediate release of Cortez Mack."

"Mr. Swingum, do you have anything else?" asked Judge Janklow.

Pouncing on the opportunity, Prosecutor Swingum added "Your Honor, according to the arrest papers, Mr. Mack resisted arrest, forcing the arresting officers to use a taser to restrain him during the execution of the warrant. Furthermore, at the time of arrest for the crime he has been charged with, Cortez Mack was in the presence of known gang members and in possession of crack cocaine, according to the police report. I think that makes him a risk to the community. On behalf of the government, we oppose any type of bond of release for the defendant."

"Any final words, Mr. Soprano?" asked Judge Janklow.

"Yes, Your Honor. My client did not resist arrest. In fact, I have proof that the arresting officers used excessive force during the arrest of Cortez Mack," said Mike Soprano, and he held up a video tape that showed Young Mac being tased and handcuffed.

"Last, but not least, my client is not a member of any gang. He's not a drug dealer, he just happened to be in the wrong place at the wrong time. That's all, Your Honor.

"Does that tape show your client being arrested?"

"Yes, Your Honor."

"I will review the video in my chambers and then make my decision," said Judge Janklow.

15 minutes later Judge Janklow emerged from his office.

"All rise," said the Marshall.

"You may be seated. After reviewing the tape it appears the arresting officers failed to identify themselves at first contact with the defendant. I won't go as far as to say if it was or was not excessive force – we can go over that in the motions hearing. After carefully reviewing the evidence, I have decided to release Defendant Cortez Mack on a signature bond. Mr. Mack, upon your release you will be required to check in with a pretrial hearing officer and follow any and all regulations he gives you. Failure to show up to court following your release shall result in a $25,000.00 fine along with a stiffer sentence on any time imposed by the Court. Do you understand, Mr. Mack?"

"Yes, sir, Your Honor," replied Young Mac, relieved to be getting released.

"Good. A pretrial hearing will be set for exactly one month from today. Does that work for you, Mr. Soprano?

"That will be fine, Your Honor," replied Mr. Soprano.

"Court adjourned," said Judge Janklow.

The prosecutor and Agent Wilson were upset. Prosecutor Swingum was angry that he didn't get his way; Agent Wilson was upset he never got a chance to interrogate Cortez Mack. Now that he knew he and Saheed were affiliated, he promised himself he would apply as much pressure to the boy as possible. To make matters worse, he hated that Dago lawyer, Mike Soprano. Mr. Soprano had made him look stupid more than once in different drug trials. "Not this time," he told himself.

The defense was happy with the outcome of the hearing. They got what they asked for, that was only because Judge Janklow and Mike Soprano were good friends. Mike was friends with all of the federal judges in D.C. Most of them played golf together at the D.C. Country Club, where Mike was a member.

Young Mac was taken back into custody. He had to be released through the booking process.

Saheed thanked Mr. Soprano, then he and True went to celebrate Young Mac's release by rolling up blunts of Hydro as fat as they could roll them and smoking until they couldn't handle anymore . . .

CHAPTER TWENTY NINE
County Hospital, Downtown Distribution City

One week later . . .

Agent Wilson had been waiting impatiently for Dr. Stanchfield to call him. When the call came, Agent Wilson didn't waste any time getting to the hospital, anxious to start interrogating Quincy Smith.

As Agent Wilson walked into Polo's hospital room, Polo noticed the badge around his neck and said "listen, man, I don't remember anything about being shot. The last thing I recall is getting in my car, so don't even waste your breath asking me questions about who shot me."

"That's too bad you don't know who tried to kill you. I did plan on asking you about that, but I'm here in regards to the nine ounces of crack cocaine, the 9 millimeter, and the bullet proof vest that were in your possession at the time you were shot."

"Damn," Polo said to himself. He had been so medicated for the past three weeks that he had forgotten all about that. "Excuse me, Officer, what's your name?

"Call me Agent Wilson."

"You FBI?"

"D.E.A."

"OK, Agent Wilson, I don't know nothing about no guns or drugs."

"You're in a lot of trouble; I can help you, brother."

"I don't know what you're talking about. I want a lawyer. Fuck this bullshit."

Growing irritated with the small talk, Agent Wilson said "Motherfucker, you got caught red-handed. I wouldn't give a fuck if you hired the dream team; your black ass is going to prison. A lawyer can't help you, God can't even help you. I'm the only person who can save your ass from doing life in the Federal prison system. With your record, you will never get out. And I'll personally make sure you go to the worse super-max in the country. Work with me and this little issue will be forgotten about."

Polo knew he was fucked and he wasn't trying to see life in the penitentiary for nothing.

"Forgotten about?" he asked.

"Forgotten about, I won't even bring it to the prosecutor's attention," Agent Wilson said.

"All right, I'll tell you what you want to know. Just promise me I won't go to prison."

"I promise," said Agent Wilson, laughing to himself about how this nigger turned into his snitch so fast.

"What do you want me to do? What do you want to know?" asked Polo.

"Oh, we've got plenty of time to discuss that, my friend. Right now, I want you to get some rest. I'll be by to see you tomorrow," Agent Wilson said, and then left the room.

As Polo lay in his bed deep in thought he knew he had just agreed to sell his soul to the devil.

CHAPTER THIRTY
North Side, Distribution City

Saheed was shook; it had been over a week since Kiesha disappeared. He decided to take that trip to Miami. He figured a little sunshine would take his mind off the stress and help clear his thoughts.

"Say, True, I'm flying to Miami for a few days. Do you wanna come?"

"Hell, yeah. When we leaving?"

"The plane leaves at 10:00 tonight."

"Ya'll just gonna fly to Miami, nigga? Y'all can't just leave the Mac," said Young Mac.

"Nigga, you know you can't leave town, unless you ready to go back to the county jail," said True.

"Shit, I may as well be in the county. I can't smoke, I can't leave town, I gotta check in every week. This shit is crazy," said Young Mac.

"Just make sure you do what them people tell you to. I need you out here promoting your music and enjoying the fruits of your labor," said Saheed.

Young Mac's album "Death before Dishonor" sold 10,800 albums in the first week, according to Soundscan. That was over $85,000.00 to be divided amongst them.

"Speaking of the fruits of my labor, when do we get paid?" Young Mac asked Saheed.

Royalty checks come every thirty days. It's gonna take two or three more weeks before we cash in.

"They need to come on with it. I got shit to do," said Young Mac.

"Check it, homie. Your album sold over 10,000 already. You got $20,000.00 and some change coming from that alone. I can give you an advance and just recoup when the check clears," said Saheed.

"How much and when?"

"Shit, I can advance you twenty G's before I catch my flight," said Saheed.

"That's love," said Young Mac, happy to finally get some money from the hard work he had been putting in.

"I gotta run, handle some shit. I'll call you and we can meet up. True, go pack your bags, G," Saheed said.

Just like that he had laundered $20,000.00. He would give Young Mac $20,000.00 in drug money and when the royalty check came that would be an extra 20 G's in the bank. Legal money. Saheed suddenly knew where to invest the stacks of illegal money he had accumulated over the years.

*****

As the plane landed in Miami, Saheed was focused. He was also deep in thought. He was putting a plan together that would consist of him making some power moves that everyone affiliated with him could benefit from. After a few days of fun in the sun he would go to work.

As the plane taxied up to the terminal, Saheed couldn't wait to get off the plane and get behind the wheel of the Rolls-Royce Phantom Drop-Head Coup he had reserved and was waiting at the airport. Even though it was a rental, he promised himself he was going to have some fun in that car. Especially since he was paying over a grand a day just to floss. He hadn't even told true about the car, he wanted to see his face when he got behind the wheel.

"Man, them Bloody Mary's got me tipsy," said True, who had been drinking Bloody Mary's non-stop the whole flight.

"I'm ready to smoke me a blunt and relax," replied Saheed.

"You got somebody picking us up?" asked True.

"Naw, we gonna rent a car," Saheed said as they exited the plane.

Taking out his cell phone, Saheed called Rose.

"Hello," she answered in her sexiest voice.

"What's up, baby?"

"Hey, Big Daddy, I was wondering when you would call."

"The wait is over. What you doing?"

"I'm just lying around, playing with my pussy and thinking about you."

"Do you miss me, baby?"

"Daddy, I miss you *sooo* much."

"Where you at?" asked Saheed.

"I'm in Miami, where else would I be?" Rose replied.

"Where *at* in Miami?"

"At the Holiday Inn on South Beach."

"What room?"

"333."

"I'll be there in an hour."

"Saheed, quit playin' so much," said Rose, getting excited.

97

"One hour, baby. Make sure that thang is hot and wet when I get there," Saheed said and hung up the phone. He didn't tell Rose he was on his way down. He wanted to catch her by surprise.

They got their bags, then went and got the keys to the Rolls-Royce. When they got to the car, True said "you ballin' out, ain't you?"

"Nigga, get used to it. From here on out, this is how we living."

When True saw the suicide doors open up on the coup he almost shit himself.

"Let me drive, Saheed."

"Now I know you're drunk."

"Come on, fam," True pleaded.

"You can drive later, cousin. Get in the car, let's ride out."

The car drove like a dream.

"I could get used to driving this," said Saheed.

"Real talk, me too," replied True, anxious to drive.

Saheed called his old friend, Suave.

"Hey, Suave, what it do, Amigo?"

"Saheed, my friend. How was your flight?" Suave knew Saheed was flying into town.

"The flight was cool, I just left the airport."

"Good. I'll be home in 30 minutes. Do you remember how to get to my house?"

"I got the address, I'll find you. Give me an hour; I'm going to make a quick stop."

"You must be going to see Rose," Suave said.

"You already know," was Saheed's reply.

"That's a good bitch, she's loyal to you."

"I'll see you in an hour," said Saheed, trying to read in-between the lines of Suave's comment about Rose.

Pulling into the Holiday Inn parking lot, Saheed parked the Phantom Coupe facing the ocean. Both he and True were captivated by the view of white sand, girls in bikinis and the great Atlantic. True had never seen the ocean before.

"Look at that cruise ship over there," True said, pointing his finger.

"Calm down, I see it, homie. When you gonna stop pointing your finger all the time? I told you, speak to me – all that pointing puts others in our business, looking like ET with that bullshit."

"Man, fuck you," replied True, jokingly.

"Here, roll a blunt. I'll be right back," said Saheed as he tossed True a sack of buds and a pack of Swisher Sweet cigarettes, then walked off into the hotel.

Knocking on the door to room 333, Saheed waited patiently for Rose to open the door. When she did, she was dressed in a string bikini, her beautiful bronze-colored breasts were pouring out of her top. She jumped on Saheed and was hugging him like he just saved her life. Hugging her back, Saheed walked her back into the hotel room. His eyes took in everything, from the stack of cash on the dresser to the rolled up dollar bill on the side of the bed.

"Saheed (sniffling), I'm so glad you're here. I missed you, Daddy."

Picking up the pile of money on the dresser, Saheed asked "is this everything?"

"Yeah, it's all there, Daddy, $22,000.00."

"I thought you would have made more than that."

"Well, I did a little shopping and I sent my mother a few dollars (sniffle)."

"Rose, you know I love you and what you do for me. You also know you don't have to lie to me."

"I know, Saheed, I don't have anything to hide."

Stuffing the bills into his pockets, Saheed grabbed Rose by her jaw, looked her straight in the eyes and said "Rose, tell me you ain't been getting high again."

Rose was caught off guard. She wondered how the hell Saheed knew she was high. That pussy-licking bastard Suave must have snitched on her, she told herself. She decided to tell Saheed everything.

"Saheed, listen, Daddy, I'm sorry. I've been using a lil' cocaine to help me get through this shit."

"Bitch, you know how I feel about you getting high. Where have you been getting it from, huh? Suave?"

Rose nodded her head "yes."

"Bitch, I can't hear you," said Saheed, looking like he was going to kill somebody.

"Yes, Saheed, Suave has been giving me drugs every day. He's always trying to talk me into moving in with him. He said I need to stop fucking with you and let him be my man."

"And what did you tell him?"

"I told him I'm your bitch and I won't leave you for him."

"Did you fuck him, Rose?"

"No," Rose lied, "but he ate my pussy."

"Bitch, that motherfucka got HIV! You need to take ya trifling ass to the doctor. You better pray you didn't contract the disease from that dirty dick motherfucker"

Rose started crying; knowing she had let Suave hit the ass raw and he came inside of her.

"I'm sorry, Daddy. Saheed, I'm sorry," she cried.

"Bitch, you're supposed to be down here on business. Instead you down here getting high and fucking for fun."

"I'm sorry," she cried.

Saheed knew Rose well enough to know she fucked Suave. "You fucked him, didn't you, Rose?"

She nodded her head "yes" and braced herself to be slapped. Instead she got an unexpected hug from Saheed. "Calm down, you'll be all right," he said as he embraced her. Saheed was playing mind games with Rose. He only said the nigga Suave got HIV because he wanted to see her reaction. He knew Suave would try to put Rose down with the stable of hookers he already had working for him. Suave was as smooth as they came and even though he didn't need Rose it was in his nature to make a play for her. To Suave it was a sport and he felt he was the best in the game. Saheed didn't know if his pimp friend, Suave, had HIV or not. He knew Suave had a high class escort operation in Miami, that was the only reason he sent his silly bitch Rose down here. If he knew she would start getting high when she came down, he never would have sent her.

"Well, me hitting that any time soon is out of the question, you need to call and make a doctor's appointment. I'm about to go check that nigga Suave. I'll be back, don't leave," Saheed said, walking out the door with the money still in his pockets. He was almost to the elevator and could still hear Rose crying.

Walking back into the parking lot, the first thing Saheed noticed was True standing outside the Rolls-Royce talking to four gold-digging beautiful Latin women. Saheed got in the car and lit the blunt True had rolled. Inhaling the smoke, he looked at True, who held up one finger in his direction, indicating he wouldn't be much longer talking to the women. Saheed looked closely at all the women and noticed they all had bodies that put the women back in D.C. to shame.

Stuffing the money Rose gave him in the glove compartment; he looked up at her hotel room and saw her staring down at him. When she realized he saw her in the window, she closed the shade.

True got in the car and reached for the blunt. Saheed passed it to him and said "I see you ain't wasting no time getting it going."

"I ain't got no time to waste. But for real, bitches ain't shit. Them hoes seen the Rolls-Royce and just like that they ready to do whatever," said True.

"They were looking good though."

"You ain't lying; I plan on having my way with them as soon as we get posted. They wanna kick it later."

"That's why we're here, to kick it until the sun comes up," said Saheed. He was still thinking about Kiesha, unable to get her out of his mind.

Pulling up to Suave's mansion, Saheed still couldn't believe how far Suave came in life. He used to be broke, now the nigga was a millionaire."

"Saheed, my Amigo, what's up?" Suave said, giving Saheed a hug at the front door.

"Que pasa, Suave? This is my homeboy, True."

"What's up, True?"

"I'm chillin' man, nice to meet you," True said as they shook hands.

Walking inside Suave's multi-million dollar home, True was impressed. The house reminded him of Tony Montana's house in the movie Scarface.

"So, Saheed, did you bring some Chronic down with you?"

"You know I did."

"Blaze that shit, holmes. I haven't been able to find any good Chronic in days," said Suave.

As True rolled up a couple blunts, Saheed and Suave talked about old times and brought each other up-to-date on what was going on. Saheed chose not to say anything to him about giving cocaine to Rose. He knew she got high by choice, not force. He had already broke her from her habit once before, it was looking like he would have to do it again.

When True finished rolling up the blunts, Suave said "let's go smoke out by the pool."

Walking outside to the backyard, True's dick got hard when he saw the two women lounging naked next to the pool. They seemed to be working on their sun tans.

Suave hit the Kryptonite and started coughing hard.

"Damn, that's some good weed. Sell me some."

"I only brought my personals; I'll smoke it with you though."

"You gonna have to mail me some of that when you get home," Suave said.

"I got you," replied Saheed.

As they smoked, Suave noticed True staring at his hoes so he asked him, "you like what you see?"

"Ain't no question," True answered.

"What one looks better to you?"

"I would have to say the one on the right."

"Miranda," Suave said, followed by something in Spanish that neither True nor Saheed could comprehend. The girl on the right got up and approached them. As she stood there with an attitude, Suave told her "this is my friend, True. Take him to the guest room and show him what Miami is all about."

She smiled and grabbed True's hand, then walked him towards the house. Saheed called True's name. When he turned around, Saheed tossed him the condom he had planned on using with Rose. True caught the Magnum rubber, and then he and Miranda disappeared into the house.

"Rose tells me you got some good coke?" Saheed said. Caught off guard by the comment, but always quick on his toes, Suave responded "this is Miami, what do you expect? But that's what I wanted to talk to you about. I got some kilos I need to get rid of ASAP."

"You a drug dealer now?" Saheed laughed. He didn't believe that at all, Suave had never sold drugs.

"No, I ain't no drug dealer, that's the problem. I got 40 keys and don't know what to do with them."

"What the fuck you doing with forty bricks?" Saheed asked, interested in where this conversation was going.

"Check it out. My little cousin Emanuel had robbed some fucking Haitians for fifty of them. To make a long story short, they ended up killing him. When I went to clean the house out he was renting from me, I found his stash."

"I'm sorry about your cousin."

"Hey, that's life. You live by the sword, you die by it. But what I'm getting at is that I know you can get rid of the shit up there in D.C."

"You're right, I could. But I don't even sell coke anymore – the city's on fire right now."

"Saheed, I understand, but hear me out. I got millions, I don't need the money. I'm going to take the proceeds and give them to his mother. I need you, Amigo. I don't trust anyone else enough to deal with them like this."

"How much do you want for them?" asked Saheed.

"Saheed, you're like a brother to me. I'll give them to you. Just give me half of what you make."

"50/50?"

"Straight down the middle," said Suave.

Even though Saheed didn't want to sell anymore cocaine, this was an opportunity too good to pass up. Doing a quick calculation in his brain, Saheed realized he would make $800,000.00 from the forty kilos at $20,000.00 each. He could sell them cheaper than that and get rid of them in a month easily.

"All right, Suave, we could make something happen. Let me chill for a couple days, and then we'll figure out how to get the shit up to Distribution City."

"I knew I could count on you."

"Always," replied Saheed.

"Hey, listen. When your boy gets done with Miranda, I'll take y'all to my condo overlooking the ocean. It's over on South Beach. Y'all can stay there until you leave."

Suave had come up after he moved from Distribution City where he was raised. He and Saheed were childhood friends. He had left town broke. All he had at the time was a snow bunny with hustle and the clothes on his back. He ended up in Las Vegas, where he started pimping hard. That's how he made his first million. He invested in real estate and built his fortune flipping houses. Suave owned property across the country and overseas. Even though he didn't need to, he continued to work them hoes out of his love for the game.

CHAPTER THIRTY ONE
North Side, Distribution City

Young Mac and Black were inside Chico's Custom Car and Rim Shop looking for the proper rims to put on the S550 Mercedes-Benz Young Mac had just leased. Even though he didn't have any credit, when he flashed the $10,000.00 to the Mercedes' dealer, the greedy car salesman pushed his pen and made it happen. Young Mac promised to return soon and pay the car off in full.

"I like those 22" Davins with the wood grain inside the chrome," said Young Mac.

"Yeah, I think those are the ones you should get," replied Black.

"Say, Chico, you got them wood grain Davins in stock?" Young Mac asked Chico, the owner of the rim shop.

"Yeah, I got a set for you. I'll give you a good deal."

"What's a good deal?" Young Mac asked.

"$7,500.00 with tires," said Chico.

"I got $6,500.00 for you right now."

"Amigo, $7,500.00 is as low as I can go. That's $1,000.00off."

"All right, Chico. How long will it take for you to put them on my Benz?" asked Young Mac, still finding it hard to believe that his first car is a brand new Mercedes.

"Not long, Amigo. Two hours at the most."

"Let's do it," said Young Mac. Then he cashed Chico out $7,500.00 for the rims. Even after buying the jewelry, the rims and the down payment on the Mercedes, Young Mac still had about $30,000.00, with more on the way. He had the hottest album in D.C. and he knew he would be a rich man soon. After his album reached 20,000 units sold, Kross Kountry Distribution agreed to upgrade his distribution deal from regional to nationwide. When that happened, he told himself wouldn't nobody be able to stop him. He was thinking for a moment that he should save twenty five G's and pay Saheed back for his lawyer fees, but he decided to handle that later. After all, that would take up damn near all his money. He couldn't believe he owed Saheed $45,000.00. A few weeks ago, he had never seen $10,000.00 of his own money, now he felt like he was balling out of control.

*****

Agent Wilson watched with envy as Young Mac pulled out of Chico's Custom Car and Rim Shop in the new Mercedes. He had been following him ever since he left his mother's house early in the morning, in the hopes that he would lead him to that nigger Corey James, a/k/a Saheed. Now that he saw him doing business with Chico, he wondered if there was a connection. Chico had been under surveillance for the last seven months. It was rumored that he was the biggest importer of methamphetamines in Distribution City. The D.C. Task Force was one snitch away from securing an indictment against the burrito-eating cocksucker.

Agent Wilson continued to follow Young Mac from a distance.

*****

Young Mac dropped Black off at his truck and went to go check on the marijuana plants Saheed left him to babysit. He was feeling like he was the next Jim Jones or even Jay-Z as he drove across town in his new car. People were breaking their necks to get a good look at his whip. He decided he would get custom plates that said "THE MAC."

Pulling up to one of Saheed's weed houses, he parked and went inside. Everything was in order. Seeing a half of a blunt sitting in an ashtray, he got an urge to smoke it. Unable to resist temptation, he smoked it until it burnt his fingertips and lips. Right when he got done smoking, his cell phone rang. He looked at the caller ID and saw it was Saheed.

"Yeah, what it do?" he answered.

"What's up, Mack'n?" asked Saheed.

"Nigga, you the one in Miami, tell me what's up."

"You sound high; tell me you ain't been smoking."

"I don't smoke. Anyhow, everything's cool. When y'all coming back?"

"We'll be back in a few days. I was just calling to make sure everything is straight back home." By "back home" Saheed was referring to his weed houses.

"Everything's cool. I'm at the house now, about to make my rounds," replied Young Mac. He had two more houses to go check on.

"All right, lil' homie, I'll see you when I get back."

"All right then," said Young Mac. He didn't even want to ask what was popping in Miami since he couldn't be there. Plus, he knew he would find out when they returned.

When Young Mac left to check on the plants at the other houses, he was oblivious to the fact that he was being followed by Agent Wilson, who was writing down every address he stopped at.

CHAPTER THIRTY TWO

South Beach, Miami

Saheed's days in Florida flew by and it was time to get back to Distribution City and go to work. Saheed worked things out with Rose, he explained to her that he made up the story about Suave having HIV and went on to lecture her about being more careful about the decisions she made. That was right before he told her it was time for her to go back to Distribution City.

When told she would be driving back with Miranda (Suave's woman) in a rental car, she started to act a fool. Not because the car was loaded with cocaine (he didn't tell her that), she just didn't like that bitch, Miranda. Saheed quickly put her in check and when he told her he was going to spoil her when she got back, she decided to go with the flow. She assumed there were drugs in the car. She knew Saheed was a hustler but decided not to question her man. They had left hours ago. The plan was to stay in Miami until the women made it home safely.

True, Suave and Saheed were at Suave's condo sipping champagne and smoking blunts.

"Say, why don't you call them gold-digging broads you met when we first got down here?" Saheed said to True.

"Man, I forgot all about those Beezy's, I'm calling them right now," said True, as he picked up his phone.

"Suave, you gonna have to get that money back down to Miami on your own time," said Saheed.

"Don't worry about that. My auntie, Emanuel's mom, lives in D.C. I told you, I'm giving it to her."

"That's your business. Just make sure you come pick it up when I call you." replied Saheed.

"Nigga, you know I'm never late when it comes time to collect."

"You ain't never lied," said Saheed, remembering how Suave would be quick to collect anytime he won a bet.

"When are you going to get your gambling operation back up and running?" asked Suave.

"I think I'm done with all that. The shit's too up and down, causes too much stress," said Saheed.

"Say, what's the address here, Suave? The ladies want to come over and lounge with us," said True.

Suave gave True the address, who gave it to the gold-diggers before hanging up the phone, then said "the bitches are on the way, it's three of them."

"I hope they're on business when they get here. I'm ready to fuck sumn!," said Saheed as he held his dick.

"Oh, they'll be on business. I've never had a woman come to the condo and not come out of her panties. It's something magical about this place," said Suave as he observed his own lavishly furnished home away from home.

They smoked another blunt while they waited for the ladies to get there. When they arrived, they were all in swimsuits and short skirts. Everyone was introduced and the sexual tension was high. After an awkward moment of silence, Suave spoke up saying "would y'all like some champagne? I've got Ace of Spades and Cristal."

"Say, Papi, we would love some champagne. But what I really need is an ecstasy pill. You wouldn't happen to have any, would you?" asked the big booty Columbian girl named Veronica.

"Matter of fact, Mommi, it just so happens that I got a few pills lying around. Does anyone else want one?" asked Suave. The other women, Stacy and Kim, both said they wanted one too.

"Yeah, let me get one of those, homie," said True.

When he said this, he looked at Saheed, who was shaking his head in disappointment. True didn't give a fuck, he was ready to party.

"What about you, Saheed?" Suave asked.

"I'm straight, player," said Saheed, realizing it was going to be a long night. He didn't like being around a bunch of high motherfuckers. Suave left the room and came back, handing out ecstasy pills. Saheed watched as they all swallowed the pills at the same time with a drink of champagne.

Less than an hour later, Stacy, Kym and Veronica were all pussy poppin' and giving lap dances to Young Mac's "Shake It, Baby," like they were working at a strip club. Saheed watched as Veronica, the big booty Columbian, lie on the couch with one leg in the air, and smacked her coochie. Making eye contact with Saheed, she signaled for him to come join her. He sat on the couch next to her as she slid her thong off. Saheed and the others watched as she began rubbing her clit and sliding a finger in and out of her wetness. Unable to just sit and watch any longer, Saheed reached out and removed Veronica's hand from her thong. Then he started finger fucking her like the professional he was. True and Suave watched with jealousy because even though all the women were bad, Veronica was the baddest and they both wanted to get her. They watched Saheed play with America's next top model for a moment, but their attention was diverted when Kym and Stacy assumed the 69 position in the middle of the living room floor and started licking on each other.

In the meantime, Saheed wanted to eat Veronica's pussy but he wasn't about to play himself like that. Instead, he grabbed her hand and led her out to the balcony overlooking the ocean. He bent Veronica over the rail and slapped her on her fat Columbian ass. Pulling out his sword, he put a condom on and entered her.

"*Oh, Papi!*" Veronica moaned repeatedly as Saheed worked her with the biggest dick she ever had inside her. The longer they had sex, the better it felt to Saheed, causing him to start beating it up to the best of his ability. As he continued to fuck her it sounded like she was crying, so he grabbed a fistful of her long hair, pulling her head back. When he did this, he noticed tears streaking down her face, so he stopped and pulled out.

"You OK?" he asked.

"Papi, don't stop! You make me feel so . . . it's unexplainable. Just fuck me, Papi!" she panted, grabbing Saheed's hard dick and sliding him back inside of her, instantly causing her to have another orgasm. The contractions from her vaginal walls caused an explosion deep inside of Saheed as he blasted off. He leaned on her, kissing her neck, as he slowly pulled out. Veronica's body had such a firm grip on him that the condom almost came off. Fortunately, Saheed grabbed it before that could happen. Heading to the shower, he walked back in the house, only to see True having sex with Kym missionary style on the couch. Minding his own, he continued to the shower. As he walked past the bedroom, he heard Stacy saying "Hell, no, motherfucker, you ain't fucking me in my ass, that shit hurts," with a Spanish accent.

Saheed laughed, remembering how the hoes back in high school used to call Suave an ass-hole bandit.

Saheed ended up having sex with Veronica six times that night. That woman was insatiable. He even had sex with her in the Rolls-Royce after they went to the store to get some more condoms. When Saheed woke up the next afternoon, the women were gone. True was missing his Rolex and swearing he would kill that bitch Kym if he ever caught her. Saheed looked at his phone and saw he had a text message from Rose saying she was home. She was right on schedule. Time to go to work.

CHAPTER THIRTY THREE
United States Courthouse, Downtown Distribution City

U.S. Attorney Herbert C. Dicks had called a meeting with Mayor Bucks, Police Chief Hoskins, and the head of the D.C. Task Force, Agent Wilson.

After everyone was seated in the conference room, U.S. Attorney Dicks started the meeting off saying "gentlemen, today a grand jury handed down indictments against 26 members of the Blood gang organization, with charges ranging from cocaine conspiracy to murder, amongst other things. These indictments will make headlines when the media hears about them, reason being that it is the largest drug conspiracy ever brought before the courts in Distribution City's history."

"That's great news, Mr. Dicks!" said Mayor Bucks.

"How were you able to secure the indictments?" Agent Wilson asked.

"Last week a gang banger named Rashad Thompson was arrested for charges ranging from attempted murder to felon in possession of a firearm. When the charges went federal, he agreed to cooperate in exchange for leniency."

"He must have done a lot of co-operating," said Police Chief Hoskins as he wiped sweat off his forehead. Chief Hoskins was Distribution City's first black police chief. Chief Hoskins was hired in an attempt to calm allegations of racism within the police department. He was also on Tank's payroll.

"The punk told us everything he knows and he knows a lot," said Mr. Dicks.

"What did he have to say?" Agent Wilson asked, very interested.

"He gave us critical information on the leadership of the Blood organization, as well as information on a few different unsolved murders."

"Has your office made my homicide unit aware of this information, Mr. Dicks?" Chief Hoskins asked.

"Yes, Chief, they were fully briefed earlier today."

"Out of curiosity, may I ask what unsolved murders we are talking about?" said the Chief.

"Well, Chief, the two Jane Does taken from the house fire on the southside last week, he helped us identify as LaTasha Long, a member of the Bloods, and the second victim was a woman they had kidnapped earlier that morning in an attempt to find her boyfriend."

"Why did they kill her?" asked Agent Wilson.

"According to our informant, they went to this woman's house to kill her boyfriend, only to find he wasn't there. They abducted her in an attempt to track him down. At some point in time, the woman who was kidnapped and this deceased woman, LaTasha Long, had a confrontation and Miss Long ended up cutting her throat, killing her. When a high-ranking member of the gang named Smoke returned to the house where this woman was being held and saw what Miss Long allegedly had done, he allegedly shot and killed her. Then he allegedly turned the gun on my informant and forced him and another member of the gang to assist him in torching the house in an attempt to destroy any evidence linking them to the crime."

"We know who Smoke, also known as Tyrone Love, is – the Task Force has a file on him an inch thick. Supposedly he's second in charge of the Blood gang."

"I'm aware of that, Agent Wilson, and Mr. Love has been named in the indictment," said U.S. Attorney Dicks.

"Did he say who this woman's boyfriend was? Or why they wanted to kill him?" asked Agent Wilson.

"Oh, you are going to love this," said U.S. Attorney Dicks, and then continued, "Her boyfriend's name is Saheed and they want to kill him in retaliation for the murder of Stanley Patterson, also known as June. And he just happens to have been the nephew of Terrance Patterson, also known as Tank, the leader of the Blood gang in Distribution City and mastermind behind their drug empire." U.S. Dicks paused to catch his breath and let the magnitude of what he was saying sink in. Then he said, "My informant tells me Tank was personally involved in the kidnapping and he's willing to testify in court in exchange for the witness protection program for himself and his family."

Sweating profusely, Chief Hoskins asked "I take it that this Tank character is included in this indictment?"

"Yes, Chief, he's the number one man on our hit list and has been for a long time. Now we have him by the balls. He's been indicted under the Rico laws – 848 kingpin statute for continuing a criminal enterprise, conspiracy to distribute over ten thousand kilos of cocaine, money laundering, kidnapping for the benefit of a gang, and murder for the benefit of a gang."

"All of this behind one man's testimony?" asked Chief Hoskins, digging for more information.

"No, Chief. All this comes from years of investigation. We have a witness list a mile long. Although this Rashad

Thompson's testimony, along with recently provided information from Quincy Smith, also known as Polo, are like nails in the coffin for these guys."

"Mr. Dicks, is this the same Saheed who we previously discussed?" asked Agent Wilson.

"Well, Agent Wilson, I will leave that up to you to figure out."

Mayor Bucks added enthusiastically, "when the majority of those charged are arrested, we will call a press conference and I want everyone present in this room in front of the news cameras."

CHAPTER THIRTY FOUR
South Side, Distribution City

After discretely meeting with Police Chief Hoskins, Tank realized it was all over. He was prepared for this day. He called a meeting with all his top soldiers so they themselves could prepare for what happened next. He let Smoke and the others know that Rashad Thompson, also known as Raw Money, and Polo were both working with the feds and we are the main cause of the indictments.

"I never thought Raw Money would cooperate with them people, never thought he would snitch," said Smoke.

"What we gonna do about this shit?" asked one of the soldiers.

"We're going to make an example out of him," said Tank.

"How are we supposed to do that if he's in federal custody?" asked the same soldier.

"We take it out on his family," replied Tank.

*****

The Hit Squad, led by Smoke, pulled up in a van with no license plates in front of Raw Money's mother's house. It was broad daylight as the four masked gunmen rushed the front door and kicked it open. Raw Money's mother screamed as the intruders entered her house. She was still screaming when Smoke slapped her in the jaw with the barrel of the 357. he clutched in the palm of his gloved hand. The blow knocked her unconscious and she fell to the floor instantly. They went room to room and rounded up everyone in the house and brought them to the living room, lining them up next to each other on the floor. All together was Raw Money's mother, his thirteen-year old brother, his ugly-ass woman, and their two year old daughter. After tying their hands behind their backs, Smoke looked at one of his soldiers and pointed his gun at Raw Money's mother. The soldier understood. Standing over the woman, he fired two rounds into the back of her head; the bullets tearing into the woman's skull caused blood and pieces of bone to fly back into the shooter's face and clothes. He fired one more shot into her back, aiming for her heart. Even though he missed her heart, it didn't matter – she was already dead.

Her terrified thirteen-year-old son tried to get to his feet after watching his mother get murdered but was knocked down by a bullet to the back of his head. Two more shots followed, one in his head and one in his heart.

As Raw Money's daughter screamed at the top of her lungs, she could barely be heard over the cries of her mother, which came to an abrupt end as the third soldier sent two hot bullets through her temple and one through her spine.

The three soldiers, with blood on their hands, looked at Smoke as the child continued to cry. He was thinking to himself, after what just happened to this child's mother and her daddy being a snitching-ass rat bastard, she would be better off dead. Acknowledging his soldiers staring at him, he put the revolver to the back of the child's head and pulled the trigger, silencing her cries. The little girl was no longer crying, but her jaw was quivering, until Smoke pulled the trigger again, sending her to heaven. He put one more bullet through her innocent heart just to make his point.

Dipping his hand in the pool of blood on the floor, he walked over to the wall and spelled "Blood "– with the warm blood of Raw Money's family."

They then fled the scene. All this happened in less than ten minutes.

*****

While all this was happening, Tank was already on his way out of town. He had safe houses across the country and several aliases with identification to match. He had millions of dollars spread out in different places from bank accounts overseas to stash houses in different states. Money was the least of his concerns. His plan was to get to Mexico and from there go to the Caribbean. He owned a large six-bedroom house in Jamaica and had a couple of smaller ones in the Bahamas.

CHAPTER THIRTY FIVE
International Airport, Distribution City

"Look at this hot-ass nigga," Saheed said as they approached Young Mac who was sitting inside his S550 Mercedes.

"That shit looks like a space ship on twenty-two's," said True.

Young Mac popped the trunk so they could put their suitcases inside. Getting in the passenger seat, Saheed said to Young Mac, "I see you're riding in style. Whose car is this?"

"Nigga, this is *my* car, why you asking crazy questions?"

"Just tell me this Mackin', how did you come up on a brand new Benz? You don't even have a driver's license."

"What can I say? Cash talks and bullshit walks a thousand miles. But for real though, I dropped ten G's on it down at the dealership and the money hungry motherfucker that sold it to me made it happen."

Saheed's first thought was that the transaction definitely got reported to the FEDS. He made a mental note to give Young Mac a receipt for the twenty grand he advanced him and take the necessary steps to cover his own ass on paper. That way if they were ever investigated regarding this incident they wouldn't have anything to worry about. He didn't give Young Mac any shit about being so careless about his spending because the money he gave him was supposed to be legit.

"Where y'all niggas going? I got this bitch waiting on me," stated Young Mac.

"Take me to my crib, we can drop True off on the way," said Saheed.

"So what y'all niggas do in Miami?" asked Young Mac.

"I'll tell you about it later. I wanna talk to y'all about a move I'm about to make that concerns both of you," said Saheed.

"I'm listening," said Young Mac.

"Here's the plan, my niggas. I got a few hundred thousand dollars I'm going to invest into the Death Before Dishonor album."

"For promoting the album?" asked True. He had thought Saheed was about to speak on the shipment of cocaine that he already knew of.

"Yes and no. I'm actually going to go store to store, city to city, buying up copies of the album. The reason for this is to recycle the cash and make it clean, allowing me to do as I please with it."

"That don't make sense. You'll lose a lot of bread," said True.

"I will lose money, you're right about that. But I'm just looking at it as the cost of doing business. Initially I will take a sizeable loss, but in the long run it will be profitable for me. After the money comes back to me via Kross Kountry Distribution, I will be able to spend and invest as I please."

"So what you're saying is, we won't get a cut from the albums you buy with your money?" said Young Mac.

"That's the reason I'm bringing this to your attention. You won't get a cut but you will benefit from the albums sold and the publicity it will generate. It's a win-win-win situation for all of us," said Saheed.

"Hey, it's your world, I'm just rapping in it," said Young Mac, not exactly sure if he liked Saheed's idea or not.

"It's all good," said True seeing the genius of the plan.

They rode in silence until they pulled up to True's house. As True got out, he told Saheed he needed some weed and would call him later. True grabbed his suitcase and Young Mac pulled off in a hurry. He was ready to drop Saheed off and go get the groupie he had waiting on him.

"The more I think about it, the more I like your plan, Saheed. The more albums sold on Soundscan the better."

"You know I would never get over on you, my nigga. I will be keeping track of every album I buy with my money. On top of that, I ordered 10,000 copies of the album to sell out of the trunk of the car. The copies that I buy from the store will be resold out of the trunk along with the others, that will recoup some, if not all and more, of the money I'll be giving up to Kross Kountry Distribution and the record stores," said Saheed. Then he dropped another jewel on Young Mac.

"So say I got caught with $20,000.00 cash. I can claim that I made that from the albums and police wouldn't be able to confiscate my bread."

"That's the best game I heard all week," said Young Mac.

"Last, but not least, we will be spreading your name, your name turns to fame and that fame will turn into cash money," Saheed preached, getting Young Mac hyped.

"That's what I'm talking about, let's do it!" replied Young Mac.

They pulled up to Saheed's house. He grabbed his bags out of the trunk and told Young Mac he would catch him later.

When he got to his front door there was a business card lodged in the screen. It was from the officer who took the missing person's report Saheed filed about Kiesha.

Walking inside, he set his bags down and called the officer immediately. Unable to reach him, he left a message asking the officer to return his call as soon as possible. His gut told him something was terribly wrong. He had a feeling she was dead. If she died while he was out tricking off his dick he wouldn't be able to forgive himself.

CHAPTER THIRTY SIX
North Side, Distribution City

Saheed's phone call wasn't returned until the next day. When the call finally came, the investigator said he came across some information and that he wanted to talk to Saheed in person. When the investigator asked Saheed to come to the precinct he reluctantly agreed.

As soon as he got off the phone with the investigator, he called Mike Soprano, who instructed Saheed to meet him in his office so they could go over to the precinct together, which was only a few blocks from Soprano's law office.

Inside the police station, Saheed and Mike Soprano were led to a conference room. Five minutes later the investigator walked in with none other than Agent Wilson. They took a seat at the table. After an awkward moment of silence, the conversation began with the investigator saying "Mr. James, I'm sorry to inform you that the body of Kiesha Adams was recovered in a house fire on the south side of D.C. a few weeks ago. The body was positively identified through her dental records."

Saheed sat speechless, not wanting to believe what he was hearing.

Mike Soprano spoke up saying "how did you know to check Ms. Adams' dental records against the remains found?"

The investigator looked to Agent Wilson who said, "We didn't until a few days ago when an informant explained to me that he participated in a kidnapping of a woman from the north side of town. We checked the date he gave us with all missing persons reports and Kiesha was the only one reported around that time. We decided to compare Kiesha Adams' dental records with the body we recorded and they were a perfect match."

Agent Wilson looked Saheed directly in the eyes as he said this. Saheed's worst fears just became reality. His blood turned cold thinking about Kiesha and their unborn child. Still, he sat without saying a word or showing any emotion.

"Why was she kidnapped? Asked Mike Soprano.

"According to my informant he and the suspects went to Miss Adams' residence with the intent of murdering her boyfriend, who goes by the name of Saheed." Agent Wilson paused to see Saheed's reaction. When there was none, he went on, saying, "But when they arrived at the house, her boyfriend wasn't there so they kidnapped her with the intention of using her as bait to get to him. She was taken to a known crack house on the south side of town. Inside of this crack house a woman named LaTasha Long allegedly cut Ms. Adams' throat while she was in handcuffs, killing her."

At the mention of LaTasha's name, Saheed knew the Bloods were responsible.

"Is this woman in custody?" asked Mike Soprano, with a disturbed look on his face.

"Unfortunately no. Shortly after Ms. Adams was murdered, LaTasha Long was shot and killed inside the house. She was murdered during an altercation behind what she did to Ms. Adams. In an attempt to hide evidence of the crimes committed, the house was set on fire with the two bodies inside," said Agent Wilson, still staring at Saheed. He didn't care about his loss. He was about to try to get him to cooperate with him.

"Who are these suspects you refer to?" asked Mike Soprano.

"They are all members of the Blood gang. And according to my informant there is a Fifty Thousand Dollar hit out on your client," stated Agent Wilson.

"Wait a minute. My client's name is Corey James. You said they are looking for a man named Saheed."

"Mr. Soprano, your client *is* Saheed. We know who he is. Right now all we need is for him to help us with our investigation so we can bring the killers to justice," said Agent Wilson.

The conversation was going on as if Saheed wasn't even present in the room, so Saheed spoke up saying, "my name is Corey James. I don't know what you're talking about when you say I'm Saheed. I'm Corey James, get it right."

"Whatever," said Agent Wilson, upset he didn't get Saheed to admit to his street name. "Just tell me what you know about the death of Stanley Patterson. You probably know him as June."

"What the hell is this, an interrogation? Gentlemen, this interview is over," said Mike Soprano as he jumped up from the table.

"Listen Corey, Saheed, whatever, the fuck your name is. There's evidence Kiesha was tortured before her death. I don't know if you're aware of the fact she was pregnant. Not only did they kill her, they killed her child. All we want is justice. Help us put the killers away," yelled Agent Wilson in a desperate attempt to get some information out of Saheed.

"Like I said, this thing is over with, Agent Wilson. Stay away from my client. If you wish to contact him, call my office."

With that said, Mike Soprano and Saheed left the police station. On the way back to his office, Mr. Soprano told Saheed he would find out all the details about the murder of Kiesha and get back to him. Saheed told him about his previous encounter with Agent Wilson and Mr. Soprano explained to him there wasn't anything that could be done about that since there wasn't any record of the incident taking place. They shook hands and went their separate ways.

*****

Saheed was fucked up in the head after hearing about the death of Kiesha and his unborn child. Tears fell from his eyes as he drove to his weed spot where he had stashed the kilos of cocaine the night before. He had met up with black earlier in the day and agreed to sell him five kilos for $85,000.00 - $17,000.00 each as long as he bought at least five. He decided he would still make the sale because even though he was hurting, he understood life goes on and he wanted to get rid of the dope as quick as possible.

As a tribute to Kiesha he decided right then that he would stop drinking and smoking weed. She would always beg him too as long as he knew her. It was time for him to handle his business.

CHAPTER THIRTY SEVEN

Saheed met with Black and sold him the five kilos. He took the cash to the storage locker and put it inside the stash spot in the Cadillac with the rest of his money.

He then went to pick up True so they could go eat dinner with Miranda and Rose at the Seafood Room.

True jumped into the rental car and without saying a word he fired up a blunt, took a couple of puffs, and tried to hand it to Saheed.

"I'm cool, dog," said Saheed.

"What you just say?" True replied, not believing what he heard. He had never seen Saheed say "no" to weed.

"I'm done smoking that shit."

"Yeah, right, you will be back smoking tomorrow."

"Say, man, Kiesha's dead. Them Blood niggas kidnapped and murdered her."

"Damn, that's crazy. How you find this out?"

"I reported her missing. Police found her body in a burnt down house over south. I'm thinking it was the same house Lil' Skitzo was killed in front of."

"The same house we saw burning on the news?" asked True.

"Yes, sir."

"That's crazy. Look, I'm sorry about your loss. Them niggas gonna pay for that."

"You're fucking right they gonna pay. I'm gonna cut that nigga Tank's nuts off and shove 'em down his momma's throat."

"You know I'm down Saheed, just let me know. It's whatever."

"I'm going to make the funeral arrangements tomorrow."

"Let me know, homie."

"I need you to help me get rid of this coke."

"That's what I wanted to tell you. That nigga Capone wants to buy a brick, said he gots 23 stacks for it."

"Capone?" said Saheed. He knew Capone but he always seemed like a corner hustler, not the type of cat who purchased kilos.

"Yeah, Capone, believe it or not the nigga done stepped his hustle up. He bought a half a key from me out of that brick you gave me," True said.

"The shit's on deck. I'll bring you two bricks later on; you can sell one to Capone and grind the other out."

"Yeah, that's what's up. I'm going to run through that shit."

"We'll handle that after we eat. Don't speak on the situation with Kiesha in front of Rose. I don't want her getting scared."

"I won't speak on it. I'm trying to see if Miranda wants to come hang with me tonight," said True, thinking with his dick again.

"Let Rose tell it, it sounds like she wants to choose you and quit fucking with Suave."

"Suave would be highly upset if I knocked his hoe," said True, thinking about that scenario.

"Shit, Suave isn't trippin' off that hoe. That man can have damn near any woman he wants."

Pulling up to Rose's mother's house, Saheed hit the horn and the women came out, both of them looking like a couple hundred thousand dollars. The women got in the car and were making small talk as Saheed drove to the restaurant. Rose spoke up saying, "Daddy, this bitch Miranda got some game. You should have heard her talking to that cop who pulled us over in Tennessee."

"Don't go there, Rose," said Miranda, as she laughed, thinking about the incident.

"Ya'll should have seen this bitch go to work. Instead of just accepting her speeding ticket she begged him to let her go with just a warning. When he refused to do so and told her he already wrote it, she convinced him to erase the motherfucker in exchange for a BJ," Rose laughed as she said all of this.

"Say it ain't so, Miranda," joked Saheed.

"I'm telling you the truth, Daddy. This bitch went back to the squad car and sucked that funny looking cop's dick right there on the side of the road!"

"I didn't get no ticket though, did I, bitch?" said Miranda. Even though Miranda didn't have any shame in her game, Rose had irritated her by speaking on her business in front of True.

"Rose, you act like you never sucked my dick on the highway," said Saheed playfully, trying to ease some of the building tension.

They made it to the Seafood Room and everyone was enjoying their dinner except for Saheed, who had lost his appetite thinking about Kiesha. He looked up to see Big Swing walk in with some fine-ass brunette. Saheed and Big Swing had been doing business for years. Saheed hadn't spoken to him since he changed his number, but he was just the man he needed to speak to.

As Big Swing and the woman with him waited to be seated, Saheed excused himself from the table so he could go holler at him. Big Swing was surprised to see Saheed. They talked for a minute, and then exchanged phone numbers. As they were speaking, Big Swing's date was studying Saheed from head to toe, as she licked her lips seductively. Saheed didn't pay her much attention, but he noticed the looks she was giving him. The host came to seat them and Saheed told Big Swing he would call him tomorrow, and went back to his table.

Back at his table he could see the three were having a good time getting drunk, as they ordered drink after drink.

"Say, man, me and Miranda are going to get a room in the Hyatt for the night." The Seafood Room was attached to the Hyatt Hotel.

"Yeah that's cool we'll just handle that first thing in the morning." said Saheed. He didn't want True trying to handle business after he had been drinking. Anyhow, True and Miranda left and checked into the hotel so they could get their freak on.

On the way back to the car, Saheed said to Rose, "Baby, you said you like them new Mustang convertibles."

"Yeah, I think they're cute."

"Well, tomorrow I'm going to the car lot to get you one. What color you want?" asked Saheed.

"I don't know."

"First thing in the morning we can go pick one out for you."

"Oh, Saheed, you really love me, don't you?"

"I wouldn't be buying you a brand new car if I didn't," said Saheed as he thought about the twenty years she would have been facing if the police would have found all of those kilos. Then his mind drifted to the suitcase full of money Rose brought to his attention. On top of that, she had made him a lot of bread over the years. She deserved a lot more than a Mustang, he thought to himself as he got in the rental car with Rose. He had spoken to his people at Kross Kountry Distribution earlier that day and they told him he would receive his first payment tomorrow, Young Mac had sold 26,000 albums in the first month. A check for $128,000.00 was scheduled to be deposited into his account at 9:30 a.m. That was $16,000.00 for True, who would be paid in the form of cocaine. Saheed decided he would give him a kilo, the nigga should be happy with that. $32,000.00 was Young Mac's but since he was in debt almost 50 G's he wouldn't see any of that, which meant the whole check belonged to Underworld Entertainment, and he had $128,000.00 to do with as he pleased.

Saheed's thoughts were interrupted by Rose unzipping his pants and pulling out his soft penis. Without saying a word she put it in her hot mouth. She loved to suck his dick every time she drank. She continued to give him head all the way back to his house.

CHAPTER THIRTY EIGHT
North Side, Distribution City

Saheed woke up in his bed next to Rose. Grabbing the remote he turned on his 42" plasma TV, turning the channel until he found the morning news. He tried to watch the news every morning so he could keep up with what was going on in his world.

He caught the headlines just as they started. The president of the United States just signed a three-hundred billion dollar war bill that congress had just passed, he and the Secretary of Defense stood there shaking hands and smiling like they both had just hit the lottery.

Then a story came on about a shortage of funds for education and how it may be the cause for a number of public schools being shut down. Next was a little bit of talk about how the new jail that was built downtown was set to open next week on schedule.

"That's some silly shit," Saheed said to himself as he was thinking if they took a small portion of the money that was spent on wars overseas, or even the war on drugs, and spent it on education, there wouldn't be much of a need for all these new jails and prisons that were being built across the country.

"In other news, 26 members of the Blood gang organization have been indicted on a number of federal charges." Hearing this, Saheed turned up the volume as he listened intently. "We now go live to a press conference in progress with U.S. Attorney Herbert Dicks and Mayor Bucks." The screen went to the press conference in front of City Hall, where Mr. Dicks was speaking into a microphone saying, "A Federal Grand Jury has returned indictments against 26 members of the Blood gang for conspiracy to distribute Cocaine. Some of these guys have been indicted also for murder and federal weapons violations. 24 of the 26 indicted have been arrested and are currently in custody. These indictments are the direct result of operation F.A.L.C.O.N., which stands for Federal and Local Coalition Overtaking Narcotics. Operation F.A.L.C.O.N. was put together by me and Mayor Bucks, along with the help of Chief Hoskins. To this day, operation F.A.L.C.O.N. has resulted in over 300 indictments and counting. I want to thank the D.E.A. and the D.C. Task Force for the hard work they put in every day. Also, the D.C. Police Department for striving to make this city a safer place for us all."

U.S. Attorney Dicks stepped away from the microphone and Police Chief Hoskins took his place. He began by saying, "Operation F.A.L.C.O.N. has been very successful during its short existence. I want to point out that these indictments against the Blood organization have not only gotten the worst of the worst gangsters off our streets, it has dismantled quite possibly the biggest drug operation Distribution City has ever seen. Furthermore, I want to make the public aware that we are still looking for Stanley Patterson, also known as Tank." He paused and held up one of Tank's mug shots for the cameras. "He is the alleged leader of the Blood gang and the mastermind behind their drug empire. He is considered armed and dangerous. We also have an arrest warrant for Tyrone Love, also known as Smoke," Chief Hoskins said, holding up a mug shot of Smoke. "He, too, is considered armed and dangerous. There is a $20,000.00 cash reward for information leading to the arrest of either of these two criminals. If you see either of these men do not, I repeat, *do not*, try to confront them. Find the nearest telephone and dial 9-1-1- immediately. Thank you."

It was Mayor Bucks' turn to speak. He cleared his throat and said, "Citizens of Distribution City. I think we will all sleep a little easier tonight because of law enforcement doing their job in an attempt to make us and our city safer. I promise you we will not let up on these criminals. When we are finished, you won't have to worry about catching a stray bullet from a drive-by, you will be able to take a walk without worrying about being robbed or attacked by some junkie. We are taking this city back from the gangsters and low-lifes that have plagued us for too long. (Sniffle) I want to thank all aspects of law enforcement involved in operation F.A.L.C.O.N. Thank you."

"Oooh," Saheed heard Rose moan, diverting his attention from the television to her. She had pulled the covers down so Saheed could see her masturbating, her hand was visibly wet as she played with her clitoris and dipped her pointer and middle fingers in and out of her fat monkey. Saheed watched her as he thought about where his condoms were, remembering they were on the nightstand next to her. He lay down on top of Rose, taking one of her nipples into his mouth as he reached for the condoms.

"Yes, yes, Saheed," Rose panted. "Take me, take this pussy."

He put the condom on while teasing her breasts with his tongue and lips. With the condom on he started rubbing the tip of his extra hard dick against her wet, hot and throbbing pussy.

Unable to stand Saheed playing with her, she grabbed his wood and shoved all of him inside her, pulling on his waist, making sure he went deep. Saheed began thrusting forcefully in and out, knowing Rose liked it rough. She was so wet and hot it felt like he was having unprotected sex. It felt so good he had to stop and make sure his condom hadn't broken. It didn't so he kept beating it up.

"Yes, Saheed, just like that, Daddy."

"Give me my pussy!" She liked for him to talk dirty to her.

"Oooh, I'm about to cum, oooh," Rose said, breathing heavily.

"You're so nasty, but this pussy's so good."

"ooooh, I'm cumming, I'm cumming on your dick," said Rose as she released her cream all over him.

"Make me come, baby," said Saheed.

"Cum on my face, Saheed," Rose said as she started rolling the pussy and throwing it back at him, intensifying the feeling for both of them and causing herself to cum again.

"I'm about to nut, baby."

"I love you, Saheed, oooh, give it to me," she moaned in pleasure.

Feeling like a volcano was about to erupt from inside of him, he pulled out of Rose's love and took the condom off just in time as spurts of hot, white fluid sprayed Rose from her waist to her neck. Saheed laughed at the sight as he tried to regain his composure and catch his breath.

"Thank you, Saheed," she said.

"What you call me?" he asked.

"I mean, thank you, Daddy," she replied as she started to get up.

"Hold on, don't move," said Saheed as he grabbed his cell phone. "This is a Kodak moment. Smile for the camera."

Rose put on a Kool-Aid smile, displaying her pearly white teeth and said "cheese" as Saheed took her picture. Rose continued to lie there and look stupid, so he told her, "go get in the shower, bitch."

"Why I gotta be a bitch?"

"Whatever, go get in the shower. We got things to do."

Rose got up and rushed to the shower, thinking about the Mustang convertible. She wasn't tripping off being called a bitch; she knew Saheed didn't mean no harm. It actually turned her on every time he referred to her as bitch and he knew it.

CHAPTER THIRTY NINE
South Side, Distribution City

Smoke wasn't sure what to do next. He had just received a phone call telling him that his face was on the news and that there was a $20,000.00 reward out for him. He had already heard about the police sweep that locked up a lot of his niggas, most of them owed him a lot of money. Tank had all of his cash stashed away somewhere and he was nowhere to be found. Smoke swore to himself that if Tank left him hanging he would murder the son of a bitch.

He couldn't believe this shit; it was all good just a week ago. All he knew was he had to make some moves quick.

He couldn't go home, his wife had let him know the feds raided their home and took the $60,000.00 he kept there. She was broke.

All he had to his name was the $8,000.00 in his pocket and five kilos of cocaine, which he needed to get rid of immediately and get the fuck out of town. He had a cousin in New York who could hide him out; his only problem was getting there. He knew if the FEDS caught up with him he was never coming home. He vowed that there would be high speeds and shoot-outs before he went out like that. He rolled over and slapped Shonda on the ass.

"Wake up, girl," he hollered. Shonda had been his bitch for years. Even though he was married, she still loved him to death and would do anything for him, or so he thought.

"What, nigga?" she asked groggily, as she stretched and yawned.

"Get up and fix some breakfast. Then I got a few errands I need you to run," said Smoke.

Shonda crawled out of the bed butt-naked and walked into the bathroom. Smoke watched her dark chocolate ass jiggle with every step as he reminisced about the hot sex they had last night. Shonda came out of the bathroom and walked straight to the kitchen to fix some breakfast out of bacon and eggs. She loved to eat so cooking didn't bother her. What bothered her was this nigga Smoke thinking he could just keep using her all these years, like she was just a dam fool. All those years he had been cooking dope and stashing drugs at her house – she was tired of it. She was tired of his empty promises and being dogged by the nigga. She knew he had a lot of drugs stashed inside her couch; she just needed him to leave so she could disappear with it.

"Fuck Smoke," she said out loud to herself, thinking about how he penetrated her asshole the night before and kept going as she begged him to stop. "The nigga done violated me in too many ways, too many times. Taking his stash would make us even," she reasoned to herself.

She brought him a plate full of toast, bacon and eggs as he still lay in the bed.

"So what do you need me to do, baby?" asked Shonda.

"I need you to go pick up that nigga Felon and bring him over here," he said.

"Smoke, you know I don't like no niggas at my house, especially with you keeping shit up in here."

"Just do what the fuck I tell you to, Shonda. Damn."

"OK, I'm sorry," she said.

"You know where he lives. Go over there and bang on the door until he answers. The nigga probably asleep. Tell him I said come over."

"Why don't you call him?" asked Shonda.

"Baby, just do what I tell you to do, shit!" said Smoke. As he walked to the bathroom she heard him mumble, "dumb ass bitch."

She heard him get in the shower and seized the opportunity to steal his stash. She quickly got dressed, then went and got the drugs out of the couch. Throwing the packages in a Macy's bag, she nervously ran to her car, put the bag in the trunk, got in the car and drove away. If she knew there was a cash reward for Smoke, she would have called them people on his crazy ass. When Smoke came out of the shower, he was ready to fuck something.

"Shonda!" he yelled, but didn't get an answer. For a second he thought she maybe went to pick up Felon but realized she would have said something to him. He went into the living room and saw the couch cushions on the floor. Digging in the couch he realized the coke was gone.

"That dirty bitch!" he shouted. Looking out the window he noticed her car was gone.

"*Shit!*" he said to himself, realizing he had to move around because she probably turned him in.

He threw his clothes on and grabbed his pistol, making sure there was one in the chamber. He made his way out to his car, watching for the police.

He was never one to cry but if he was the type he would be bawling like a bitch right now. He was hurt. It seemed as if overnight his life had fallen apart. First Tank betrayed him, now this bitch Shonda thinks she can get me. Fuck this, he thought to himself. Thinking Shonda probably went to her brother's house, he started driving in that direction. If he didn't get his dope back he would kill everyone he knew she cared for. His thoughts were interrupted by the gas light coming on.

"This is some bullshit," he said, then drove to the nearest gas station.

As he was filling his tank he started worrying about somebody recognizing him and calling the police. He was hotter than fried fish grease and thought about just getting on the Greyhound with the eight G's in his pocket. He knew that would be stupid because the feds would have notified the bus station and airports to be on the lookout for him.

*****

Maniac had just left the hospital downtown after getting his wound checked up on – the doctor said it was slightly infected and gave him a prescription for some antibiotics. He also informed him that he was HIV positive. When he asked the doctor how long he would have to wear the shit bag, he was told possibly forever. He refused to believe what the doctor told him. He was driving home, mad at the world. He was wishing death on every woman he ever fucked, along with all the Blood gang members in D.C. When he spotted Smoke at the gas station, it felt like Christmas. He parked and pulled his 9-millimeter Ruger with the 30-round clip out from under the back seat where he had it hidden.

He waited for Smoke to leave the gas station and started following him from a distance. Maniac didn't watch the news and he wasn't aware of what was going on with Smoke and the rest of the Blood gang, the streets weren't talking yet. If he had known what was going down, he wouldn't have done what he did next.

With his hat pulled low, almost covering his eyes, he pulled behind Smoke at a traffic light and ran into the back of his bumper, expecting Smoke to pull over. When he did, Maniac was going to pull up next to him and blast that flip-flopping piece of shit.

Instead of pulling over, Smoke hit the gas, causing his tires to squeal as he turned the corner. Smoke had thought the car was following him and when it ran into his bumper that only confirmed his suspicions. As he sped away, the car started chasing him – he thought it was an undercover cop on his heels.

When the driver of the car behind him started shooting at him, he knew it wasn't the police. They wouldn't be so reckless. When his rear window shattered, he grabbed his 40-caliber Glock and started shooting back through the already broken rear window.

Bluuka, Bluuka, Bluuka, the Glock kicked hard as he fired with one hand and kept the other on the steering wheel. Paying more attention to whoever was shooting at him than the road, Smoke jumped the curb and slammed into a giant oak tree, smashing his head through the windshield. Miraculously, he held on tight to his gun.

Maniac stopped his car when he saw the accident and was running up on Smoke's wrecked vehicle to finish the job.

In major pain but still alert, Smoke pulled his head back through the windshield and went to get out of the car. Forcing the door open, his eyes met Maniac's, who was running towards him with a big ass pistol pointed at him.

Maniac saw the driver's door fly open, and then made eye contact with Smoke. He saw Smoke try to aim his pistol at him, so he squeezed the trigger on the Ruger as fast as he could. *Bang, Bang, Bang, Bang, Bang, Bang.*

Smoke had his breath knocked out of him as multiple hollow-tipped slugs tore holes into his chest. He attempted to return the favor. *Boom,* he fired his gun, only the bullet went straight into the ground as he was no longer able to aim. "I let this nigga kill me," was his last thought as a hollow-tipped 9-millimeter slug caught him directly in his left eye, knocking him out of the game.

Maniac continued to fire his weapon as he walked closer to Smoke. He could see Smoke's brain was splattered all over the car. He knew he was dead. Still, he kept shooting him in the face until there was nothing left of it and his clip was empty.

"Die, bitch," Maniac said, then turned and ran to his car. He jumped in and fled the scene.

"Damn, I got a lot accomplished today," Saheed thought to himself. Since waking up early that morning and having sex with Rose, he had already gone and bought Rose a new car. When they got to the Ford dealership and were looking at the new Mustangs, Rose noticed the new Camaros across the street at the Chevy dealer and said that was what she wanted. Saheed bought a new Camaro for Rose, paid in full. Even though he put it in his name, she was happy. With Rose out of his way, he went on about his business. He was able to hook up with True and give him the two kilos. He explained the situation to True, letting him know that one kilo was his share of the "Death Before Dishonor" album sales and the other he owed him $17,000.00 for.

Saheed then met up with Big Swing, who bought two keys for $34,000.00 cash. Big Swing had wanted to buy four but Saheed didn't trust him like that because the nigga was shady. So he told him he could only sell him two at a time. Even though Saheed knew Big Swing's money was good, he knew the game and knew that even cats you're cool with will switch up and put a bullet in your back if the price is right.

He was on his way to meet up with Black and Young Mac, who seemed to be attached at the hip ever since Young Mac leased that Mercedes. Black said the car was a "pussy magnet" and said something about getting one for himself.

When Saheed pulled up on Young Mac's car, he saw they had three women in the backseat of the Benz. Saheed parked and as he approached them he noticed one of the ladies was Pocahontas. He had a quick flashback of her deep throat and his dick got hard instantly. He greeted them and Pocahontas was quick to speak, saying "hey, Saheed, you can't call a bitch?"

"I've been busy," he replied.

"No, you've been missing out," she replied, licking her lips seductively.

Saheed laughed at her comment and turned his attention to Young Mac, who was obviously high.

"Damn, boy. Your eyes is red as shit," said Saheed.

"We been smoking all day. I'm higher than the gas prices," Young Mac said as he laughed at his own comment.

"Nigga, you stupid. Them people will lock your ass up. You think they playing with you?"

"Yo, chill, Saheed. I gave him the game. All he gots to do is drink a bottle of Test Pure before he takes the piss test and he will test negative," said Black, inserting himself into the conversation.

"Both y'all is dumb niggas. The feds can tell if you drink that shit. The way to pass is by drinking a few gallons of water beforehand and when you go take the drug test you piss out pure water," said Saheed.

"Yo, you hear about them Blood niggas? 26 of them niggas got indicted," said Black, changing the subject.

"Yeah, saw it on the news this morning. Two of them are on the run – Tank and some other nigga."

"There's only one on the run now. The other nigga's name was Smoke. He got killed this morning," said Black.

"Oh, yeah? How you find this out?" asked Saheed.

"Yo, I got my ear to the streets and you know how the streets be talking," Black said.

"So what y'all about to do? I got to make funeral arrangements for Kiesha," said Saheed, saddened at the thought of having to bury his boo.

"Yo, we just lounging. I put all my business on hold. With them Blood niggas locked down I'm guessing there's about to be a drought and I'm trying to cash in when it hits," said Black.

"OK, I'll catch up with you niggas later."

"Hey, Saheed, I'm trying to ride out with you," said Pocahontas from the back seat.

"Not today, I'm hard at work," he replied.

"Bitch, you're coming with us, what the fuck's wrong with you?" said Young Mac.

"Nigga, who the fuck you calling a bitch? You got me fucked up."

As Saheed walked back to his car he could hear Young Mac and Pocahontas arguing. He got in the rental and drove away. He had to go check on his marijuana crops and make arrangements for Kiesha's funeral.

*****

Agent Wilson was bored. He had been following Cortez Mack and his Mercedes around all day. All he seemed to do was drive around meeting women. When Young Mac met up with Saheed, his dick got hard. Finally he was back on his trail. That didn't last long – in less than a mile he had lost him.

133

"*Fuck!*" screamed Agent Wilson, pounding on the steering wheel.

Out of frustration he decided to take the rest of the day off. He wanted to get some sleep before the clan meeting he had scheduled for later that evening.

*****

After pulling out of the hood where he had met Young Mac, Saheed, being the cautious person he was, watched his rear view mirror closely. After about a half mile he suspected he was being followed so he drove like he was Jimmy Johnson through the side streets of Distribution City, making it impossible for anyone to follow him without blowing their cover. He made a mental note to tell Young Mac not to bring the Benz anywhere near him or his spots until shit cooled down.

"Hot ass stupid motherfucka," Saheed said to himself, thinking about the mistakes Young Mac seemed to keep making.

Walking into his weed house, Saheed walked straight to his grow room. He instantly realized it was time to harvest the crop. He could tell by how all the of the buds' hairs had turned from blond to red, which meant they were ready.

Unplugging the grow lights, Saheed grabbed some scissors and started on the laborous task of cutting, trimming, and hanging the marijuana. He could tell it was going to be a large yield and it was going to take up the rest of his day. He was tempted to smoke a blunt but resisted the urge and chose not to.

His cell phone started ringing. Looking at the caller ID he saw it was True calling.

"What it do, my nigga?" he answered.

"Saheed, I just got robbed!" exclaimed True.

CHAPTER FORTY ONE
North Side, Distribution City

After receiving the phone call from True, Saheed stopped what he was doing so he could meet True at the studio. When he got there, True was waiting on him.

"Tell me what happened," was the first thing out of Saheed's mouth.

"After I got that work from you earlier, I went and put that shit up at my crib. Capone had been blowing my cell phone up wanting to buy that kilo."

Saheed cut him off saying "Capone robbed you?"

Not believing what he was hearing – True and Capone were like family and Saheed didn't think he would cross True like that.

"Yeah, Capone. Let me tell you how it went down. So I go meet up with the nigga and we agree to do the transaction at his spot in the hood. I went to get the brick while he went and got his money together. We met back at his spot. As soon as I come in the door, the nigga lights a blunt then passes it to me. I start smoking and he starts talking about how the last shit didn't cook up right and how he lost a few ounces," said True.

"That's bullshit, that shit was A1. That nigga must not have known what he was doing," Saheed interrupted.

"No, he knows how to cook but I put two ounces of cut on his package. He says he lost three so I'm thinking he was trying to hustle me for an extra ounce."

"You know how niggas do, tell me how it went down," said Saheed, impatiently waiting for the rest of the story.

"So, anyhow, I know this shit I got for him now is pure. He starts talking about he wants me to cook some for him to make sure it's good before he buys it. I'm thinking, shit's all gravy; he's got a bag of money on the table. So I'm like, whatever. I took an ounce out of the brick and set the rest on the table next to the money. Meanwhile, he's in the kitchen getting the shit I need to cook the dope. Anyway, to make a long story short, I'm cooking up the ounce of crack and he's standing over my shoulder. When it was done, I went to the sink to put the cold water on it. I told the nigga to come look and he didn't answer. When I turned around he was gone, so was the money and the coke. I walked into the living room and the front door was hanging open."

"So you saying the nigga just ran out the house?"

"That's what happened. I pulled out my pistol and ran outside. The nigga was nowhere to be found."

"What I tell you about turning your back to a motherfucker when you're selling dope? You're lucky that nigga ain't kill you."

"I know, I put my guard down being that that was the homie," said True.

"Business is business, True, remember what I told you about when you put your guard down? You get hit."

"I know I fucked up. I got the money to cover the loss though. I just can't believe the nigga betrayed me."

"That's a petty nigga for you, petty niggas do petty shit."

"Man, fuck that. I'm burning the nigga on sight," said True.

"That nigga Capone on some dope fiend shit. The $17,000.00 he just put you in the hole wouldn't even cover lawyer fees for a murder charge," said Saheed.

"I know, it's the principle. I got love for that man; I would *kill* for that nigga. And he wants to try to play me…. I'm killing that bitch," said True, getting angry.

"This is a perfect example why I don't do business under the influence. That shit takes you off your square."

"Check it out, Saheed. I know where the nigga is at right now. I'm 'bout to go handle my business. I just wanted you to know what's poppin'," said True, as he pulled out his pistol and pulled back the slide, putting a bullet in the chamber.

Saheed could tell by the look in his eyes the boy was serious.

"Well, let's do it then, what we waiting on?" said Saheed, pulling out his new Glock model 19. He pulled the slide back and it made a *click-click* sound as the armor piercing bullet went into the chamber.

"Where you get that?" asked True.

"Suave gave it to me. I stashed it in the rental with the cocaine."

"I need one of those," said True, looking at his raggedy Ruger.

"I'll get you one, but for now what you got will work."

"Oh, I'm good with this, I just like Glocks," said True.

"Don't we all? Fuck all that, how you know where Capone's at?"

"I've been fucking his baby's momma for the last few months so I called her. She answers but she's acting like she can't talk. I ask, 'is that nigga over there?' and she says 'yeah.' This was right before you got here. He couldn't have told her what's going on. Silly bitch," said True.

"Well let's go pay them a visit and get your shit back," said Saheed, ready to put in some work for his little homie.

"Let's do it," True replied.

*****

North East, Distribution City

It was still light outside as Saheed and True approached the block where Capone's baby's mother's house was located. They didn't really have a plan other than to just run up in the house with their guns drawn and make Capone give the drugs back and take whatever money he had.

True directed Saheed into an alley and they stopped directly behind the house where Capone was hiding out. They knew he was there because his car was parked out front.

They couldn't see the house because the garage was in the way. Saheed took the keys out of the ignition.

"I'm putting the key in the ashtray." He did this in case of emergency and True had to drive for some reason, he would know where the car key was.

True and Saheed both pulled ski masks over their faces and put gloves on their hands.

True got out and Saheed followed him into the backyard. True, having prior knowledge of the house layout, knew the back door was a raggedy piece of shit that didn't even have a deadbolt – the only lock was on the door's handle. Knowing this, True ran straight to the door and kicked it right next to the handle, causing it to swing open. Rushing in they ran straight into Capone and his baby's mother. They were both sitting at the kitchen table, naked with crack pipes in their mouths and a pile of crack on the table in front of them. As True and Saheed stood with their pistols pointed at the two, Saheed laughed at the sight of Capone and his lady naked, smoking crack together and looking scared to death. Both of their eyes appeared as if they were going to pop out of their heads. They were scared to move or make a sound, partly because of the effects of the crack smoke. Capone started to stay something when True smacked him in the forehead with his pistol, knocking him to the floor. Then he kicked Capone's baby's momma in the breast, knocking her out of her chair. She screamed as she landed on the floor next to Capone.

"Bitch, shut the fuck up," said True, disgusted with the fact he had been fucking a crack head and not knowing.

"Where that shit at?" said True, before he slapped Capone again with the pistol.

"Aaagh," yelled Capone after being hit with the gun. "It's on the table, take it."

"Nigga, I ain't got time for games," said True. Then he put the nine to Capone's kneecap and pulled the trigger. *Blam*, the 9-millimeter round tore through Capone's knee, causing him excruciating pain.

"Sir, I swear that's everything, on the table," Capone lied through his pain. If he wasn't so high he would have realized the masked man was True and thought of a better lie than that.

"Nigga, you wanna play? Let's play then," True said, and shot him in his other knee.

"Aaagh," Capone screamed out like a bitch. "Sir, I swear, that's everything. Don't shoot me no more," he said as he started crying along with his baby's mom.

"Nigga, you got balls. I see I'm a have to put a bullet in them." Placing his gun against Capone's nut sack, he was about to pull the trigger when Capone's baby's momma screamed, "nooo, stop, please! The shit's in the cabinet above the sink. Just take it and leave," she cried.

She couldn't let her man get his nuts blown off; she planned on having more babies and wanted all her children to have the same father. True opened the cabinet and found the kilo that was stolen from him. It was torn open and a small chunk was missing – that was probably the dope that was on the table. As True stood there, relieved to get his dope back, Saheed snatched Capone's baby's mother by her weave and put his Glock to her forehead.

"Bitch, where the cash at?" he screamed in her face.

"Oh, my God!" she cried. "Don't kill me; I'll get it for you."

"Get up," Saheed ordered.

As he marched her at gunpoint out of the kitchen, Capone was in major pain as he bled out of both his shattered knees on the kitchen floor. Through his pain he thought about beating his baby's momma's ass for giving up his money and his coke. He would have made them niggas kill him before he gave it up. His thoughts were interrupted by a hot stream of piss hitting him in the mouth as True emptied his bladder on his face and his bullet wounds.

Saheed came back into the kitchen holding a bag that True assumed was full of Capone's money. Saheed laughed when he saw True pissing on Capone.

"Come on, let's go, nigga," said Saheed as he scooped the pile of crack off the table into the bag with the money.

They ran out of the house and got into the car. When Saheed started it up, he looked at the clock and noticed they were in and out in seven minutes.

Driving back to the north side, Saheed told True to lie his seat down so it only looked like one person in the car.

"I can't believe you was fucking that smoked out bitch, let me find out you, smoking," Saheed laughed.

"Man, fuck you. I ain't know that bitch smoked," replied True.

"You burnt out. I can't believe you pissed on him."

"The nigga lucky I didn't blow his dick off, even worse kill him and that crack smokin' hoe."

z z z z z

North Side, Distribution City

"$23,000.00 exactly," said True when he finished counting the money they took from Capone.

"So the nigga could have just paid for the brick and avoided all this drama," said Saheed, shaking his head.

"Stupid ass nigga, I can't believe he was smoking crack."

"Only God knows what these cats out here be on. This just goes to show you can't underestimate the next man's greed," said Saheed.

They divided up Capone's cash, $11,500.00 each.

"That nigga knows where my house is, I got to clean it out and relocate," said True.

"Go get your shit and bring it to my grow house on 47th, you can stay there. Matter of fact, you can take shit over for me."

"You bullshitting," True said, not believing what he heard.

"Real talk, I just harvested a crop today. You can have the next one. All you gotta do is pay the bills and the house note. I've been too busy to take care of the plants anyhow, it's all yours."

"That's love, Saheed. I appreciate that, I appreciate everything."

CHAPTER FORTY TWO
Distribution City Cemetery

Saheed watched as Kiesha's casket was being lowered into the ground, his face was without expression but he was crying on the inside. He was in extreme pain for causing the death of the only woman he ever loved. Knowing that Kiesha and his unborn child were tortured before being savagely murdered was driving him crazy. He knew if he ever saw Tank he would kill him on sight, whatever the cost may be – he would suffer the consequences.

They were forced to have a closed casket service due to the damage the fire caused to Kiesha's body.

Black, True and Young Mac attended the funeral, along with some of Kiesha's coworkers and a few of her distant relatives, it was a small gathering.

Saheed spared no expense on the funeral, buying the finest of everything money could buy. He picked out a purple casket since that was Kiesha's favorite color and a large marble headstone that had a picture of her face engraved into it. The sky had been covered all day by dark gray clouds. After they finished lowering the casket, it started raining hard. Unable to keep his emotions in check any longer, his tears mixed with the rain as he started crying for his baby. He was wishing he could trade places with Kiesha. He knew it should have been him being laid to rest.

*****

South Side, Distribution City

At the same time Kiesha was being buried, Maniac was burying his dick deep inside Kendra, Black's cousin. He had been having sex with her ever since he got out of the hospital, after they both had been shot outside of the church at Lil' Skitzo's funeral. Lucky for her she only suffered a minor flesh wound. The bullet had gone in and out. After a few stitches and a bottle of pain pills, she was back to normal with a barely visible scar.

Maniac knew he was wrong for fucking her, especially without protection after the doctor told him he was HIV positive, but being that they had already been having unprotected sex he told himself that she would have already contracted the virus. He was right.

"Oh, baby, you're the best," Maniac said after cumming inside of Kendra.

140

She just stared at him with a smile on her face. He had been dicking her down so well she was starting to fall in love with him.

Putting his clothes on he said to Kendra, "I'm going to run to the liquor store, do you want anything?"

"Yeah, grab me a bottle of Alize and a pack of Newports."

"OK, give me some money," Maniac demanded, with his hand out.

Kendra rolled her eyes in disgust as she reached down on the side of the bed to grab her purse. She took out a twenty dollar bill and gave it to him while thinking to herself, "Why do I keep getting involved with these petty ass niggas?"

Maniac took the bill from her, rubbed her breast, and said, "I'll be right back, don't bother getting dressed."

Then he left to go get some liquor and smoke the sherm stick he had in his car. As he got in the car he grabbed the PCP-laced cigarette and lit it up. Inhaling, then exhaling, the smoke, he began to feel the effects immediately. The wet was stronger than the watered down stuff he was used to smoking.

"That boy from Kansas City gots some gorilla piss!," Maniac thought to himself. When he had bought the sherm stick he had watched as the dealer from K.C. dipped a brown cigarette in a vial containing a thick yellow liquid that reminded him of honey, the water he was used to was clear and looked like water, living up to its name.

"That boy from K.C. is going to put these other cats out of business." Maniac said to himself as he felt the drugs effects throughout his entire body.

He started his car to go to the store. Five minutes later he was driving the wrong way down a one-way street. He was so high he didn't know where he was or what he was doing. It wasn't long before he side-swiped a parked car, and then crashed head-on into an oncoming SUV. The accident smashed the front end of his car and broke two of his ribs. Maniac was so high he didn't feel any pain.

Maniac jumped out of the wrecked vehicle and started running down the street.

"Hey, come back!" the elderly driver yelled out of the window of his SUV before calling the police on his cell phone.

Running down the street, Maniac didn't realize he was just in an accident or even know why he was running. All he knew was he was hot, so he peeled his shirt off and continued to run. The cool rain on his skin felt good but he was still burning up so he stopped running in the middle of the street and took his pants off. A car drove by, honking his horn, and he took off running again, leaving his pants and shoes behind. He wasn't wearing any underwear so he was asshole-naked with some socks on, running down the street in the middle of rush hour.

Responding to an emergency call about a hit-and-run, Officer Gabinski was en route when he saw a naked black man running down the street towards him. Officer Gabinski turned on his emergency lights and pulled the squad car in front of the man. When he did this, the man stopped and stared wild-eyed through the windshield at Officer Gabinski.

Officer Gabinski had been trained on how to deal with the mentally ill and after 30 seconds of watching the crazed man in front of him he recognized him as Jamal Sanders, also known as Maniac. He assumed he was high on PCP, being that he was known to smoke that shit.

Officer Gabinski realized this was a prime opportunity for him. He called for back-up and got out of the car with his 9-millimeter Berretta aimed at Maniac's chest.

"*Put your hands up now!*" screamed Officer Gabinski.

Looking at the fucking pig with the gun pointed at him was making him mad. When the white boy started shouting at him, Maniac didn't hear a word he said. All he heard was a voice telling him to take the gun and kill the cracker. Without thinking twice about it, Maniac rushed the officer.

When Maniac refused to put his hands up, Officer Gabinski thought "he must know I'm going to kill him." When he started running towards him, Officer Gabinski didn't hesitate to pull the trigger. The bullet struck Maniac in the heart but he continued to run towards Officer Gabinski, who then squeezed the trigger again, shooting Maniac in his face. Even though he was already dying the second bullet took his life and caused his body to collapse face-first onto the pavement. His head slammed hard with a thud into the wet concrete right in front of Officer Gabinski's boots. He looked at the dead black man and said "die, nigger."

CHAPTER FORTY THREE
Open Field, The Middle of Nowhere

The full moon shone bright through the cloudless night, the stars seemingly obeying its every command. One hour north of Distribution City a very large cross was being burned. Approximately twenty men dressed in white hooded robes, one dressed in red, formed a circle around the blazing structure. As the fire engulfed the wooden cross, the men devoured can after can of German beer.

"Brothers," Agent Wilson began his speech, "I thank you for coming on such short notice. Tonight is a night for celebration. As you are all aware, Brother Gabinski did the Brotherhood and the world a favor last week when he shot that nigger to death. Gabinski, as the Grand Dragon of the D.C. Chapter, I thank you on behalf of the Ku Klux Nation. It's an honor to have you amongst us."

"Whoo-hoo! Good shootin', Gabinski!" shouted one of the robed Klan members with a country accent.

"Kill a nigger, get a paid vacation. Must be nice," said another member. He was referring to the paid administrative leave Officer Gabinski received. Standard procedure in police shootings.

"Brothers," Agent Wilson resumed, "according to the National Study done by the N.A.A.C.P. and others, Distribution City ranked number one for the highest amount of racial profiling. Even though the population is 70% white, 75% of the traffic stops have been of people of color. I want everyone to give themselves a round of applause."

After the hand clapping and yelling stopped, Agent Wilson, also known as the Grand Dragon, continued. "We all need to keep up the good work and continue to keep the pressure on them chinks, spics, and especially those fucking niggers."

"What's up with the drugs?" asked one of the Klansmen.

"Everyone's package will be given to them at the end of this meeting," said the Grand Dragon.

"Good, because the demand for them there methamphetamines is unbelievable. We're all going to be millionaires real quick," said the same Klansman.

Agent Wilson had managed to start a Ku Klux Klan chapter in D.C. two years earlier. It consisted only of his closest buddies in law enforcement, including two county prosecutors and a federal judge. Since then they had formed a drug ring that was

143

impenetrable. They confiscated large quantities of illegal drugs and resold them for a 100% profit. Even the members not involved in the actual dealing of the drugs received an equal share of the proceeds. They had no fear of being caught, because they felt they were above the law.

After debating minor issues for 15 minutes, the Grand Dragon brought the meeting to an end, shouting "White Power!"

"White Power!" the others replied in unison.

"White Power!" screamed the Grand Dragon.

"White Power!" the others hollered back at him.

Afterwards, the confiscated drugs were distributed accordingly and the Klan members dispersed.

CHAPTER FORTY FOUR

Over a week had passed since True had shot Capone in both of his knees. Since then, Saheed had been focused on laundering his money. With his help, "Death Before Dishonor" album sales had surpassed 20,000, according to Soundscan and was now scheduled for nationwide distribution.

The downside to Underworld Entertainment's distribution deal was that they were responsible for all promotional costs, including touring and video budgets. Saheed was set on getting a video shot for Young Mac's single "Shake it Baby" within the next month. He knew that having a hit video was the most important piece of the puzzle, being that the album was going to be distributed nationwide. By seeing an artist's video, consumers got a visual image to put to the song. Saheed knew there was no better promotion than a video. A video gave the artist a chance to sell himself to those who otherwise would be uninterested. It was a proven fact that a hit video generated more album sales than an artist going on a nationwide tour. With all the legal troubles Young Mac was going through, going on tour was out of the question. At the rate Young Mac was rolling, the only place he was going was jail. Every time Saheed had seen him in the past week, Young Mac was higher than the North Star. Saheed had tried to talk to him but was unable to get through to the boy. He was letting the money and his new position in life go to his head.

For the past week Saheed had been sending Rose from store to store, city to city, and even out of state to purchase copies of Young Mac's album. He instructed her to then turn around and sell them everywhere she went for $5.00 to $10.00 each, whatever she could get. Being that Rose was a beautiful woman in a brand new Camaro, she had no problem getting people to buy them. Using her hustle skills and charm, she was able to sell almost as many copies of the album as she bought every day. Saheed had received the shipment of 10,000 copies of the album and was selling thcm out of the trunk of his car also. On top of that, he had a street team of young cats from out of the hood working for him. They would be out at any given time in different parts of the city, putting posters up and harassing people to buy the CD for $10.00, of which they got to keep $5.00 for themselves.

Between himself, Rose, and the young boys working for him, they had sold almost 1,000 copies underground in the first week. Saheed was surprised. He was also satisfied with the 1,500 albums sold online at www.UnderworldEntertainment.com. He needed to go talk to his friend at the university so she could rearrange the website for him and make it possible for people to purchase only the songs they wanted for 99-cents apiece. None of the albums sold underground or online were registered on Soundscan but all the funds came back to Saheed and to him that was all that mattered.

Saheed was scheduled to receive another check from Kross Kountry Distribution in a few weeks. He told himself that when it came he was going to buy himself that new Lexus LS 46Oh, the one that parked itself.

As busy as he had been with his music, he still managed to keep the cocaine moving. He was down to 21 kilos. Since everyone was saying it was dry in the streets, Saheed had started to go up on his prices and put some cut on the coke. He could easily mix in an extra five kilos of cut with the dope he had and no one would complain. If he did that he would make an extra hundred Gs but he decided not to be greedy. He just wanted to hurry up and get rid of the drugs and move on with his life. The FEDS were busting people's heads left and right. With so many suckers in the game snitching, Saheed didn't want to sell drugs any more. Even though the money was outrageous and he was balling out of control, it wasn't worth it to him. Saheed knew if he ever got caught he would do his time before he turned snitch, even if it meant spending life in prison or the death penalty.

He was on his way out to Black's house to see what he wanted. Black had called him and told him to come over but didn't say what he wanted. Saheed was hoping the nigga wanted to buy another five bricks. They never talked business on the phone. Pulling up to Black's house, he saw Black look out the window. When he got to the door, it swung open before he could knock.

"Saheed, my favorite nigga," Black joked, obviously high. His eyes were bloodshot red and the house smelled like weed.

"What up?" Saheed said as he shook Black's hand and stepped in the house. He saw Young Mac passed out on the couch.

Black saw Saheed looking at Young Mac and said "that nigga's hung over from last night."

"Where's the Benz? I didn't see it outside."

"Ah, we got it impounded last night. Police pulled me over, realized I was drunk. They let us go but impounded the car."

"They let you go?" Saheed asked, amazed. "That's a blessing."

"I know it is. I was fucked up. We kicked it last night though, check this out," said Black as he walked over to his entertainment center and pushed "play" on a video camera that was hooked up to the TV.

When the video came on, Saheed instantly recognized Pocahontas and one of the cum freaks that was with her the night he met her. The two women and Black were all sitting around with drinks in their hands. Obviously Young Mac had the camera. Saheed could tell because his hand swung into view and he recognized the Rolex on his wrist.

"Hold on," Black said, and hit fast forward on the camera. As the video played in fast forward, Saheed watched as Young Mac turned the camera around on himself. He was saying something, but something else caught Saheed's eye.

"Rewind that back to where the nigga turned the camera on himself. I want to hear what he said."

He did so and pushed "play" on Young Mac's close-up. Instantly he knew why Saheed told him to rewind the tape. Clearly visible was a powdery white substance on the side of his nose and inside his nostrils.

"So that's what y'all be on," said Saheed, realizing where the change in Young Mac's attitude was coming from.

"We just be kicking it, relax," said Black, then pushed fast forward again on the tape. When it got to the part he wanted, he pushed "play."

The camera showed Pocahontas going down on her friend. After a few minutes of this, it showed Young Mac coming into the picture. Pocahontas stood up and Young Mac began having sex with her friend. Then Black came into view. He wasn't wearing any clothes. Pocahontas began performing oral sex on him.

"*Damn, nigga!* What the fuck happened to you?" Saheed asked.

"What you talking about?" asked Black.

"I remember you were 225, all muscle. Now you look like the Black Skelator, you ain't nothing but skin and bones," Saheed said before he started laughing at his boy.

"Yo, fuck you, you're just mad I had your girl on her knees giving me some boss head."

"That ain't never my girl, player. She do got some boss head, though."

"You ain't lying," said Black, "and that pussy good."

Saheed continued to watch the video as Black laid back on the couch and Pocahontas started riding him. Young Mac and the other girl were still doing their thing in the background.

"You hate to wear a condom," said Saheed.

"Yo, Saheed, you just do you and I'm a do me."

Saheed shook his head back and forth from left to right, thinking to himself "that nigga Black's crazy." At the same time he was erasing Pocahontas' number out of his cell phone.

"I know you ain't call me over here to watch this amateur porn. What's the business?"

"Yo, what you talking about, amateur? Nigga, I'm professional."

"What the fuck ever. What's the word?" asked Saheed.

"Yo, I need five more of them things."

"I got you faded, when you want them?"

"Shit, I'm ready right now," said Black.

"I can go grab them and bring 'em back over here if you want me to."

"Yo, that will work. I'll be right here waiting on you."

"Give me about one hour," said Saheed.

"Same price, right?"

"$85,000.00 for five, you know the deal."

"I can't beat that with a pistol. You want the money now?" asked Black.

"Yeah, that would make it easier and less complicated."

Black got up and went upstairs to get the cash. Saheed focused his eyes back on the TV. He watched as Black and Young Mac switched women. He looked on as Young Mac mounted Pocahontas and entered her in a doggy-style position. He wasn't wearing a rubber.

"These niggas is crazy, burnt the fuck out!" Saheed said to himself.

Just then Black walked back downstairs holding a small Nike sports bag. He tossed it to Saheed.

"$85,000.00, no need to count it," said Black.

The money was arranged in thousand dollar bankrolls with rubber bands around them. After counting it twice, Saheed said, "This is only $83,000.00."

Black laughed and said, "Yo, I knew you were going to count that shit." Then he tossed him the other two rolls of money.

"You play too much, player," said Saheed as he was thinking about how far they came from teenagers selling petty crack on the street corners to selling birds. As he got up to leave, Black said, "one hour, don't be bullshitting."

Saheed slapped Young Mac on his face, waking him up.

"Get your shit together, homie," he told him.

Saheed returned to Blacks house forty-five minutes later with 5000 grams of cocaine.

CHAPTER FORTY FIVE

Polo's head was pounding; he was suffering from a migraine headache. After he was shot, being exposed to bright lights or loud noises would trigger the migraines that would last for hours.

He had a plate in the back of his head covering the hole in his skull. The surgeon told him it was a miracle he even survived, and without brain damage it was unexplainable. He had to wear a shit bag that was constantly getting on his nerves and he walked with a serious limp due to the bullets that tore through his legs.

He didn't know who shot him but had a feeling it was Saheed who pulled the trigger.

He had been out of the hospital for a week and as fucked up as his life was, this Agent Wilson dude was making it worse. He had already helped him get them Blood niggas indicted and was scheduled to testify against any of them that went to trial. He had told him about a couple of murders committed by the Black Mob, causing a good friend of his who was about to get out of prison to get charged with murder and sent back to the county jail. Every time he tried to tell Agent Wilson he didn't know anything else, he was threatened with being charged in Federal Court on drug and weapons charges. There was no way he was going to Federal Prison. He would set his own brother up before he let that happen.

"Tell me more about this Saheed guy," said Agent Wilson.

"I already told you everything I know about him," pleaded Polo, wishing Agent Wilson would stop talking so loud – his head was killing him.

"Look closely at this picture. You sure that's him?"

"I'm 100% sure that's him, he's the one who shot and killed June."

"You said you believe he's the one who shot you?"

"I said I have a feeling it was him," replied Polo, getting irritated from being asked the same questions repeatedly.

"Listen, I need you to say that right before you were shot you recognized Saheed's face and that he was the shooter." Now this white man wanted him to lie for him again. This wasn't the first time he asked him to tell a lie. He lied and said he bought some dope from half of them Blood niggas that were indicted, even though he had only dealt with a couple of them.

"Fuck, Saheed, being that I wasn't able to kill the nigga. I hope the feds give him life," Polo thought to himself.

"Man, I'll say what you want me to say and tell you everything I know about him. Shit, I can even tell you the name of the bitch who braids his hair."

"With your testimony, we will be able to put him away forever, get revenge for your dead homie. Wouldn't you like that?" asked Agent Wilson with a big smile on his face.

"You putting me into the witness protection program after this is all over, right?"

"Oh, yeah, sure. I'll get you set up in a nice big house somewhere where nobody knows your name," Agent Wilson said, then started laughing.

Polo went on to give another recorded statement identifying Saheed as a drug dealer who was responsible for the murder of Stanley Patterson, also known as June, and the one who attempted to murder him.

Armed with the hearsay evidence from the Blood members who were cooperating and Polo's statement, Agent Wilson was ready to bring his case against Saheed to the District Attorney's office.

Even though Saheed hadn't sold all of the cocaine he got from Suave, he had gotten rid of more than enough to pay Suave his half of the proceeds. Suave didn't call Saheed about his money, Saheed appreciated that. He decided to pay the man now, instead of making him wait until he got rid of everything. If he ever needed a loan, he knew he could count on Suave. He dialed Suave's number.

"Que pasa, mi amigo?" Suave answered the phone.

"I'm chillin', what's up with you?" replied Saheed.

"I'm getting ready to put this hoe in my past, if she keeps coming up short with my cash, that's what's up."

"You're crazy, man," Saheed laughed in response.

"Speaking of hoes, would you believe Miranda ain't never come back home? I don't know where she's at."

"Nigga, she's still up here in D.C. Her and True been laid up every day on some lovebird shit."

"For real, that bitch is tripping. That's all she wants is a boyfriend. I told her about that shit. Matter of fact, I done told her twice. Mark my words, Saheed, she'll be back because she needs pimpin' in her life."

"I hear you, P. So when you coming to D.C.? I thought you were going to come home and visit your people," said Saheed, indicating to Suave he had his money for him.

"Shit, I planned on coming up tomorrow. Look, I'll call you when I get off the plane," said Suave.

"OK, I'll be waiting on you."

"All right, my friend," said Suave.

Saheed hung up the phone and started laughing at what Suave said about Miranda wanting a boyfriend. If that's what she was looking for, that's what she got in True. That nigga True was acting like he wanted to get married to the hoe.

Saheed decided to call True and see what he was up to. After the first ring, True picked up.

"Hello," he said, answering the phone.

"What's up, lil' homie?" asked Saheed.

"Ain't shit, me and Miranda just relaxing."

"You know what I just realized?" asked Saheed.

"What's that?"

"I just realized you ain't nothing but a rest-haven for a hoe. A whore's boyfriend," joked Saheed, attempting to piss True off.

"Man, fuck you!" said True, getting upset behind Saheed's disrespecting him.

Saheed laughed, and then said "look at your situation, man. You laid up with a bad-ass bitch who just made the next man some major money. You're treating her like a queen while she plays you like a trick. When she gets tired of you, or vice versa, she'll be back to putting money in the next man's pocket," said Saheed, still laughing at his lil' homies' foolish ways.

"What the fuck ever. It's too early for your bullshit. What's up?"

"All I'm saying is you need to be trying to get some money out of that slut, she's a fucking gold mine."

"You're on bullshit, I'll call you later," said True, then he hung up on Saheed.

Saheed knew he was on some bullshit, but he liked to amuse himself. He decided to call Young Mac and fuck with his mental. After four rings Young Mac answered.

"Yeah."

"What is it? You're up kind of early for a rap star or haven't you been to sleep yet?" Saheed said sarcastically.

"Whatever motherfucker, I'm down here at the free clinic getting my dick checked out. One of these trifling hoes done burnt Da Mac," said Young Mac.

"You sure you ain't burnt yourself? Because you were looking like the trifling one on that video that Black has over at his house."

"Man, fuck you; it was probably your bitch, Pocahontas, who burnt me."

"I told you, she ain't none of mine. I bet you put that rubber on next time, won't you?"

Damn right, all that raw sex ain't cool. I fucked around and learned the hard way," said Young Mac, meaning every word he said.

"You better pray you ain't learned too late and get your blood checked. That HIV shit is going around the town."

"I'm about to get checked for everything. Say, I gotta go, the nurse is calling my name."

"Check it out; I need you to come holla at me today. We're about to get paid again and we got moves to make," said Saheed.

"I'll call you when I get out of here."

"Later," said Saheed.

"One-hundred," replied Young Mac, and then the line was disconnected.

Saheed was on a roll so he decided to call Black. After getting his voicemail he called again and got an answer.

"Yo, what's popping, yo?" asked Black, breathing heavily into the phone.

"Nigga, you sound like you getting some pussy or something."

"Me and Rita are just getting some early morning exercise."

"Who the fuck is Rita?" asked Saheed.

"Yo, you know who Rita is. Rita, say good morning to Saheed."

"Good . . . ooooh . . . good morning, Saheed, aaah . . ." she moaned as Black kept stroking her. Saheed instantly recognized the voice of Pocahontas.

"Yo, now you know who Rita is?" asked Black.

"Dig this, Black. I was calling to put you up on game. Young Mac down at the clinic right now and he said he thinks that bitch burnt him," said Saheed laughing, knowing what was coming next.

"Yo, what you say?" Saheed heard a slapping sound and then Rita let out a scream. "Now that you say that, this bitch does smell kinda funny and my shit feeling weird," said Black, knowing Rita's scent was past funny, more like rotten fish.

"Sounds like she burnt you, too. Niggas better start wrapping it up," said Saheed, getting inside Black's head.

"You scandalous, bitch. You burnt me!" said Black, and Saheed heard another slapping sound. Then he heard Rita saying "hit me again and it's on you, dirty bitch." Saheed heard another slap and Rita screaming some more.

"Yo, I'm a call you back," said Black, then hung up the phone. Black was known to slap a bitch; the nigga didn't have too much respect for women. Thinking about Black's lifestyle, he realized the man didn't even really respect himself. He couldn't the way he put himself out there with all them different women.

Saheed got on his laptop to check out how many albums had been sold. According to Soundscan, the "Death Before Dishonor" album was approaching 35,000 sold. In less than two months they sold almost 40,000 units. If Young Mac was on a major label, they would probably be thinking about dropping him from their roster for having those kind of numbers, but for a first release from an independent record label, those numbers were beautiful, Saheed told himself. Now that the album was being distributed nationwide, Saheed needed to get that video out of the way immediately. It should have already been done. He was thinking about how he could have already sold a hundred thousand units if the video was done and how much money he was missing out on. Kross-Kountry already owed him another six-figure check. He hadn't spent any of the money from the last check besides buying that Camaro for Rose. He told himself it was time to buy a nice house on the lake and a new whip, when his thoughts were interrupted by his phone ringing. It was Black calling.

"What's up, player?" asked Saheed.

"Yo, this bitch just cut me. I had to knock her out."

"Where she cut you at?"

"The bitch sliced my face with a razor."

"You better go to the doctor and get stitched up."

"That's what I'm about to do," replied Black.

"While you're there, get your dick checked," Saheed said, then started laughing at his boy.

"Yo, fuck you! I'll call you later."

"Hit me later," Saheed said, and then hung up.

*****

County Hospital, Downtown Distribution City

After getting off the phone with Saheed, Black had looked at Rita who was knocked out cold from him punching her in the temple. He poured some cold water on her face in an attempt to wake her up. After she regained consciousness, she saw Black's bloody face and apologized. He said he was sorry for putting his hands on her. He dropped her off at a cab stand on his way to the Emergency Room and they agreed to never speak to each other again.

Since then, the doctor had to give him 66 stitches on his face. The cut seemed to follow his jaw line all the way to his chin. It would definitely leave a scar.

The doctor also gave him a shot of antibiotics and a prescription for some pain pills. He was told he had Gonorrhea and Chlamydia. He was ready to leave except he had taken an HIV test that the doctor had said only took 20 minutes. That was 35 minutes ago and to Black it seemed like the longest 35 minutes of his life.

When Dr. Stanchfield returned to Black's room, he had a solemn look on his face. Black knew it meant bad news.

Dr. Stanchfield cleared his throat and said, "Mr. Williams, there's no easy way for me to tell you this. According to the quick test, you are HIV positive."

"That can't be right!" said Black, feeling like he had the breath knocked out of him.

"Mr. Williams, these tests are 99% accurate. We're sending a sample to the lab for further analysis. The lab will only confirm what we already know. I'm sorry."

"I'm gonna die," said Black, with tears in his eyes. He had no idea where he may have contracted the virus.

"Mr. Williams, it's not the end of the world. With treatment you can live a significant amount of time, longer than without. In the last five years, the medical community has made great advances in the fight against AIDS."

"This is crazy, doctor," said Black, tears running down his face.

"This is reality, Mr. Williams. Every day young men and women like yourself are diagnosed with HIV. It's an epidemic that has to be stopped."

CHAPTER FORTY SEVEN

The next day, Suave caught a plane to Distribution City like he said he would. He rented a Cadillac Escalade then went to meet Saheed at the Rib House for lunch. After they ate, Suave followed Saheed to go pick up his money.

The cash was at one of Saheed's weed houses, where he and Young Mac had been up until almost dawn counting and recounting the loot. During that time, they decided to shoot the video to "Shake it Baby," in and outside of Lucy's Cabaret. They agreed to find the best looking women possible for the video shoot and planned to do it the next week.

Once they made it to the house, Saheed showed Suave around and he was very impressed by the sophistication of the grow operation. He wanted to learn how to grow it himself so Saheed gave him a book called "The Marijuana Bible," and told him the book would teach him everything he needed to know.

He then gave him a good suitcase that held Sauvé's share of the money, the same suitcase he had taken from Icy Waters. There was the $90,000.00 that Saheed had taken from Icy Waters' house, all in ten and twenty dollar bills divided into thousand dollar stacks. They were taking up a lot of space and making the suitcase look like it held a lot more than it did. The rest of the money was made up into five and ten thousand dollar bundles of different bill denominations. Altogether there was $340,000.00 total.

"Damn, you got rid of that shit quick," said Suave.

"I still got almost half of it left. I just wanted to get you out of the way so I wouldn't have to worry about it."

"I appreciate it. I always know I can trust you," said Suave.

"I got a gift for you," Saheed said, then left the room. When he came back a minute later he tossed Suave a large plastic bag full of Hydro.

"What's this?" asked Suave after catching the bag.

"It's half a pound of Purple Kush and half a pound of Kryptonite, same stuff I brought with me to Miami. You said you wanted some, there it is. A token of my appreciation."

"Good looking out, my friend," said Suave. Then he opened the suitcase. Saheed thought he was putting the weed in there. When he started pulling out the thousand dollar stacks, Saheed didn't know what he was doing. Suave pulled out forty Gs altogether and set the cash on the table. Then, unexpectedly, Suave said, "this is for you, Saheed, a $40,000.00 bonus."

"Suave, that's unnecessary," said Saheed, not believing what he was hearing. Suave had always been good people but never the type to give money away.

"I'm not trying to hear what you're talking about," replied Suave, then went on saying "I still got three hundred thou right here in the suitcase. I'm going to give my aunt two and keep one for myself. Take that as a token of my appreciation," said Suave as he looked Saheed in his eyes.

After they were finished, Suave left to go give the money to his aunt and they agreed to meet up later that night.

Saheed had some extra time on his hands so he decided to go look at some cars. He drove straight to Lexus of D.C. and told the dealer he wanted to test drive the Lexus LS 600h. As he test drove it and the dealer pointed out all the options available, Saheed fell in love with the car.

One hour later, Saheed was driving out of the dealership in his new Lexus. It was all black with black leather. The dealer explained that the black-on-black was rare and hard to come by being that only so many cars were made with that combination.

Being that Saheed had very good credit, he could have bought the car but he decided to lease it instead because he didn't want to commit himself to the $115,000.00 they wanted. He could buy it later if he wanted. Riding in his new car, he felt like his position in life had been upgraded. The feeling didn't last long.

After driving around for awhile he rolled through the hood to see what was up with his lil' homies and to see how many CDs they had sold. Along with the CDs, he had given a couple of them young boys some Hydro to sell. He knew he had to stay on top of them or them lil' niggas would fuck his money off.

After making his rounds he stopped in the neighborhood convenience store. When he came out, Agent Wilson was sitting on the hood of his Lexus.

"Get the fuck off my car," Saheed demanded.

"Some nice wheels you got here, boy," replied Agent Wilson, not budging from his position.

"What the fuck do you want? I have nothing to say to you."

"I'll tell you what I want; I want my piece of the fucking pie."

"I don't know what you're talking about," said Saheed, getting nervous as his heart started pounding.

"Don't play stupid with me. I know all about Underworld Entertainment and your deal with Kross Kountry Distribution. I know about the six-figure check you received and about the one that's on the way," said Agent Wilson.

"So what the fuck are you saying?"

"What I'm saying is, when you receive the next payment, your black ass is going to pay me the sum of $50,000.00 cash. If you don't pay, we're going to find so much crack cocaine inside your vehicle that you will spend the rest of your life sweeping floors inside of a Federal Prison," Agent Wilson said with a smile.

"That's extortion."

"Call it what you want, but those are your two options. If you try some slick shit like turning me in, my boys got me covered and your ass will be doing life," Agent Wilson bluffed. Being greedy, he decided to extort Saheed on his own.

Thinking quick Saheed said, "All right, I'll pay. How do I get in touch with you when I get the cash?"

Agent Wilson had been anticipating the question and handed Saheed a piece of paper with a number written on it.

"You got two weeks. If I don't get my money by then, it's all over with for you," said Agent Wilson, getting off the car. "In the meantime, we'll be watching you."

Saheed didn't reply, he just got in his car and drove away. He didn't have any intention of paying that motherfucker a dime. He just needed to come up with a plan.

He had no idea that while he was in the store, Agent Wilson had planted a GPS tracking device under the rear bumper of his car.

CHAPTER FORTY EIGHT
Downtown Distribution City

A week had passed since Saheed's run-in with Agent Wilson. He still wasn't sure how he was going to handle the situation.

He was trying to stay focused on the task at hand – the filming of Young Mac's video – and not let his thoughts distract him.

He had hired a film crew from the University of Recording Arts for the video shoot. Being that he was cool with the owner of Lucy's Cabaret, he was able to rent the place out for a few hours. It wasn't cheap.

They had spent the entire week searching for the best looking strippers possible who would be willing to do the video, not one of the women they found turned them down. Most of them agreed to do it for free; they just wanted to get their face on television.

Suave decided to stay in town for the video shoot. He had been trying to catch up with Miranda all week but with True's help she managed to avoid him – until now.

Saheed had been expecting Suave to check her on sight. Instead he was ignoring her like he didn't know who she was. Occasionally he would glance in her direction. Miranda and Rose were both shaking their goods, along with about 15 other strippers; all were dressed in high heels and hoe gear. G-strings were everywhere, along with short skirts and fishnet stockings.

The cameras were rolling as Young Mac rapped away and his hit single "Shake it Baby" played repeatedly in the background.

Saheed, Suave, Black and True were lounging in the VIP section, surrounded by dancers. Bottles of champagne and Cognac sat at the table in front of them. The film crew kept a camera pointed in their direction so they would be shown at different times throughout the video. Saheed made sure they got him pouring champagne across the ass of two of the dancers as they pussy-popped on each side of him. His diamonds looked like fireworks as they reflected the light in the club. He had bought True, Young Mac, Black and Suave all Underworld Entertainment chains. They were representing to the fullest for him and his company tonight.

After hours of listening to "Shake it Baby," Saheed had a headache and he was glad it was over. All they had to do now was record the end of the video that showed all the dancers piling into the cars out in front of Lucy's Cabaret.

Parked in a row was Young Mac's S550, behind that sat Saheed's Lexus looking flawless on the 22" rims he had purchased the day before, behind him was True's cocaine white 750 BMW that he had leased for $10,000.00 down from the same dealer Young Mac had got his car, and last in line was Suave in his rented Cadillac Escalade.

The cameras rolled as the women all squeezed into a vehicle of their choice and were driven off into the night. At least that's how it would appear in the video. In reality, they were driven around the block. After recording this scene twice and pulling back around the block, the director hollered "cut, that's a wrap!" then smiled, knowing he was going to turn his film into a hit video and finally make a name for himself.

As everyone got out of the vehicles, Saheed heard Suave's voice boom, saying "bitch, get in this motherfuckin' truck!"

He turned around and saw Miranda running towards the Escalade. As she ran past True he asked her, "hey, where you going?" Without stopping, she barely slowed her pace as she looked back at him and said, "I'm sorry, True, I gotta go," then blew him a kiss before hopping into the Escalade. Suave had told Saheed that as soon as they were finished shooting the video, he had to hit the freeway and head back to Miami. He decided to drive home because of the $100,000.00 and the pound of weed in his possession. Saheed had vacuum-sealed the money and the weed, then they stashed it in the door panel earlier that day. As the Escalade started to pull away, it stopped right in front of True. The driver's window dropped down and Suave stuck his head out the window. With a mean mug on his face and looking True in his eyes, Suave hollered out loud enough for everyone and their momma to hear, "nigga, *this* is pimpin'!" Then he pulled away, leaving True standing there looking dumb. Saheed had watched this transpire and he knew True would never see Miranda again. He approached his lil' homie and said, "come on, let's go kick it."

They were all oblivious to the fact that Agent Wilson and his partner were down the block taking pictures.

*****

After the video shoot, everyone went to the After Party down at the Embassy Suites. Saheed had rented out several rooms and filled each one with bottles of liquor.

Saheed had invited everyone he was cool with and before long the rooms were packed with people. Some of them weren't invited; they had just heard about the party and decided to show up. Everyone was having a good time. Each suite consisted of two or three rooms, so there was plenty of action. Some of the hustlers got a dice game going in one of the backrooms; plenty of money was exchanging hands. In another room, some of the strippers decided to practice their profession and started getting their hustle on. Some of the ballers had their money out and were tricking big. Black was among them.

In the suite next door, the atmosphere was more relaxed. People were just kicking back, lounging, and getting their drink on. Saheed looked over at True, who was looking like he had the blues.

"What's wrong with you?" Saheed asked True, knowing the man was sick over Miranda going bad on him.

"I'm cool," True lied. "I think I drank too much," he was really thinking how he'd like to kill Suave and live happily ever after with Miranda.

"Let me find out you're stressing over that hoe."

"I ain't thinking about that bitch," said True, telling another lie. Then he took another swallow of Hennessey. Saheed knew True was full of shit but decided not to press the issue. He changed the subject, saying "I think that video is going to be hot. I want you and Young Mac to go down and help them people edit the film tomorrow."

"Yeah, that sounds like a plan," replied True.

The conversation was interrupted by Rose, who approached Saheed with a super-bad white girl behind her. Saheed had been eyeing her all night. She had a body like Ice T's wife, Coco. Rose sat on Saheed's lap and said, "Daddy, this is Sarah. Sarah, this is my daddy, Saheed." Rose then leaned down towards Saheed's ear and whispered, "come in the back room, I have a treat for you."

Saheed look at Sarah, who was staring at him were her bright green eyes saying "come fuck me." Sarah licked her lips seductively as Rose stood up and grabbed her hand. They walked away, with Rose leading Sarah to the back. Saheed look at True, whose jaw had dropped at the sight of all that ass swishing towards the back room.

"I'll catch up with you in a few," Saheed said to True.

"In a minute," True replied.

Saheed had gotten up and was walking towards the back room. He was harder than a steel pipe and ready to get his freak on. He checked his pockets, double checking for his condoms. Satisfied, he entered the back room and locked the door behind him.

Rose and Sarah were sitting on the edge of the bed and began kissing after Saheed locked the door. Saheed watched as these two freaks of nature tongue kissed like they were deeply in love with each other. Slowly they began undressing one another. Being that they were both already barely clothed, it didn't take long before they were completely naked. As Rose began sucking on one of Sarah's large, pink nipples, Sarah asked Saheed, "Do you like what you see?" Then she let out a soft moan as Rose slid a finger inside her.

Looking at her slim waist and large curves, Saheed answered her saying, "of course I like what I see, you're dripping sex." Then his curiosity got the best of him and he asked, "Damn, girl, what's your measurements?"

"Last time I checked they were 38-23-40. I work hard for this body, it's all natural."

Rose was tired of the small talk and her pussy was throbbing so she laid back on the bed and spread her legs wide open, then said to Sarah, "this what you want, white girl?" She then dipped her middle finger in her wetness and stuck it in Sarah's mouth. After sucking Rose's finger like a lollipop and removing all the juice, Sarah whispered to Rose, "that's what I want baby" before going down on her. She started kissing Rose on her inner thighs, and then worked her way inside, not missing an inch with her soft lips. She slipped her long tongue inside Rose, causing her to come in her mouth. Rose grabbed Sarah by her blond hair and started grinding her coochie hard into her face.

Saheed was loving every minute of the show. He took out his cell phone and started recording the action with the built-in video camera.

After about two minutes, Saheed couldn't stand it any longer. He took off all his clothes then put a condom on. Sarah still had her face buried between Rose's legs; her ass was high in the air begging for attention. Walking behind her, Saheed smacked her softly on the ass. Palming her ass with both hands, Saheed entered her, going all the way in and forcing her walls to expand and accommodate him. Saheed then grabbed her small waist and pulled her against him, as he pressed forward, going as deep as possible. Sarah acknowledged him by moaning loudly and rocking her ass back and forth. Saheed looked at Rose, whose eyes seemed to be in the back of her head.

"Oooh, Saheed, you feel gooood!" Sarah moaned. "I'm loving it!"

Still holding her by the waist, Saheed started driving into her with force as he made eye contact with Rose, who now seemed to be studying him.

"Oh, oh, my God, Saheed, I feel you in my stomach."

Saheed didn't respond as he pounded at her insides with short, quick thrusts.

"I love it, it's the best, I . . ." Sarah was cut short by Rose grabbing her head and giving her a mouthful.

"You like this pussy, don't you, bitch?" said Rose as she rolled her hips and came all over Sarah's face.

"I, I, I love it, Rose," said Sarah as she released her love juice onto Saheed's long and thick magic stick.

As Sarah's sugar walls contracted tightly around him, Saheed let out a loud groan as he filled the tip of the Magnum rubber with hot semen. Sarah could feel the heat and asked him, "You like that, daddy?"

Her calling him daddy caught him off guard. Saheed, out of breath and still recuperating, just slapped her ass in approval as he pulled out. He then went into the bathroom and got in the shower.

*****

In the suite next door, Black was talking with Young Mac.

"Yo, I beat that bitch Rita's ass for burning me," said Black.

"Good, that's what she gets. Bitch burnt me too. I'm a smack the shit out of her when I see her," said Young Mac.

"Yo, I'm trying to fuck that sexy dark skinned girl."

"You better wear a rubber, hoes these days trifling."

"Yo, I learned my lesson," said Black, holding up some condoms and showing them to Young Mac. He then thought about the situation. Dr. Stanchfield had called him and told him that the lab results not only confirmed he was HIV positive but that he had full-blown AIDS. He was in denial.

"I hope so. Better to be safe than sorry."

"Yo, whatever," said Black, then he staggered off drunk, looking for the dark skinned stripper who said he could hit it for $250.00.

After he found her, they chose the bathroom to have sex in. Black sat on the stool and pulled out his meat. He put the condom on as the woman got naked. He reasoned that if he wore a condom the girl wouldn't catch his infection. The pretty-faced dark skinned woman straddled him and began riding his dick. Her vagina was dry, causing friction. It wasn't long before the condom broke. Both she and Black were too drunk to realize it.

It wasn't until Black busted a nut and she climbed off him that they realized what had happened. By then it was too late. She had just become the next person to contract HIV. Of course, she didn't realize what happened so she just washed up with a rag and went on about her business. Black, on the other hand, knew what he did and it made him feel fucked up, but he wasn't about to tell the girl. He couldn't risk people finding out he had that sauce.

*****

Around the same time Black finished up with the hooker, hotel management showed up with the police to end the party and kick everyone out. It was fun while it lasted.

Saheed woke up the next afternoon in his own bed. The first thing he saw were Sarah's large breasts soaking up the sunlight that made its way through the blinds. He rolled over and looked at Rose, who was snoring lightly in her sleep. After getting kicked out of the hotel, Saheed and the two women came back to his house to finish what they started. They ended up having sex until 9:00 in the morning – around that time they all passed out from exhaustion.

Ironically, Saheed thought how Kiesha probably rolled over in her grave as he had sex with the two women in the same bed they used to share. He almost shed a tear thinking about her, his unborn child, and what should have been. His phone started ringing so he got up to see who was calling. It was Black.

"Yeah," said Saheed, answering the phone.

"Yo, wake up, man. They got Young Mac."

"What are you talking about?"

"Yo, last night after the party, Young Mac came back to my crib and fell out. Well, this morning he said he had to go take a piss test down at the Federal Building. I rode with him because we planned on going to eat breakfast after he came out. Problem is, he never came out."

"*Fuck*, I told that dumb motherfucker don't be getting high," said Saheed. He hated waking up to bad news; it always seemed to set the pace for the day.

"The nigga said he wouldn't be but 15 minutes. I've been waiting on his ass for over an hour."

"Where you at now?"

"I'm sitting in this nigga's car around the corner from the fucking Federal Building," said Black, getting all animated as he talked.

"Come scoop me from my house. We'll go grab some food and figure this shit out," said Saheed, as he made eye contact with Sarah.

"Yo, I'll be there in ten minutes," Black said, then hung up the phone.

"I'm hungry, too," said Sarah, as she reached out and grabbed Saheed's morning wood. It wasn't until that moment that Saheed realized he was naked. As Sarah attempted to take him into her mouth, Saheed stopped her and said, "Not right now, sweet mouth, I gotta do something.

Sarah, not being a person used to accepting "no" as an answer, replied "this won't take long," and before Saheed could say anything he could feel the back of her throat.

Sarah was right, it didn't take long. As Sarah finished swallowing the last drop, Saheed couldn't believe he let this broad suck him off without a condom on.

"Breakfast is my favorite meal," she said as she lay back down in the bed.

Saheed looked at Rose, who was still snoring, deep in dreamland somewhere. After the crown he got from Sarah he was in a slightly better mood as he got in the shower.

15 minutes later he was riding in Young Mac's Mercedes with Black. After Black finished telling him the story again he called the Sicilian.

"Soprano Law Office," said Mike Soprano's secretary.

"Mike Soprano, please."

"One moment," said the secretary.

Three minutes later Mr. Soprano answered, saying "Mike Soprano."

"Mike, it's me, Corey," said Saheed.

"Yeah, what's up?"

"I think Cortez got detained down at the Fed Building. He went in for a UA and never came out."

"I'll call and see what's going on. Call me back in a half hour." Then Mike Soprano hung up without waiting for a reply.

They went to the Pancake House and grabbed something to eat. After finishing his food, Saheed called the Sicilian back.

"Mike Soprano."

"It's me, Corey, again."

"Here's the deal. Cortez Mack has been detained for testing positive for THC and cocaine."

"Can you get him out?" asked Saheed, already knowing the answer.

"I could try, but they're not going to let him go."

"So he's going to have to fight this from the inside?"

"That's the way it looks. He's got a Motion hearing next week. I'm going to try to get the case thrown out."

"Do everything you can, Mike. I need him out," said Saheed, seriously.

"Call me Monday. I gotta go. Don't worry about Cortez, he'll be fine," Mr. Soprano said reassuringly.

After filling Black in on the conversation with the Sicilian, Black asked Saheed "what should I do with this nigga's car?"

"Hold it down for now, he's gonna be calling soon."

Black then started to tell Saheed about having AIDS but then had second thoughts and wasn't able to get the words out.

Saheed started to tell Black about his situation with Agent Wilson attempting to play him for $50,000, but decided not to, being that he was trying to come up with a plan to kill the motherfucker. He decided there was no way he was gonna let that pig extort him.

Saheed's phone starting ringing and the caller ID said "unavailable."

"Yeah," he said, answering the phone.

"Saheed, these bitches got me down in the County," said Young Mac.

"I already know. I just got off the phone with Soprano. He said you're going to have to chill until you go to court next week."

"This is some bullshit. We get paid today, right?"

"You already know. The money should be in my account already; I haven't had a chance to check on it. I just woke up," said Saheed. He hadn't even thought about the money that was supposed to be deposited into his account that morning.

"You need to get on that ASAP."

"I'm a get on it Mack'n. I told your ass about that bullshit you and Black was on. Look at you now. At least we got the video done."

"Fuck the video, Saheed. I'm in jail. I need to get out immediately," said Young Mac, stressing over his incarceration.

"You piss in your bed, you gotta sleep in it. Just chill out. Mike said he's going to try and get your case thrown out at your Motion hearing."

"Yeah, all right, I'm going to chill. Do you think you can set up a bank account for me?"

"I should be able to do that. I'll need your information though," said Saheed.

"Call my moms and get it from her, and call that nigga Black and get my car."

"He's with me now, hold on," Saheed said, then passed Black the phone. They talked for a minute then Saheed got back on the phone and said "I'll just park your car in my garage."

"Yeah, that's cool. Listen, I gotta go. Handle that for me and I'll call you later," said Young Mac.

"One hundred," said Saheed, hanging up the phone.

He thought about the ten kilos he had left. Big Swing had told him last night at the party he wanted to buy four of them. That would leave him with six.

"Say, how much work you got left?" Saheed asked Black.

"Yo, I still got damn near two bricks. Shit's been going slow the last couple days. I think I gotta go back down on my prices." Black had been charging his customers $25,000.00 a key ever since the Bloods got indicted. They weren't happy about it and now seemed to be getting their work from someone else.

"Check it out, I got four left. Do you want them?" Saheed asked him. He said he only had four because he was going to give two bricks to True. They were for the money he owed him from the album sales. True could pay him back the difference. They had talked about it the night before. True was cool with it because he was coming out ahead. It was a win-win situation. True was more than happy to help out his big homie.

"Yeah, I want them. But like I said, I'm still sitting on two of them thangs. I'll be ready in a day or two."

That didn't work for Saheed. He was tired of selling cocaine.

"Look, I'll throw them to you, just get me my bread."

"Yo, it's nothing, I got you," Black replied, nonchalantly.

By the end of the day, Saheed had gotten rid of the last of the cocaine. He sold Big Swing the four bricks he wanted for $68,000.00. Black owed him $68,000.00 for the four bricks Saheed gave him on consignment. True owed him $34,000.00, when Saheed did the math, he had made approximately $400,000.00 off the 40 kilos. With the six figure deposit he received that day, he had over two hundred and fifty thousand dollars in the bank. Altogether he had $600,000 in dirty money, add that to the money in his account and he had a close to a million.

He was proud of himself, knowing he started with nothing and made the money on his own. But he wasn't content and knew this was only the beginning.

Agent Wilson was pissed as he walked out of the interrogation room with blood on his hands. He had gone into the room so he could interview a young Indian punk who was supposed to have ties with the Native Mob.

The little dude had some big balls. Instead of giving Agent Wilson information on members of the Native Mob, the little bastard spit in his face, with most of the spit landing inside of his mouth. To Agent Wilson, being spit on was the most disrespectful thing a person could do to him. After being spit on, he didn't waste any time coming across the table and punching the handcuffed teenager in the mouth. The boy started talking shit, causing Agent Wilson to completely lose his temper and start beating on him. Agent Wilson didn't stop punching the boy until a sheriff's deputy pulled him away and the boy had a broken jaw and the majority of his teeth knocked out.

He thought about the time he stomped out that nigger Saheed for spitting on him. Just then his prepaid cell phone started ringing. The only person with the number to the phone was Saheed; he had bought it just for the occasion.

"Saheed," Agent Wilson answered, then said "I must've thought you up, tell me something good."

"I got your money," replied Saheed.

"And it's about time. Me and the boys had planned on coming to see you tomorrow."

"What the fuck ever. How you wanna do this?" asked Saheed.

"Call me at 9:00 tonight and I'll tell you where to come," said Agent Wilson before hanging up the phone. With Saheed calling him back at 9:00, that would give him enough time to get a Judge to sign an arrest warrant for the murder of Stanley Patterson, also known as June. Agent Wilson's plan was to get the $50,000.00 from Saheed, then arrest him the next morning for murder. If he hadn't planned on extorting Saheed, he would have already arrested the piece of shit.

*****

North Side, Distribution City
After talking to Agent Wilson, Saheed hung up the pay phone and jumped back into his Lexus.

Saheed knew this might be his last day on earth and he was prepared to go out in a blaze of glory. He thought about just paying the money, something he could easily do, but he had a gut feeling that racist pig Agent Wilson was going to double-cross him in some kind of way, he just didn't know how.

In his trunk he had an AK-47 with several hundred rounds of ammunition inside multiple clips. He knew the 7.62 rounds would tear through police body armor in the event of a shoot-out with the law. He also had the Glock-19 on his hip. The clip was filled with Teflon-coated armor piercing bullets, also known as cop killers. In Saheed's mind there was no turning back now. He drove to Kiesha's gravesite. He would wait there until it was time to call Agent Wilson back. He chose to go into the cemetery because he hadn't been there since Kiesha's funeral and knowing what he was about to do he didn't want anyone knowing his whereabouts in the event he ever had to make up an alibi.

*****

South Side, Distribution City

Agent Wilson was paying close attention to the dot on the screen off his laptop computer. Through the GPS tracking device he placed on Saheed's bumper, he was able to follow his movements in real time. Being that the Lexus had a built-in GPS system, he could have tracked Saheed without placing his own device on it, but in order to do that he would have needed a warrant and he didn't need all the extra attention, not to mention other people in his business.

He glanced at his watch – 6:55 p.m. Soon he would be $50,000.00 richer. Even though he already had a couple hundred thousand, a man could never have enough money.

At 9:00 p.m. on the dot, his prepaid phone rang.

"Right on time, I like that in you," said Agent Wilson.

"Fuck the small talk, let's get this shit over with," replied Saheed.

"Watch your mouth, boy. Now listen closely. Bring the money down to the southeast docks on the river. You know where that is?"

"Yeah," answered Saheed.

"Good. When you get down there, follow the signs that direct you to the boat launch. Drive until you get to the parking lot and park. Make sure you drive that nice Lexus of yours.

When you see a set of headlights flash on and off three times, get out and walk the money to the vehicle. Do that and you won't have any problems."

"I'll be there in 30 minutes."

"Don't be late, and make sure you're by yourself," said Agent Wilson. Then he hung up the phone.

*****

After getting off the phone with Agent Wilson, Saheed drove into an alley and grabbed the ass-kicker out of the trunk; placing the AK-47 on the back seat he continued his drive to go meet Agent Wilson. Agent Wilson wanted to make the transaction down at the boat launch on the river. That was fine with him. He was familiar with the area. He knew that there wouldn't be anybody around to witness what was about to go down. Ever since a modern boat launch was built a few miles away, nobody used the old site any more. The parking lot was surrounded by thick trees on three sides; the only opening was the river. Saheed's only concern was Agent Wilson might have shooters hiding in the back of the bushes. It was a chance he would have to take and he was prepared to bang till his death.

Agent Wilson was parked in the dark shadows of the parking lot. He studied the computer screen intently. He watched as Saheed got closer to his location. He thought about how this dumb nigger would be going to jail in the morning for murder. He had shown the evidence he had to his Klan brother, Bruce Phillips, who was a prosecutor for the county. He agreed to take the case and told him they wouldn't have any problem getting a conviction with Polo/Quincy Smith's testimony. When they took the evidence before Judge Rivers, she quickly signed the Arrest Warrant.

Agent Wilson watched on his computer as Saheed made his way down the final stretch to the boat launch. He thought to himself, maybe he should have brought some back-up, and then quickly dismissed the idea. Saheed had too much going on for himself to try to kill a federal agent. Besides, the Sig-Saur 9-millimeter was all the back-up he needed. That nigger is no match for me, Agent Wilson arrogantly convinced himself. He shut the computer off and waited for Saheed's Lexus to pull into the parking lot.

After pulling into the apparently deserted parking lot, Saheed backed into a secluded parking space and waited. As he scanned the area, his heart was beating a million miles a minute. Although he was nervous, he remained calm. Out of the shadows in the corner of the parking lot, a set of headlights flashed three times.

The moment of truth. Grabbing the nylon backpack filled with doughnuts, Saheed pulled his hood over his head and stuck the Glock in the pocket of his hooded sweatshirt and got out of the car, leaving the keys in the ignition.

Agent Wilson watched as Saheed's silhouette approached his truck. The man was a shadow in the night. As fear gripped him, Agent Wilson wrapped his finger around the trigger of his pistol.

As he walked towards the truck, Saheed heard Agent Wilson say "come to the driver's side."

As he got closer, he noticed the driver's side window was open and Agent Wilson had a pistol pointed at him.

"I got your money," said Saheed. "I just want to make it home."

"Do as I say and you will live. Slowly hand me the bag," Agent Wilson commanded.

Reaching out with his left hand, Saheed extended the backpack out in front of him. At the same time, his right hand grip tightened around the Glock pistol he had pointed at Agent Wilson through the sweatshirt.

Agent Wilson reached out for the bag with his left hand, keeping the sig pointed at Saheed with his right. Thinking to himself, "it's now or never," as soon as Agent Wilson's hand touched the backpack, Saheed pulled the trigger.

As he reached for the sack of money, something didn't feel right, almost like a sixth sense. His brain was screaming at him to just shoot the nigger. He already knew he would get away with hit. On impulse, he squeezed the trigger, firing directly into Saheed's chest.

As pain shot through his chest, Saheed fell to the ground unable to breathe. "I fucked up, this bitch is gonna kill me. What a fucked up way to die," Saheed thought to himself as he lay on the concrete.

At the same instant he shot Saheed, a bullet tore through his Adam's apple and severed his spinal cord. Paralyzed from the neck down and choking on his own blood, Agent Wilson knew it was all over.

Catching his breath, Saheed couldn't figure out why he was still alive. Pointing the Glock at the driver's door, Saheed slowly got to his feet. He could see blood spatter on the windshield and realized he hit the motherfucker. He heard a gagging sound. He pointed his pistol in the window and saw Agent Wilson was a bloody mess. He smiled as he focused the glow in the dark sights on the man's forehead and pulled the trigger. He didn't need a doctor to tell him Agent Wilson was dead. Still, he continued to fire shots into his head and body. The slugs that hit his body armor cut through the Kevlar like a hot knife through butter.

Being that it was dark out, the flashes from the gunshots almost blinded Saheed. But as he ran back to his car he could clearly see the hole in his sweatshirt. His bulletproof vest saved his life. He knew if Agent Wilson had been using the same kind of bullets he was, they both would be dead.

Jumping into the Lexus, he fled the scene like a bat out of hell.

CHAPTER FIFTY ONE
North Side, Distribution City

After the shooting, Saheed decided to lay low in one of his grow houses. He had taken the battery out of his phone, making it impossible for anyone in the world to locate him. To calm himself down, he had smoked a blunt of Kryptonite and ended up passing out.

Waking up at almost noon the next day, he wasn't sure what his next move would be. He turned on the television just in time to catch the beginning of the 12:00 news.

The murder of Agent Wilson was the top story. The anchor woman was saying that the body was discovered after 11:00 P.M. the night before by a D.C. police officer who was patrolling the area. He went on to say that the body was that of a member of law enforcement but that the name of the officer was being withheld from the public until the family could be notified of the tragic event. Then the anchor woman said there was an ongoing investigation and that no other information was available at that time.

He thought about reporting the Lexus stolen but then realized that wouldn't be necessary being that he didn't have any plates on the car. As much as he didn't want to, he decided he would return the car to the Lexus dealer and pay the costly termination fee for canceling his lease. Better to be safe than sorry.

Saheed thought about how he had to be ready for anything. If Agent Wilson's law enforcement friends knew he was responsible for his death, they may try to murder him. At the same time, it appeared Agent Wilson was working on his own, being that he didn't have anybody backing him up. Saheed was glad he didn't have to use his AK the night before, he was even happier to be alive.

Turning on his I-phone, he dialed Rose's number. When she answered, Saheed said "hey baby what's up?" "You're what's up, big daddy. I've been missing you since last night," replied Rose.

"Yeah, everything is cool with me. What are you doing?"

"Oh, me and Sarah were about to go to the mall and grab some lunch. Are you hungry?"

"Dig this baby, Sarah's cool and all that but I don't feel comfortable with her all in our mix like she's part of the family."

"That's what we want to talk to you about. Sarah says she wants to join the team and get down with us," said Rose, assuming Saheed would be pleased hearing this.

"Alright, listen, y'all go get something to eat, grab something to go for me. I'll be waiting on you when you get back to the house and we can talk about it then."

"OK, daddy. Will Chinese food work?"

"Yeah, that's good," said Saheed, then he hung up the phone.

After changing clothes and stashing the murder weapon in the attic, Saheed got in his Lexus and made his way over to the house he called home.

Pulling into his driveway, he parked his car. As he was about the get out, a caravan of cars and trucks paraded down the street and stopped in front of his house, blocking the Lexus in the driveway.

Saheed looked through his rear window and saw at least ten white boys pointing pistols at him. He thought about the AK-47 in the trunk, it was useless to him at the moment. "*Fuck*," he said to himself, wishing he would have left it on the back seat.

He knew if those white boys didn't kill him, he would never see the streets again. First degree murder of a federal agent – it was over with.

"Put your hands up!" screamed one of the white men.

Doing what the man said, Saheed put his hands in the air.

"With your left hand, slowly open the door and get out of the car," demanded the same voice. Saheed did as he was told.

"Keeping your hands in the air, I want you to very slowly walk backwards."

Complying with the officer's orders, Saheed stepped backwards, taking his time, hoping these pigs didn't start shooting. He continued to walk backwards in the direction of the voice until he felt what he assumed was a gun pressed against his spine.

"Do you have any weapons on you?" asked the officer.

"No," he responded to the voice talking to him.

"I'm going to handcuff you," said the officer with the gun in his back.

Grabbing Saheed's left arm and pulling it behind his back, he put on a handcuff. Then he grabbed his right and did the same.

With his hands cuffed behind his back, Saheed said, "can you tell me why I'm in handcuffs?"

"We have a warrant for your arrest. You've been charged with murder," said the officer.

"That's crazy, I haven't killed anyone!"

"Read him his rights, Johnny," said the officer to one of his comrades.

As Saheed was being read his rights, he looked around and saw some of his neighbors looking through their windows. He saw Rose coming down the street in her Camaro.

"We're about to search your house. Anything in there we should know about?" asked the same officer who put the handcuffs on him.

Saheed said nothing as he thought about what he had in the house. There was nothing except the two pistols he had stashed under the kitchen floorboard where his money used to be. He doubted they would find them; still he was glad he moved his cash. Saheed watched as a squad car pulled up.

"Johnny, go put him in the patrol car. They're going to transport him downtown."

Grabbing Saheed by his arm, the swine named Johnny was bending Saheed's arm at a funny angle as he roughly shoved him over into the D.C. police car. As Saheed sat in a cramped and twisted position in the back of the car, the cop got out to talk with the others. While they conversed, Saheed looked at Rose and Sarah, who appeared to be arguing with some of the police. He watched as one of the plain-clothed officers, probably a detective, pulled the AK out of the trunk of the Lexus. He didn't really care about that because he wasn't a felon and being that the high-powered rifle was the semi automatic version, he could legally possess it.

The cop got back in the vehicle and drove away. On their way down to the County Jail, the cop behind the wheel was talking shit – Saheed just ignored him.

CHAPTER FIFTY TWO
County Jail, Downtown Distribution City

After six hours in a holding cell without being allowed to make a phone call, Saheed was taken upstairs to an interview room.

Inside was the officer who had handcuffed him at his house and the plain-clothed, bald-headed cocksucker who Saheed watched pull the AK out of his trunk. Saheed sat down at the table.

"I'm Officer Anderson," said the officer who had cuffed him. "This is Detective Russell."

Detective Russell seemed to cut Officer Anderson off when he began reading Saheed his rights.

After Detective Russell finished, Officer Anderson said "state your name for the record."

"Corey James."

"What is your occupation?" asked Detective Russell, thinking Saheed was going to cooperate or maybe say something to incriminate himself during the interrogation.

"I can't answer any more of your questions without the advice of my lawyer." Saheed always said this when police tried to get information from him, every time it seemed to back them off.

"Fair enough, you're fucked anyway," said Officer Anderson, upset he didn't get any information from Saheed. He knew once a lawyer got involved there would be no statements made. He was aspiring to be promoted to detective and a murder confession would have helped him greatly.

As the two pigs left the interrogation room, Saheed heard Detective Russell say to a corrections officer, "Take him up to long term housing. He's going to be here for awhile."

"*Damn, I fucked up,*" Saheed thought to himself.

*****

"Stand for count," shouted the C.O.

It was time for the morning head count. Saheed woke from his sleep and stood by the door in his cell. He couldn't wait to get out of his cell and call the Sicilian. After the detective tried to interview him the day before, they had finally allowed him to make a phone call. He had called Mike Soprano then, but got his voicemail and was forced to leave a message.

After count, a trustee came past each cell and handed each inmate a small carton of milk, a stale pastry, and an orange. Breakfast was the same thing every day inside D.C. County Jail.

30 minutes later, the cells were unlocked. Walking out of his cell, the first person he saw was Young Mac. The County Jail housed State and Federal inmates, they even held offenders for the I.C.E. (Immigration and Custom Enforcement) – they brought them all together like they were one big happy family.

"Saheed!" said Young Mac as he approached Saheed smiling.

"You look stressed out, lil' homie," said Saheed, shaking Young Mac's hand.

"Man, these bitches got me fucked up in here. What the fuck you down for?"

"They say murder. I don't know what the fuck's going on."

"You ain't talked to Soprano? I can't never reach that muthafucka. He's always in court or out of the office on some bullshit," said Young Mac.

"The man be busy. I'm a call him right now." Then Saheed walked over to the phone and tried to call him. It was only 7:30 in the morning so he doubted he would get an answer. He was right.

As he hung up the phone a corrections officer opened the door and began reading names off a list in his hand. "Daquan Carter, Corey James, Wayne Jenkins, line up for court."

Walking up to Young Mac, Saheed said, "Pray for me." Then he and the other two men followed the sheriff's deputy out of the housing unit.

*****

As he was led into the courtroom, he was surprised to see Mike Soprano sitting at the defendant's table.

"Hey, Corey, how you holding up?"

"Mike, tell me what's going on. I don't even know why I've been arrested," said Saheed, playing dumb with his attorney. He knew damn well what he did.

"I spoke briefly with the prosecutor. Apparently you're being charged with murder in the death of Stanley Patterson."

Saheed was unable to suppress his smile. He was very relieved. He thought they had him for Agent Wilson's murder. That explained why he wasn't in Federal Court.

179

"That's crazy, Mike. This is some bullshit. I didn't kill that man, didn't even know him," said Saheed, looking like he was telling the truth and sounding convincing.

Mr. Soprano didn't believe him. Saheed always screamed innocent and played ignorant, even when he was caught red-handed. Mike Soprano didn't care if his clients were guilty or innocent; the only thing that mattered to him was the money. His job was to win trials and get charges dismissed – that's what he did best. He had been doing it for over 30 years.

"Just be cool. Right now this is a bail hearing. I'm going to get you out."

Banging his gavel, the Judge said, "Mr. James, you have been charged with second degree murder and two counts of attempted murder. The purpose of today's hearing is to discuss bail. Does your client understand, Mr. Soprano?"

"Yes, Your Honor," replied Mike Soprano.

"Prosecutor Phillips," said the Judge, giving Bruce Phillips the green light.

"Your Honor, on March 1st, Stanley Patterson was shot to death as he rode in a vehicle driven by his friend Quincy Smith. Mr. Smith was the intended target of Mr. James when the deceased Stanley Patterson was struck by a bullet and killed. On August 15th, Mr. James committed a drive-by shooting in another attempt to murder Quincy Smith. In that incident, Mr. Smith was shot multiple times in the head and body. He survived." Bruce Phillips paused and smiled at Saheed, then went on saying, "Upon his arrest, Mr. James was found with an AK-47 assault rifle in the trunk of his car. Your Honor, apparently Mr. James is a threat to the community. Therefore, we ask the Court to set bail in the amount of one million dollars."

"Thank you, Mr. Phillips, the Court will take that under consideration. Mr. Soprano," said the Judge, giving the Sicilian the opportunity to do his thing.

Springing into action, Mike Soprano stood up and began by saying, "Your Honor, my client is dumbfounded by these allegations against him. My client is a law abiding, tax paying citizen. I know Mr. James and consider him a personal friend. Personally, I do not believe he is capable of committing these crimes. The rifle found in the trunk of his car is legal, any adult with a clean record can walk into a gun store and purchase one, no permit required. At this time, Your Honor, I ask the Court to impose a reasonable bail in the amount of $50,000.00 and respectfully consider my client innocent until proven guilty."

"Thank you, Mr. Soprano," said the Judge. "After hearing from both sides and given the nature of the offense, the Court has decided to set bail in the amount of $250,000.00. Court adjourned." Then the Judge slammed his gavel, bringing the hearing to an end.

Turning to face Mike Soprano, Saheed said, "Call your bail bondsman, I got the money. Just get me released." He was relieved to get such a low bail, out of $250,000.00 he only had to pay 10%. 25 G's was nothing for his freedom.

"I'll call him as soon as I leave," said Mr. Soprano.

"Thanks, Mike, I appreciate everything."

"Come straight to my office when you get released, I'll be there all day."

The deputy came to escort Saheed back to the holding cell. As he got up, he saw Rose and Sarah for the first time sitting in the front row. Rose was crying, probably thinking he wasn't going to get out. He waved to her as he thought "that girl is dumb."

*****

Four hours later Saheed was released and back on the streets. He went straight to Mike Soprano's office. Inside the office, Mike Soprano said to him, "Corey, to beat these charges it's going to take a lot of hard work, so I'm going to have to charge you a $50,000.00 fee. Anyone else, it would be $100,000.00."

"That's all right, I'll get you your money," said Saheed.

From there he went to meet the bail bondsman who told him "your lawyer is the only man who can call me and have me put up a million dollars of my own money just on his word alone."

After transferring $25,000.00 from his business account to the bail bondsman, the man said "state law says that a house has to be put up as collateral anytime the bail amount is over $60,000.00, but since Mr. Soprano told me not to worry about it, I'm not going to worry about it. Being that you're not gonna run from the charges, I won't have to hunt you down." The bail bondsman was also a bounty hunter.

Driving Rose's Camaro with her in the passenger's seat and Sarah in the back Saheed drove to the impound lot to pick up his Lexus. Before parting with Rose he told her, "I need you to go place some new ads on Eros.com, advertising you and Sarah as a double date, and get a profile posted of just Sarah by herself. It's time to super grind. We gotta stack this money like never

181

before," said Saheed, thinking about the 75 G's the trial was about to cost him. Even though he had the money, it was still a lot of bread.

"Daddy, we wanted to take you home and fuck you real good," said Rose, reaching for Saheed's dick.

"Later for all that. Can you handle what I asked you to do?" asked Saheed.

"Yes, daddy," replied Rose.

Driving away in his Lexus, Saheed thought to himself "I got her trained well."

He called Black to check on the money the nigga owed him but didn't get an answer. He called True, who was at the studio watching the final edited version of Young Mac's "Shake it Baby" video. Saheed went to check it out.

CHAPTER FIFTY THREE

West of Distribution City

Saheed woke up with a hangover. True had talked him into going out the night before and getting drunk. They were celebrating the success of Young Mac's video and album sales. The video got played on T.V. daily and was an Internet sensation being that the Internet version was uncut and raw. After the video began to air, album sales sky-rocketed. They now had over 80,000 sold, according to Soundscan. With 80,000 albums sold, Saheed was paid in full. Counting the dirty money he was sitting on, he had well over a million dollars and was enjoying life.

Everything was good besides his legal problems. He had Court two days earlier and obtained the Motion of Discovery on his case. The Motion of Discovery laid out the State's case and all the evidence they had against him. All they had was Polo's testimony and some hearsay evidence from some of them Bloods who turned snitch after being indicted. All they said was they had heard Saheed was the one who killed June. Mr. Soprano said the case was weak and could be won at trial. Being that Mike Soprano had won more murder trials than any attorney in the Country, Saheed believed him and had decided to pay the man his 50 Gs. They moved for a speedy trial and that was scheduled to begin in another month.

Young Mac on the other hand was fucked. At his Motion hearing, Judge Janklow had ruled that the police had performed an illegal search and seizure when he was found with the seven grams of crack cocaine, clearing the way for him to be released. But the prosecution had ten days to appeal and they did. Chief District Judge Dan Robinson overruled magistrate Janklow's decision. Young Mac was now scheduled to plead guilty to possession of seven grams of crack cocaine. That guaranteed him 60 months in the Feds. But he was promised he would be able to do his time in a prison camp and be given the drug program, which, after completed, knocked a year off his sentence. He would be home in a little over three years. He wasn't happy but didn't stand a chance at trial.

Out of the $68,000.00 Black owed Saheed, he had only paid him twenty of it back, and had been ducking and dodging Saheed ever since. Saheed had never thought his boy would pull some sucker shit like he was doing, he thought they were better than that. If the nigga needed it, Saheed would have given him the 50 G's the nigga was trying to play him out of.

Rose and Sarah were pulling their own weight. In the past month they had brought home over $30,000.00 working as escorts. They gave all their money to him and in return he was taking good care of them. They were down for their man.

Saheed had been turned out on the ménage a trois shit and refused to have sex with one without the other. They always used protection. Saheed always preached to them that the latex would keep their health good and that he believed in check-ups and Planned Parenthood.

The day after Saheed had bailed out of jail, he had returned the Lexus back to the dealer and had been driving Young Mac's S550 ever since. When Black said it was a pussy magnet he wasn't lying – he got more action in that car than he thought possible.

Since the death of Agent Wilson and being that he was the head of the Drug Task Force, the FEDS had been cracking down super hard on every drug dealer they could find. They seemed to be desperate to find his killer. The street's drug supply was at a standstill. The Bikers, the Italians, the Asian gangs, the Mexican mafia, and even the Blacks seemed to have closed down shop. The little bit of drugs that did make it to the streets were sold at a very high risk and went for outrages prices. Lots of fake drugs were being sold; people were being robbed left and right. People were turning on their friends as the streets starved. Cats in the game snitching reached an all time high. All of this caused a major spike in the murder rate. Every night, the news informed the public about the latest killing or multiple murders that took place in Distribution City. After the police raided his house, Saheed no longer felt comfortable resting his head there. He ended up renting a big house with the option to buy in an affluent suburb west of D.C. He planned on buying it after his trial. The house sat on a large lake, so he decided to lease a large boat to go with it. Every day, Saheed would go out on the water and kick it on the boat with whoever wanted to go. One day, Sarah had started talking crazy to him so he threw her in the water and pulled off. Even though she could swim, they were in the middle of the lake and she thought she was going to drown out there, but Saheed quickly turned around and got her back in the boat. He did it to prove a point to her and he hadn't had a problem from her after that.

Saheed thought about the night before. He had seen Tank on "America's Most Wanted," and all the hatred he had for that man came back to life. John Walsh was pleading for the public's help in finding him. They didn't have a clue as to where he may have fled.

Saheed was contemplating taking his boat for a spin, thinking maybe the fresh air might help his hangover, when his I-phone started ringing. He knew it was True calling by the ringtone.

"Yeah," Saheed answered.

"Saheed, I've been shot."

*****

North Side, Distribution City – 20 Minutes Earlier

True sat in his BMW outside of the corner market with a hangover from hell. He never should have drank that Patron last night. If he would have drank Hennessey like he preferred to do his head wouldn't be pounding.

He was waiting on white boy Casper, who was supposed to have already been there. He had agreed to sell him a pound of Hydro for $4,500.00 the night before. He had never dealt with Casper on a business level but knew him from around the town.

Just as he was about to leave, Casper pulled up in his white Suburban on 24" of chrome. True called his phone.

"What up? I'm here," said Casper.

"You see the white BMW?" asked True.

"Yeah, I see it."

"Follow me around the corner," True said and pulled away from the corner market.

After driving for a few blocks, True parked and Casper pulled up behind him. Getting into True's BMW, Casper shook True's hand and said "what's good, player?"

"This bomb weed I got for you," said True, handing Casper a bag containing the pound of Hydroponically grown marijuana. True grew it himself, with Saheed's help.

"That shit smells potent," said Casper, as he picked through the bag and finger fucked the buds.

"It's the best in town," said True.

"I'll take it," said Casper, and in a flash had a short barrel 44. special pointed at True's face. Cocking back the hammer he said, "I'll take that chain and pinky ring, too."

"You on some bullshit, Casper, but you can have it all. Just take it and get the fuck out of my car," True said as he thought about the 9-millimeter on his waist.

"Empty your pockets, too, bitch."

True took off his Underworld Entertainment chain and held it out for Casper. When Casper took one hand off the gun and attempted to snatch the necklace, True moved with lightning speed, grabbing the pistol and Casper's wrist with both hands. The men started wrestling for control of the gun. The white boy was strong and still had his finger on the trigger. As they grappled he sent a wild shot through the roof of the car. True twisted Casper's wrist down with all his strength, pulling the gun out of his hands. But as he yanked the pistol away it went off with a *bang*. The slug tore through True's upper thigh, missing the tip of his penis by less than an inch.

"Aaaagh, damn," True hollered after the hot steel burnt a hole through his left leg.

After losing control of the pistol, Casper knew he fucked up. Opening the door, he jumped out of the car empty handed and started running. Aiming through the open door, True squeezed the trigger on the revolver, shooting Casper square in the middle of his back, causing him to fall face-first in the dirt of somebody's front lawn. The bullet had ripped a large hole in his chest. Throwing the car in drive, True put his good foot on the gas and peeled away as fast as possible; the force of the car accelerating caused the passenger door to slam shut.

True glanced at his leg and saw blood everywhere. In a panic he found his cell phone and called Saheed. When Saheed answered, True said, "Saheed, I've been shot."

"What the fuck you mean you've been shot? Who shot you?" Saheed asked, with grave concern in his voice.

"I just want to tell you I got love for you. If I die I want you to know that," said True as tears ran down his face. They were caused by the pain of being shot and the thought of dying.

"True, where you at, dog?"

"I'm in my car. White boy tried to rob me."

Saheed instantly knew he was talking about Casper. True had told him he was supposed to get with him.

"You need to get to the hospital now, can you drive yourself?"

"I'm driving there now. I'm hit in the leg, shit hurts,"

"If you're dirty, get rid of the dirt in case the police search your car," said Saheed, relieved his ill homie only got hit in the leg. Still, he was aware it could be life-threatening. He knew someone who died from being shot in the leg.

"Fuck the police, I'm bleeding to death," but True knew Saheed was right. He thought about Casper and the time he could get for shooting him. Turning into an alley, True saw a space between two garages that looked discreet. Parking his car, he stuffed the 44 and his 9-millimeter in the bag with the marijuana and tossed it through his window into the opening. The bag landed under a bush and out of view. Driving off, he heard Saheed yelling his name through the phone.

"I'm here, man. I'm a be all right," said True, gaining control of himself and hoping what he said was the truth.

He talked to Saheed all the way to the Emergency Room. Once there, he was rushed straight to surgery.

Around the same time, paramedics arrived on the scene where Casper lay. He was dead upon their arrival.

CHAPTER FIFTY FOUR
Downtown Distribution City

The courtroom was packed with Saheed's friends and family on one side and Junes' family and friends on the other, with members of the media getting in where they could fit. The tension was high and extra security had to be called in just in case a fight were to break out, which was a common occurrence at murder trials in D.C.

Sitting in the courtroom, Saheed waited patiently for his trial to begin. A jury of his so-called peers had been selected the day before.

As he sat there he reflected back on the past year. He thought about all the money he had made, all the drama and violence, his ups and downs – it would definitely be a year he would never forget.

He wondered was it all over now? Even though Mike Soprano said he was going to win the trial, nobody would know for sure until the jury's verdict came back.

He thought about all the lives he had taken throughout the years, he thought about Kiesha and other close friends he had lost. Was this God's way of punishing him?

He knew he had a good run and that if he ended up getting life in prison that it could have been worse. He had friends who were doing life sentences, homies who had never even had a chance to experience living. He was definitely fortunate – more than that, he had been blessed.

"All rise," said the Sheriff's Deputy. Everyone stood up as the Honorable Judge Kathy Newman entered the courtroom, signaling the start of the trial.

Kathy Newman had the reputation of being merciless. She was known as being a miserable, evil bitch who always sentenced the defendant to the longest prison term allowed under the law. If Saheed lost this trial that would mean life without parole.

"You may be seated," said Judge Newman, and the trial began.

Prosecutor Bruce Phillips opened up with a twenty minute speech that assassinated Saheed's character and made him out to be an inner-city terrorist. Then he tried to make it seem as if he was a bigger threat to the public than Al Quida.

Mike Soprano countered in his opening statement. Painting a beautiful picture for the jury that portrayed Corey James as a law-abiding business man who, under the circumstances had been accused of false and trumped up charges. He told the jury evidence against his client was weak; even more, that it was non-existent, and that he would prove the man was innocent.

After going over the facts of the case, the State called their first witness, Rashad Thompson, also known as Raw Money.

As Raw Money took the stand, one of the Blood members from June's family yelled "you're a dead man, you fucking snitch!" prompting a shouting match between the two until the Sheriff's Deputies could escort the Blood gang member out of the courtroom where he was handcuffed and taken to jail for his outburst. He was charged with a felony for making terroristic threats.

Raw Money went on to tell the jury about what he heard about Saheed supposedly killing June while shooting at Polo. Nothing was mentioned about his involvement in Kiesha's death. If Saheed had known that Raw Money had participated in the kidnapping, torture and murder of the love of his life, he would have attacked him right there in the courtroom.

When it was Mike Soprano's turn to question the witness, he brought up Raw Money's criminal record and his recent arrest for attempted murder and other offenses. After exposing the jury to the fact that Raw Money was nothing but a low life piece of shit who stooped as low as lying on his people to save his own ass, Mike Soprano asked the Judge to discredit the witness' testimony based on the fact it was nothing more than hearsay.

Judge Newman agreed and discredited his testimony from the record and told the jury to disregard his statements.

The same thing happened with the next two Blood gang members who took the stand. Even though they were discredited, the jury heard every word they said and the damage was done.

"Your Honor," Mike Soprano said," it appears the prosecution's witnesses have nothing more to offer than hearsay testimony with no factual basis. Surely you won't allow this to continue?"

"The Court agrees with your concerns, Mr. Soprano. That will be all for the day. This trial will resume at 9:00 a.m. Mr. Phillips, I will not allow any more hearsay at this trial. Be prepared to present actual evidence tomorrow morning. Court is in recess," said Judge Kathy Newman, slamming her gavel.

*****

After the end of the first day of trial, Saheed, Sarah and Rose went home and had sex, sex, and more sex. They got it on in almost every room in the house. They fucked in the boat and even did their thing in the backyard of the house under the stars and pale moonlight. Saheed couldn't get enough. He knew after his trial he may not ever be able to have sex again and all he would be left with were his memories.

*****

At 8:45 a.m. the next morning, Saheed was immaculately dressed in a $3,000.00 black pinstripe suit with a black tie to match. Mr. Soprano sat next to him at the defendant's table. Even though he was dressed to impress himself, he was forced to compliment Saheed on his attire.

Saheed looked back at Rose and Sarah, who were looking good with their fake prescription glasses and women's business suits on. They both looked like educated professionals and made Saheed wish the three of them were off having sex somewhere instead of sitting inside a courtroom at his murder trial.

"All rise," said the Sheriff's Deputy as Your Honor walked into the courtroom and took her seat.

"You may be seated," said Judge Newman, and then banged her gavel twice.

The jury was brought in and the trial was back underway. Prosecutor Phillips had planned on bringing in more witnesses to say the same thing the last three informants had said, even though it was all hearsay and he knew they would be discredited. He wanted the jury to hear from as many people possible that Corey James, also known as Saheed, was the killer. Being the no-nonsense Judge that Kathy Newman was, she made it clear that she wasn't going to allow him to proceed as planned. That forced him to present the jury with the only real witness and evidence that he had, Quincy Smith, also known as Polo.

As Polo entered the courtroom and took the stand, Saheed looked calm and appeared to be unaffected by Polo's presence. But on the inside his blood was boiling. "After all the shit this nigga done started and dirt he's done, the nigga turns snitch. Bitch-raised motherfucka," Saheed thought to himself as he and Polo stared each other down.

Prosecutor Phillips began his questioning and Polo laid out the same story he had told to Tank. He told the jury how he and long-time friend, June, were riding around minding their own business when they came to a stoplight and someone in the car next to them started shooting at him, killing June. He told them how he caught a glimpse of the shooter before pulling off and recognized him as Saheed.

Prosecutor Phillips asked him, "do you see this Saheed in the courtroom today and if so, could you point him out?"

"Yes, replied Polo," he's sitting right there." Then he pointed at Saheed, who was the only one at the defense table besides Mike Soprano.

The questioning continued for the next 45 minutes and Polo went on to say "he clearly saw the face of the shooter when he himself was shot and recognized him as Saheed."

Saheed admitted to himself that Polo did sound convincing, even though he knew Polo was full of shit. There was no way Polo could have recognized his face through a ski mask.

Upon cross-examination, the Sicilian picked Polo apart. This was what Saheed paid him for. When he asked him about what he got in exchange for testifying, Polo just said he "felt obligated to do so."

When asked about the bulletproof vest, nine ounces of crack and the pistol the police found on him, Polo fumbled with his answer and Mike Soprano made it clear to the jury he was testifying to avoid being charged in Federal Court, where he would be looking at more than twenty years.

When Mr. Soprano asked him why he waited so long to tell the police who killed June, Polo couldn't answer and just sat there looking nervous.

Bruce Phillips' face turned red with anger as he watched his case falling apart. He had never lost a murder trial and he didn't plan to lose this one.

"Objection!" shouted Prosecutor Phillips.

"Overruled," replied Judge Newman. "Answer the question, Mr. Smith.

Polo continued to sit there and say nothing.

"The man is a liar. No further questions, Your Honor," said Mike Soprano, and then he joined Saheed at the defense table. With his face flushed red and feeling defeated, Bruce Phillips said "the State rests its case." Still, he wasn't giving up hope.

"That will be all for the day, Court will resume at 9:00 a.m. in the morning, at which time the defense will call its first witness," said Judge Newman, slamming her gavel.

*****

That night, Saheed and True went out and got drunk. They went from club to club and ended up inside Lucy's Cabaret. Saheed ended up leaving with a Mexican woman who didn't speak English well, but inside the Double Tree Hotel she rode him like a motorcycle. Saheed left her there while she was in a deep sleep and didn't make it home until 5:00 in the morning.

*****

It was 9:15 a.m. the next morning and everyone, including the jury, was seated.

"The defense calls Cortez Mack," said Mike Soprano.

At that time, Young Mac was brought into the courtroom. He testified in Saheed's favor, saying that he, Saheed and True were inside the studio at the time of June's murder, that Saheed was there all day with him, making it impossible for him to have killed Stanley Patterson.

A young female member of the jury was a fan of Young Mac's and couldn't stop staring at him.

During cross-examination, Prosecutor Phillips tried everything he could to poke holes in Young Mac's story but was unsuccessful. He then went on to attacking Young Mac's character and made sure the jury knew he had recently pled guilty to a drug charge.

After Young Mac was escorted out of the courtroom, Mike Soprano called True to the stand. True confirmed everything Young Mac had said – that they were in the studio that entire day working on the hit single "Shake it Baby," and that Saheed didn't leave the building around the time of June's murder. Saheed and True had made sure True had his story straight the previous night before they went out.

Under questioning from Mike Soprano, True told the jury that it would have been impossible for Saheed to have shot Polo because they were in Miami at the time. Mike Soprano then entered pictures showing True and Saheed in Miami into evidence.

Saheed prayed silently that the jury would fall for the bluff he was pushing onto them. The original photos had a date stamped on them but Saheed had cut the dates out of the pictures, and then made copies to be shown in Court, making it impossible to tell when they were taken. After cross-examination by Prosecutor Phillips, True stepped down with the aid of his crutches. He had done his job.

"The defense calls its final witness, Ricardo Gonzales," said a confident and cocky Mike Soprano.

Suave took the stand and Mike Soprano immediately went to work questioning him.

Suave went on to confirm Saheed had in fact been in Miami the week Polo was shot and told the jury he knew this because Saheed was a guest at his house.

Under cross-examination, Prosecutor Bruce Phillips used every trick he had ever learned in a desperate attempt to make Suave slip up and get caught in a lie. He knew this was his last chance.

Afterwards, both Mike Soprano and Bruce Phillips made their final arguments.

The Sicilian made an eloquent speech on Saheed's behalf and ended it saying, "Mr. James wanted to take the stand and defend his name but I told him there is no need to, being that we have proven to everyone in this courtroom that he is not guilty."

The jury was sent back into deliberation. Two hours later they sent word to the Judge that they had reached a verdict.

"That was quick," said a nervous Saheed to Mr. Soprano. Mike Soprano just smiled in response.

After the jury returned to the courtroom, Judge Kathy Newman said to the jury foreman, "Has the jury reached a verdict?"

"Yes, Your Honor," said the foreman.

Handing the written verdict to the Sheriff's Deputy, he brought it to Judge Newman. Her face wrinkled up as she read it silently, then she passed it back.

"The verdict is . . ." said the foreman, "Count One, attempted murder, the jury finds you not guilty." Shouts of joy erupted from Saheed's friends and family.

"Silence," said Judge Newman, banging her gavel.

"Count Two, attempted murder, the jury finds you not guilty. Count Three, second degree murder, the jury finds you not guilty. You have been found not guilty on all charges, Mr. James."

Inside, Judge Newman was upset with the jury's decision. Everything seemed too coincidental for her. She believed he was guilty and had been looking forward to sentencing Corey James to life on a slave plantation, also known as prison.

Rose was in tears. She thought Saheed was going to prison because she knew for a fact he wasn't in Miami when he said he was. She was happy but never would have thought Saheed was a killer.

Bruce Phillips was pissed he lost, but he understood that it was a weak case. He really wanted to win this one for his dead Klan brother, Agent Wilson.

Saheed felt like he had won the lottery. He had a Kool Aid smile plastered on his face as he hugged his family members and friends. He thanked Mr. Soprano then invited everyone back to his house for a barbecue in celebration of his victory.

CHAPTER FIFTY FIVE

Two months after his trial it was business as usual for Saheed. Only now he was able to enjoy his success. "Death Before Dishonor" sales had reached 106,000, and then slowed down drastically due to illegal downloads. Saheed couldn't complain, he felt like he had struck oil. Between his dirty money and legal funds, he had over a million dollars saved. He continued to wash his dirty money through his record company and the pizza shop he had recently opened, although it was a slow and difficult process making sure he kept all the numbers on paper intact and in order.

Rose and Sarah continued to get money in a major way. They say three is a crowd, but they were a happy family. Saheed continued to grow his plants and he had started back smoking. He had even cross-bred the Purple Kush with the Kryptonite and came up with his own personal strain of marijuana. The plants produced some of the best tasting, most potent bud he had ever smoked. He was in the process of making arrangements to go compete in the Cannabis Cup in Amsterdam later that year. He had to hurry up and come up with a name for his strain before he missed the entry deadline.

He had just signed the papers sealing the purchase of his house on the lake the day before. He was sitting in his computer room messing with the Internet, trying to figure out a way to make improvements on Underworld Entertainment's website when Sarah came in and said, "Daddy, me and Rose are about to go on this call. Do you want us to do anything while we're gone?"

"No, I'm good, baby. Just handle that business and come straight home. We're gonna step out Downtown tonight."

"OK, daddy, we'll be back after we hit this lick."

Pulling up to the address they were given, Sarah and Rose went and knocked on the door. When a black man answered, Sarah was surprised because he didn't sound black on the phone. He invited them in and as Sarah walked by the man squeezed her ass hard.

Rose looked at the man and thought he looked familiar but couldn't place the face.

"I know I said I wanted both of y'all but I only got $300.00 to spend so I'll just take her," said the young man, pointing at Sarah.

"That's cool, big boy, just give me the money," said Rose.

"Here it is," he said, handing her three big faces.

"You don't mind if I watch, do you?" asked Rose.

"Not at all," he said and led them to the bedroom. Wasting no time inside the bedroom, the man stepped out of his pants and his little penis was as hard as it could get.

"Let's do this," he said, as he slid Sarah's skirt down. "You got a beautiful body, I wanna eat you out."

"I'm sorry, honey, but I can't let you do that. It's too personal," replied Sarah.

"I want you to suck my big dick then," said the man as he lay on the bed jacking off.

Rose and Sarah both burst out laughing at the little dick trick thinking he was big.

"OK, big boy, mommy will take care of you," said Sarah after she stopped laughing. She pulled a condom out of her purse and put it on him with her mouth like Rose had taught her. She had practiced on Saheed until she got it right. Then she started doing what she did best – sucking dick. Within 60 seconds she made the man cum. She got up and put her skirt back on.

"Oh my God," said the young man, not believing he had come so quickly.

"Oh my God!" said Rose as she realized where she recognized the man from.

"Say, I got another $200.00 for some of that ass," the man said, pulling out two more bills from his pants on the floor.

Sarah started to grab it when Rose spoke up, saying "we don't have enough time, we gotta go." Then she snatched Sarah by the hand, looked her in the eye and motioned for the door, indicating it was time to go. Sarah wanted to get that money but didn't protest.

"Slow down, you just got here," said the man, getting angry.

"Sorry, maybe another time," said Rose. She and Sarah walked out of the bedroom, and then left the house in a hurry, leaving the front door open.

By the time the man had got his pants on and made it to the front door, all he could see were the taillights of Rose's Camaro as she pulled away.

"Crazy ass black bitch!" said Polo as he slammed the door shut.

"What was that about?" Sarah asked Rose as they drove away.

"I just got a bad feeling about the situation," Rose lied. She didn't want to tell her the man was the snitch who had testified against Saheed. She assumed Saheed would be ready to murder the piece of shit as soon as she told him the business and decided not to say anything to Sarah. Rose had learned a lot from her daddy. Even though she was part of the family, Sarah was kept on a need-to-know basis.

When Rose gave Saheed the scoop on what went down, he sobered up out of his weed high real quick. He complimented Rose on not saying anything to Sarah. Even though she was part of the family, he didn't trust her with his life.

As his brain raced, he formulated a plan to kill his longtime enemy, Polo.

"*Saraaah!*" Saheed yelled out for the now blond bombshell.

"Yes, daddy," she said as she entered the room.

"I need you to call Lucy's Cabaret and see if you can go to work tonight."

"I thought we were going out?"

"We can go out tomorrow. Just do what I asked you to do."

"O.K., daddy," Sarah said, disappointed. She was looking forward to her night out with Saheed. With Sarah out of the way, Saheed put his plan into action.

*****

East Side, Distribution City

Polo was sitting on his bed watching a porno, reminiscing on the good head he had gotten earlier that day when he heard someone knock on his front door. He wondered who it could be because no one knew where he stayed. Getting out of the bed, he looked out the window and saw Rose's Camaro.

"Just in time," he said to himself. He was just about to order more pussy off the Internet. Even though he had bust a nut earlier that day, he wasn't satisfied. He had been locked up in the house for months, hiding and at the same time recovering from his wounds, not being able to show his face around the town left him sexually frustrated. Once word got out he was snitching, all his bitches cut him off.

"Who is it?" asked Polo, knowing who it was.

"It's me, Cream," said Rose, using her alias that she had posted on the website Polo found her on.

Opening the door to let her in, Polo almost shit himself when someone in a ski mask stepped from the side of the doorway and put a pistol in his face.

Unable to keep his anger in check, Saheed slapped Polo in the jaw with the barrel of the Chrome 44. Magnum he chose to use for the job. The blow caused Polo to fall on his ass back into the house.

Doing as Saheed had told her beforehand, Rose closed the door and reluctantly got back into her car and drove away into the night. She wanted to stay and help her man.

"Nigga, where the money at?" said Saheed, in an attempt to throw Polo off what was really going on.

"I got two G's in my room. You can have it," Polo managed to say through his fractured jaw.

"Lie on your stomach, nigga," ordered Saheed. Polo did as he was told.

"Put your hands behind your back."

Again Polo did as he was told. He wasn't trying to get killed over two G's.

Saheed pulled some plastic ties out of his pockets. He had them linked together so they could be used as handcuffs. After tying Polo's hands together, Saheed thought about Kiesha and stomped on the back of Polo's head, driving his face into the floor. After kicking him several more times in the face, Saheed regained his composure and got back to the task at hand.

He looked at Polo's blood on his shoes and realized he shouldn't have done that.

Saheed took a plastic container out of his pocket, opened it, and removed a Hypodermic needle he had previously filled with five grams of cocaine and a little water.

He looked at Polo, who was moaning and crying like a bitch as he mumbled something about where his money was at.

Saheed put his bloody shoe on Polo's back and placed his left hand on his neck, where he felt Polo's pulse. He used his right hand and plunged the cocaine-filled needle straight into Polo's jugular vein and emptied the contents into his system. He rolled Polo onto his back, and then removed the ski mask from his face. When Polo saw it was Saheed, his eyes looked as if they were going to fall out of his head. Saheed wasn't sure if it was from the shock of seeing him or the effects of the cocaine overdose, because at that instant Polo started kicking his legs wildly like a toddler throwing a temper tantrum. After about 15 seconds of kicking his legs, he started flopping around on the floor like a fish out of water. After a minute he just laid there, staring at the ceiling, eyes wide open. Saheed knew that he was dead because he could smell Polo's shit in the air and he didn't appear to be breathing.

Saheed thought about all of the drama the man had caused him, when Kiesha came across his thoughts he blacked out again.

Cocking the hammer on the 44., Saheed put the gun to Polo's forehead, right above the bridge of his nose, and pulled the trigger. Due to the repercussion of the gunshot, blood, bone fragments, and small pieces of flesh sprayed Saheed's face and body, snapping him out of the trance that overcame him.

After killing Polo twice, Saheed knew for sure he was dead. He fled out the front door leaving the syringe and container he had brought it in. It didn't matter because he wore gloves before handling them and didn't leave any clues for the crime scene investigators.

Running around the corner to his car he slowly drove away undetected.

CHAPTER FIFTY SIX
Saheed's House, Lakeview

Over a month had passed since Polo's death. Once again, Saheed had gotten away with murder. He remembered Black saying one time that the police in D.C. didn't know how to solve murders – maybe he was right.

He thought about True killing white boy Casper and getting away with it. The detectives never figured that one out. After True got out of the hospital, he and Saheed went back and found the stashed guns and pound of weed in the alley where True had left them. Saheed was surprised they were still there, untouched, being that it was visible from the alley when you looked closely.

After visiting Polo, Saheed took his boat out on the river, along with the guns used to kill Polo, Agent Wilson, and white boy Casper. After dismantling each one, he tossed them into the water piece by piece as he sped upstream, effectively getting rid of the murder weapons.

The house was quiet. Saheed had sent Rose and Sarah down to Miami to check some of that South Florida money after business had slowed up in D.C.

Black still hadn't paid Saheed his $50,000.00. Saheed charged it to the game and took it as a loss. He still couldn't believe his boy chose a punk ass 50 G's over their friendship. He heard a rumor that Black had gotten set up in a reverse drug sting by his Mexican connection when he went to re-up, but he didn't know if it was true or not. Even though he didn't fuck with Black anymore, he didn't wish no shit like that on him.

Saheed was glad he was out of the game and didn't have to worry about shit like that anymore. He put his feet up on the couch and was about to blaze a blunt of Hydro when his living room window shattered and something landed on the floor next to him. Before he could react, there was a loud explosion and a blinding light as the flash bang went off.

Deaf from the explosion and temporarily blinded, Saheed wasn't aware of the battling ram knocking on his front door or the Federal SWAT team that stormed his house.

He was so disoriented he didn't know what was going on until one of the agents smacked him in the back of the head with a pistol and knocked him to the ground. He was quietly placed in handcuffs. Then he knew what time it was. Slowly he regained his senses as the FEDS tore his house apart like it was the neighborhood dope spot.

After twenty minutes some Irish-looking cocksucker approached him and lifted him to his feet, then said, "We have a warrant for your arrest. You've been indicted for money laundering, conspiracy to distribute cocaine, and the murder of a Federal law enforcement officer."

"Man, fuck you!" replied Saheed, then he spit in the agent's face. In response, the Irish-looking agent punched Saheed in his mouth, knocking him to the ground. Before he could continue the beating, another agent intervened and stopped his colleague from whooping Saheed's ass.

After reading him his rights, the man asked Saheed if he wished to cooperate.

With blood dripping from his mouth Saheed responded "I need to call my attorney…."

To be continued………………………

Distribution City

2

coming soon

a novel by Boss Fred